THE STRANGER

AMONG US

Second Edition

THE STRANGER SERIES

THE STRANGER

AMONG US

BRYAN M. POWELL

TATE PUBLISHING
AND ENTERPRISES, LLC

The Stranger Among Us
Copyright © 2015 by Bryan M. Powell. All rights reserved.

No part of this publication may be reproduced, stored in a retrieval system or transmitted in any way by any means, electronic, mechanical, photocopy, recording or otherwise without the prior permission of the author except as provided by USA copyright law.

The opinions expressed by the author are not necessarily those of Tate Publishing, LLC.

Published by Tate Publishing & Enterprises, LLC
127 E. Trade Center Terrace | Mustang, Oklahoma 73064 USA
1.888.361.9473 | www.tatepublishing.com

Tate Publishing is committed to excellence in the publishing industry. The company reflects the philosophy established by the founders, based on Psalm 68:11,
"The Lord gave the word and great was the company of those who published it."

Book design copyright © 2015 by Tate Publishing, LLC. All rights reserved.

Published in the United States of America

ISBN: 978-1-68142-654-9
1. Fiction/Christian/Futuristic
2. Fiction/Christian/Fantasy
15.04.27

Endorsements

I have been following the Stranger Series from the beginning, and I was thrilled when Bryan asked me to read his finished manuscript of *The Stranger Among Us*. I have to say, he certainly stretched my imagination. From the first action-packed pages to the thrilling finish, my mind raced and my heart pounded wanting to know how it all worked out. If our future is half as bright as Bryan painted it, I say, "Even so, come quickly Lord Jesus."

- Cécile Pabolcheck, reader, editor-at-large and soon to be married in Cincinnati Ohio.

When we started reading *The Stranger Among Us*, we had no idea the ride it would take us on. Bryan's three dimensional characters and imaginative scenes and action kept us reading to the very end.

- Richard and Lavonia Nelson, pastor emeritus, conference speaker, evangelist.

Acknowledgments

  To my readers, who, without your encouragement and support, I would not have carried on when discouragement and loneliness set in.

  To my alpha, beta and loyal readers who encourage me with your kind words of support.

  To the editor and publisher of the first edition, John Bell, and Vabella Publishing, who went out on a limb for me. Thankfully the limb held and we both climbed to the safety of earth where we all live.
  And for Tate Publishing being willing to publish the second edition.

Dedications

I dedicate this story to the Author and Finisher of my faith, the Lord Jesus Christ to whom be glory and honor and wisdom and power, world without end.

Secondly, I dedicate this book to my lovely and patient wife, whose insight and opinion I value beyond words.

Character Bibliographies

Emma Newton – as the Octavian Granddaughter of Mr. and Mrs. Chase Newton, her enthusiasm for King Jesus brought her in conflict with her society and one person in particular.

Professor Adoniram Christos – AKA Supreme Commander Christos. He had a vision for the world and it did not include God.

Michael and Joanna Newton – his decision to leave on their pilgrimage to Jerusalem without the protection of the caravan was a costly one.

Timothy and Joy Newton – the younger siblings of Emma Newton found themselves tested to the limit. It was their love and faith that sustained them.

Nguyen (Wynn) Xhu – A History teacher in the Edenica School of Higher Learning. Although she was an Immortal Saint, she still had feelings…and a past.

Chief Nicholas the Wise – the appointed leader of the Forest Saints. It was his responsibility to lead his tribe to the safety of the Mountain Keep and to defend it to the end.

Arthures – Chief Nicholas the Wise's right-hand man, husband and father and defender of his people.

Andorra – the leader of the hunting party and guardian of the Royal Forest of Marlborough. His responsibility was to see that anyone entering his forest without permission, never left…alive.

Saint Bartholomew – an Immortal Saint and Head of the Sanctuary of the Truth. His courage in the face of danger marked him as a condemned man.

Jamis Newton – the son of Damien and Jolie Newton. As one of the billions Eonians inhabiting a nearly perfect earth, his heart was far from perfect. When the time came for him to choose between his dream and Emma, he chose wisely.

Scriptural Premise

"Then I saw an angel coming down from heaven, having the key to the bottomless pit and a great chain in his hand. He laid hold of the dragon, that serpent of old, who is the Devil and Satan, and bound him for a thousand years; and he cast him into the bottomless pit, and shut him up, and set a seal on him, so that he should deceive the nations no more till the thousand years were finished. But after these things he must be released for a little while."

Revelation of John 20:1-3

"Blessed and holy is he who has part in the first resurrection. Over such the second death has no power, but they shall be priests of God and of Christ, and shall reign with Him a thousand years. Now when the thousand years have expired, Satan will be released from his prison and will go out to deceive the nations which are in the four corners of the earth, Gog and Magog, to gather them together to battle, whose number is as the sand of the sea."

Revelation 20:6-8

Chapter 1

Edenica School of Higher Learning

Miss Nguyen Xhu stepped to the center of the tutorium, her warm, almond shaped eyes took in the faces of her young students.

"Greetings in the name of King Jesus," her authoritative voice rang clear and strong. Smoothing out the long flowing white robe, she waited for their response. Like many other immortal saints, she was sent to a remote region in Southeast Asia to teach the young Eonians who populated it, but their time was coming to an end.

"In the name of King Jesus we greet you," echoed back the response, hollow and empty.

Her petite shoulders sagged slightly. It grieved her that her students cared nothing for the King, nor the benefits afforded them under his benign rule. She released a quiet sigh and pressed on.

"Please open your books to the section marked, The Post-Modern Era," she said.

Movement caught her attention as a student raised his hand. "Yes Jamis?"

"Miss Xhu, what is happening to our planet? The news is reporting we had an earthquake. They are saying it's the first to happen in a thousand years."

Nguyen Xhu paused before answering. She knew the answer, but didn't want to cause a panic.

"It could be attributed to a number of things," her voice

calm, her mind racing. "The earth is undergoing some, uh, changes, that's all."

"There's always the possibility of a geographical 'wobble'," interjected Emma, one of her brightest students.

A ripple of laughter started in the back of the room and swept forward like a breeze on an open field.

Miss Xhu's eyes bore a whole through the perpetrator, and the smirks subsided.

"Is that what you believe Emma?" Miss Xhu asked.

"No, not by a stretch. I believe God made the world and holds it together by the word of his power." Her quick reply drew the ridicule of her classmates.

"Yeah right, so explain why God let all those innocent people in Belorussia die. Was he asleep? Or maybe he simply doesn't exist."

Jamis, by far the institute's best athlete and class bully, enjoyed taunting the prettiest girl in school.

Emma felt her cheeks burning. "Jamis, how can you say such a thing when we've got evidence all around us that God exists?" Dressed in the traditional toga, Emma was a feisty, petite blond with fiery green eyes. She could outwit and out talk Jamis and he knew it.

He ran his hand through his curly brown hair and crossed his arms. "I don't know that, I've never seen God. Have you?"

Not missing a beat, she returned his coy smile. "Well, we are required to visit Jerusalem before our twenty-first birthday. Why don't you come with me this year and see for yourself?" Her voice carried a playful tone which drove her tormentor insane with envy, jealousy and desire.

Jamis, the twenty-two year old son of Damien and Jolie, had never made the pilgrimage and had no intention of going, not without good reason. Before he answered Emma's challenge, Miss Xhu stepped between them.

"Now you two ..." she began.

Suddenly, the ground shook, knocking her to the tile floor. She quickly scrambled to her feet. Craning her neck, she gazed through the crystalline domed tutorium. Streaks of red and orange contrails stretched across the velvet sky like bear claws. With each impact, the tutorium vibrated and threatened to collapse.

"Run!" Miss Xhu cried.

As the last student entered the subterranean tunnel, she swung the large aluminum door shut and threw the air lock.

Swoosh. The vault sealed.

The earth shook again.

"What's happening?" asked Emma, eyes wide with fear.

Miss Xhu leaned heavily against the door, panting.

"That's no 'wobble,' M, something bad is going on," quipped Jamis, his eyes searching the titanium steel tube around him.

"Quickly, we need to get down to the tram level and get to the central hover-port as fast as possible," Miss Xhu said.

"But what about all the other students?" Emma asked, a slight tremble in her voice.

Her teacher pulled away from the surface, the heat from the outside inferno made it too hot to touch. The answer was obvious.

"I don't know sweetie. All I can say is that we need to get to the tram as fast as possible. Now go!"

The frightened students followed Miss Xhu as she jogged down the corridor to the elevator. She punched in the code, and the door slid shut behind them. It jolted to life, then began its slow descent. She tried to control her breathing as she watched the numbers decrease until it reached number twelve, the transportation level.

"Everyone move quickly without pushing," she said in a

controlled tone.

The class obeyed, too frightened to speak. With a measured pace, she led them though the terminal and waited for the next automated tram to glide to a halt. The doors slid open, and she herded them in.

"Please fasten your safety harnesses before we depart," the mechanical voice sounded in the overhead speaker.

Emma slipped the harness over her slender shoulders, but struggled with the hasp.

Jamis squeezed in next to her, "Here, let me help," his breath came in short gulps. He clicked the connection, and smiled.

"Thanks…I think." She narrowed her eyes, "I could have done it."

Jamis cocked his head, his hands extended, "I was just …"

The tram accelerated to supersonic speed, pushing them deeply into their seats.

Exactly ten minutes later it slowed.

Emma looked up and ran her fingers through her hair. "I don't care how many times I've ridden that, I always get dizzy."

The corners of Jamis' mouth stretched upward, "now look at who's 'wobbling.'"

She punched him in the ribs with her elbow. "Not funny Jamis," she said, clearly irritated.

He winched, "Sorry, but I'm not buying your wobble theory, M."

The anti-g tram vibrated and dropped to the negative g-force rail beneath it, throwing everyone forward. She glanced up at him, "Neither am I."

Grabbing the seat in front of him, Jamis grit his teeth and pulled himself up. "Good thing I got your harness in place."

Emma shook her head, letting a few strands of silken hair fall across her face. "Like I said, I could-a done it."

Miss Xhu stood, gripping the seat in front of her, "Okay class, everyone remain calm. This is just a temporary power failure. We'll be up and running shortly."

The minutes extended, the environmental support system wheezed to a halt, and the temperature rose.

Her students became restless, and a low murmur broke the uncomfortable silence.

"We gotta get out of here, or we'll suffocate," Jamis said.

He released his harness and stood on the uneven floor, a moment later the ground beneath the tram heaved. Amid crunching metal and breaking glass the car buckled and collapsed on its side sending students sprawling. Jamis was thrown forward smashing his shoulder on the bulkhead. Letting out a curse, he scrambled to his feet, and shook the slivers of glass from his hair. He willed himself forward.

Overhead, an alarm pounded out an inane cadence. A jolt of adrenaline surged through Miss Xhu's veins, and she grabbed the emergency release and pulled. With a loud swoosh, the cabin door slid open.

"Quickly, everyone get out!"

In the dim light, she saw Jamis clamor over the other students heading for the door. *Coward,* she thought.

"Ladies first," she demanded.

"What do you think I'm doing?" snapped Jamis, as he and a few of his buddies jumped out and began assisting their classmates.

The frightened group gathered around their teacher while above them; a red light beat out a rhythmic pulse.

Exasperated, Miss Xhu pulled her cell phone from her waist band and moaned, "I can't get a signal this far down."

Jamis jumped up on the concrete walk and found a meter box, "We're about two kilometers from the hover-port. We'll have to go the rest of the way on foot."

As he spoke, the hum of a distant generator rumbled to a halt. The lights dimmed and a cold, dark blanket closed in around the frightened students.

Chapter 2

University of California, Berkley

Two halogen spot lights flicked on illuminating the stage as Professor Adoniram Christos strode across the platform to a crystalline podium. A respectful hush settled across the tutorium as students and instructors alike nodded to each other in whispered awe. His traditional white robe accented by a golden clasp which held a shoulder cap gathered loosely about his feet. Locks of short-cropped hair domed his noble head and his long stately neck combined to form a Caesar like figure. Two piercing black eyes bore into the camera lens as he spoke without notes. From that moment on, he captivated the world's attention.

He lowered his chin and spoke in a resonant tone. "Greetings in the name of all that is good." He addressed the world-wide audience with poise and confidence. "Today, we have embarked upon a new course. Just imagine a place where you are your own god. Where you set the agenda and everyone had to dance to your music. Such was the case under the Age of Man. In those days, mankind looked at himself quite differently than he does today. For centuries, you and your families were assigned a job, and you went about your duty until the day you died. I might add, through genetic engineering, your slave masters have manipulated your bodies to live longer, so they could get more work out of you. The ruling class doesn't care whether you are fifty or three-hundred and fifty, just as long as you can get the work done. Well, I'm here to tell you, I care. I have taken notice of your plight, and I am prepared to do something about it"

He paused to let the standing ovation play out. Minutes later he resumed his comments.

"While the governing class is living a life of leisure, we have been hard at work building their great society. And while they enjoyed the fruits of our labor, we were hard at work planning and preparing for the day when we would throw off the shackles of slavery and take back our paradise. The process has already begun. Look to the far western sky and you will see what my forces have done to the population center called Celebration. It has been reduced to glowing embers."

After another ovation, he stared into the lens of the camera and spoke.

"My goal is to unite and make our demands known within six months. If the ruling class does not agree to our terms, we will take the struggle into the streets of every population center in the world. They will listen or be crushed under the wheels of change. Let all the armories be broken open, let every man arm himself. We must prepare to defend ourselves against this ruthless regime. Do not shrink from the struggle until you have annihilated their race. First we'll turn our attention upon Jerusalem, and it will feel our wrath. Then we will attack the Holy City. When we are finished, it will be called the Unholy City, for we will defile it with the blood of saints and of angels, and yes, with the blood of god."

The professor's voice rose and thundered, and resonated within the halls of the tutorium and the hearts of his students. A soft murmur began somewhere within the assembled audience, and then it doubled, and doubled again. It grew exponentially until the auditorium reverberated with the chant. "We will overcome!" "We will overcome!"

Michael, the archangel, circled high above the tutorium—listening.

His vesture shimmered in the golden sunlight. A large, jewel studded sword hung loosely in its scabbard. Every muscle in his angelic body, taut. Without effort, he lifted his gilded wings and ascended to the gate of Heaven. His flight carried him past the mansions of ivory and pearl, past the river of life and the spreading tree branches that bore twelve kinds of fruit. He was on a mission. He slowed his speed when he neared the Mountain of the Lord and came to a stance looking up. At the top of the stairs were lightning flashes coming from within the thick cloud cover giving it an ominous appearance. He knew ensconced within the unapproachable light, sat the King of Glory, the ruler of the universe.

Michael gathered his wings behind him and lightly drifted to a stance at the bottom of a long, wide staircase. Angels of all ranks and degrees ascended and descended, each bearing a message. He joined the band of angels and began his ascent. Upon arriving, he fell on his face in worship to the king of glory. The voices of the seraphim rang in rhythmic cadence, "Holy, Holy, Holy, Lord God Almighty." The arches of the temple reverberated, and a thick blanket of smoke billowed around him.

"Step forward, Michael, my trusted archangel. What news have you from the far corners of the universe?"

Michael rose to his feet and stepped deeper into the cloud. "My Lord and my God, you alone are all-knowing, all-powerful, ever-present. There is nothing hid from your eyes. Who am I that you should ask of me, word from your creation?"

"And yet I do, I long to commune with my creation, and

you my loyal servant have been with me these long eons. What word have you?

Michael again bowed his head. "At your leave, I released the Great Serpent, and he has done as you proclaimed he would. Already the planets Edirne and Edenica have fallen, and now he has turned his sights on Earth. Even as I speak, he is calling the world's inhabitants to ratify the Declaration of Independence from the Federated Alliance of Planets. The rebellion has begun. Should I lop off his head and rid the world of this nuisance?"

Billows of smoke swirled around him as the wrath of God smoldered, then burst aflame.

"I have said in my wisdom, he will be loosed for a season. Let him be. All things are as they should be. Go now and keep watch over my children. See that none fall into his clutches."

Michael bowed to one knee, "Yes my Lord. Yours is the power, the glory and majesty forever, amen."

Around him, the seraphim and cherubim took up the chorus. He descended the staircase with renewed determination.

Chapter 3

Level Twelve...Transportation Level

"We must hurry and hope the elevators still function." Miss Xhu said quickening her pace.

The ground shook, and large chunks of rock fell from the ceiling scattering the students. Someone groaned through the dust filled tube.

Jamis pulled his cell phone from his belt and pushed a button. A greenish light appeared, and he began to search the area. He stopped and knelt next to one of his classmates. A piece of ceiling tile protruded through his skull; a trickle of blood ran down his forehead. Lifeless eyes stared at Jamis. He felt for a pulse, and shook his head. Despite the cool air, Jamis' skin grew clammy. He swayed and buckled at the waist, heaving. Tears flooded his eyes as he leaned heavily on the wall. It felt cold and hard against his skin. In the distance, he heard voices.

"Jamis! Jamis!"

He jolted to attention as someone stood over him calling his name.

"Emma?" he blinked. "What happened?"

"You blacked out, now get it together. If we don't get out of here we'll all die," her voice echoed over the din.

With Emma's help, he struggled to his feet. Dirt and dust clung to his face. He spat out the taste of bile and wiped his mouth. "Okay, I think I can make it."

They picked their way through the rubble and caught up

with their class, their faces smudged with tears, sweat and dirt.

Jamis looked at his teacher and shook his head.

"Quickly, we must hurry," Miss Xhu called over her shoulder.

The rhythmic tapping of Miss Xhu's sandals echoed off the tile floor as she led her frightened students to the elevator.

In the distance, the carriage doors beat out an inane cadence against a contorted form. Miss Xhu recoiled at the bloody site.

"Don't look," she said blocking the view from inquisitive eyes.

"Jamis, c... c... could you help?" she stuttered.

He nodded to his buddy and they pushed forward. Taking the corpse by the torn and bloodied shirt, they dragged it from the entrance and around the corner.

"Hurry, get in," Miss Xhu said, her breath coming in shorts bursts. Her fingers trembled slightly as she pushed the button. The doors slid closed, and the elevator began its slow ascent.

With every level, red lights beat out their annoying warning call. They passed level six, then five and four. Three passed and everything stopped. The elevator went black. A few girls giggled nervously.

"Okay boys," Nguyen said.

Someone pushed their way to the front of the elevator. "Miss Xhu, let me try to get the doors open." Jamis said.

She heard him groan as he struggled to force the doors open. A sliver of light cracked the darkness, and the doors relaxed out of sight. The elevator hung halfway between two floors.

"Which way, Miss Xhu, up or down?" he asked.

Her eyes switched between floors while she considered

her options, "Up!"

A few other guys pushed forward and helped the rest of the class out. As the last student cleared the elevator, the ground shook and the cable snapped sending the carriage in a free-fall.

"That was close," Emma said wiping her brow.

"Yes, too close." Then Jamis took the lead and found the stairs. "This way," he yelled over distant explosions. Grabbing one of the girls by the arm, he pulled her forward.

Emma glared at him and rushed up the stairs, two at a time. When she arrived at the main level, she stopped. Her breath caught as she looked at the gaping holes in the Central Hover Port dome. Orange light streamed down and mingled with billows of acrid smoke. Twisted bodies lay strewn throughout the concourse. The taste of bile crept up her throat, and she covered her nose trying to keep out the stench of death.

"We must hurry, if we are to escape," Miss Xhu said as she rushed down the wide concourse.

Many of the tubes leading to the departing hover-crafts were struck by the incoming missiles and burned out of control. The few that remained led to empty stalls.

Breathlessly she led her class from one corridor to another seeking anything that would fly. Light fixtures overhead popped and sent sparks and shards of glass raining down.

"There's one," Jamis cried.

A moment later the building shook with the force of another wave of missiles. The ceiling collapsed. Girders buckled, and the walls closed in burying Jamis. His face was pressed into the floor and jagged pieces of concrete, and metal jabbed into his ribs. Trying to breathe, the thick dusty air made him choke. All he could think about was getting out from under whatever was pressing down upon him. He pressed his hands into the carpet. It was wet and sticky. Blood, it must be blood. Pushing himself to a kneeling position, he realized the weight on his back, was one of his classmates. One look and he knew he was dead.

Jamis forced his feet under himself and pushed. The taste of dirt and bile filled his mouth. He tried to spit, but his mouth was too dry. No time to find a water fountain, he thought.

Looking through the haze, he saw four ghostly figures of Emma, Miss Xhu, and two other students, rising like spirits. They were nearly unrecognizable, covered in a thin layer of grey dirt.

His teacher bent over and checked on a student lying at her feet. She placed her fingers on her neck and felt for a pulse. Looking back at Jamis, he saw her shake her head.

The building swayed.

Miss Xhu coughed out a command, "We need to get out of here, now!" she cried, then wiped the blood from her hands on her tunic and ran for the only tube connecting the concourse to a hover-craft.

When the last student leaped through the door, she swung it shut, hitting the air-lock. The door groaned and sealed them in.

"Anyone know how to fly this thing?" Miss Xhu asked, between gulps of air.

Jamis stepped forward, "You'd better fasten your harness, this may be a little rough."

Miss Xhu and the remaining students quickly took their seats, tightened their harnesses, and adjusted their breathing apparatuses.

Jamis climbed into the plush captain's seat, its soft cushion absorbed his weight. He swiped his hand across his face trying to clear his vision. A panel of blinking lights, computer monitors and gages stared back at him. He sat, staring, wondering where to start. A mechanical voice roused him from his musings.

"Please select a destination." The female voice commanded.

A list of possible destinations scrolled on a monitor. He smiled to himself and touched one.

"You have selected the Providence population, if that is the destination you desire, please confirm."

Frustrated with the protocol, Jamis skipped through the additional prompts and reached for the button marked, 'Thrusters.'

His experience at flying a hover-craft consisted of a crash course he'd taken when he was a junior member of the Civil Space Patrol. His fingers shook as he fumbled with the ignition sequencer. Any number of miscalculations could result in the hover-craft crashing upon lift off.

Movement caught his eye and he glanced up. Emma's slender form gracefully slipped into the co-pilot seat. She strapped herself in with ease, reached up and threw a toggle switch.

"There, that should keep us from crashing." She sat back and crossed her arms. "What?" she asked, innocence masking her face.

Jamis' shoulders slumped. He hated it when she did that.

"Come on, let's get outta here," she chided, rocking back and forth as if that would move the hover-craft forward.

He took a frustrated breath, grabbed the yoke and throttled back. The hover-craft broke free from its tether and lurched. The ground shook. "I'm goin', I'm goin,'" he said through clenched teeth.

He nudged the space craft forward. Once they cleared the terminal, he shoved the throttle wide open and yanked back on the yoke. The hover-craft rose from the surface of the tarmac and shot into the sky amid billows of black smoke.

Emma pressed her fingers in her ears as the cabin pressurized. No sooner had their hover craft passed through a cloud, than and a shock wave swept past them. It shook violently, and Jamis and Emma gripped the yokes to maintain its equilibrium.

Looking over her shoulder, she peered through the starboard porthole. With a sharp gasp, she turned to Jamis, tears streaming down her cheeks.

"It's gone, Jamis, Celebration—is gone."

Jamis banked hard to his left and pulled up. His mouth fell open. "Who attacked us and why?" Jamis asked.

"How should I know? We need to get home as fast as possible," Emma said, her voice barely above a whisper.

Flash!

A red streak swished past them. An attack hover-craft appeared above them firing wildly. Nimble as a cat, Jamis yanked the stick to his left, and swirled around. Then he gunned the laser magnetic ion thrusters and the hover-craft accelerated to light speed, disappearing into the sky.

From Jamis' seat, he watched the cool, deep, starlit field race pass above his cockpit. He had taken the hover-craft into the exosphere far from the danger below and guided it with the skill of a seasoned pilot, but now he needed a break. He relaxed his grip on the yoke and flexed his fingers. Every muscle in his body ached. Scanning the instrument panel, he checked his trim, fuel level and speed. At this rate, it will take us forever to get to Providence. He increased the thrust and hoped the fuel wouldn't run out. As the adrenalin rush subsided, the weight of responsibility pressed upon him, he was the pilot of a stolen hover-craft with no authorization and no experience at landing it. *What would his mom and dad say to that?* he thought.

Running his hand through his hair, he shook it loose and a cloud of dirt and pebbles fell on his lap. His toga, still sticky with blood, clung to his leg. *I wonder whose blood it is.*

Fatigue weighed down on him like a lead blanket. Reaching up, he pushed the auto-pilot. The hover-craft adjusted its trim, increased its speed a notch and re-calibrated its trajectory. An automated voice spat out their new coordinates.

"You are traveling at supersonic speed. You will reach your destination in approximately three hours. The weather conditions of Providence Population Center at the time of your arrival will be a mild, 78 degrees, with a light and variable wind from the south. Humidity will be low, and it will be partially sunny. Please enjoy your flight."

Jamis shook his head, *How could she know such things?*

Chapter 4

Aboard the Hover-Craft

Professor Christos' voice echoed through the comm system. Lexus sat stunned at what he'd just listened to. He toggled the intercom, "Jamis, did you hear that?"

"Yeah, we all did. Professor Christos' message came through loud and clear." He released his comm and glanced to his co-pilot. "M, wasn't that the most inspiring lecture you've ever heard?"

Emma sat, arms crossed, red streaks like fingers crawling up her neck. "That was the most treasonous speech I've ever listened to, if you mean that!" she replied. "He is saying things that haven't been spoken for over a thousand years. All the wars, the famine, the heartache, the broken lives and man-made disasters have come from this way of thinking. Just think for a minute Jamis, we all can't be gods each having our own way. That would be like a room full of children fighting over a few toys."

Jamis' hands came up in mock surrender, "Now hold on. It wouldn't be like that. We all possess a spark of divinity. We just need to fan it a little. Then we too would ascend to become gods, and we'd get along like, uh." He paused trying to think of the right metaphor.

"Like magpies," her eyes flashed with fire.

"Mag-whats?"

"Magpies, noisy birds, fighting over a few crumbs of bread." A smirk spread across Emma's face. "You see Jamis, selfishness is what got us in this mess in the first place. Don't you remember what Miss Xhu taught us about the fall of man?"

Motion caught her attention, and she glanced over her shoulder. Miss Xhu floated to the bridge where Jamis and Emma sat.

"His message sounded like the kind of teaching which spread around the world before the dark days."

Jamis slumped back in his seat. "Yeah, I guess you're right, but it sounded so good."

Emma didn't miss a beat, "Well, I think it's supposed to sound good, but God has given us a brain, and we need to use it. Remember, we grew up on a planet teeming with life. All of it is in harmony with itself. And God doesn't demand anything of us more than our voluntary love and devotion." As she spoke, her dainty arms drew wide circles. Jamis' eyes followed her motions.

"Don't do that."

"Do what?"

"Swirl your arms around, it makes me dizzy," he said holding his forehead.

"So," she said without taking a breath, "when we get home, are you going to join us on our pilgrimage?"

"I'm thinking about it, but ..."

"Don't give me that lame excuse about getting a job flying hover-crafts, not if you get dizzy with me swirling my arms around." She did it again just to annoy him.

His color darkened to a pale green. "Okay, you got me," he said, a chuckle percolating in his chest.

"So are you coming?"

He held his hands up in mock surrender. "Maybe, uh, I gotta go."

"Go? Go where? We're in a hover craft silly."

He released his harness and pushed off, holding his stomach.

Providence Population Center

Beep! Beep! Beep!

The hover-craft shuttered as it neared its destination. A series of alarms sounded, lights blinked. Jamis bolted to attention. "What's happening, M?"

She sat white knuckled gripping the yoke, "I, I don't know, all of a sudden we began to nose down. I grabbed the stabilizer to level us off, when lights started flashing and that dumb buzzer went off."

Jamis shook his head with a half-smile, climbed into his seat, and clicked the harness. He mashed the auto-pilot button, and the bridge fell silent.

He banked hard to the port side. "Well, first of all, we need to keep from hitting those space scrapers." As he spoke, he keyed in a new set of coordinates.

"There that's better. You were fighting the auto-pilot guidance system. That's why the alarms were sounding."

Emma took her hands from the joy-stick and crossed her arms. "Okay mister know-it-all, take me home."

She sat back and gazed out the porthole at the earth below. She inhaled and let it out slowly. "It sure is good to be home."

Jamis' shook his head, "Yeah, well, I haven't landed this thing yet."

The intercom jumped to life, "Captain, I don't think I can hold her together much longer, she's gonna blow," said Lexus in his best Scotty accent.

Jamis fought to suppress a grin but failed.

"Okay Mr. Scott, just give me a little more, and I'll get this rig home."

A wave of static washed through the intercom, then cleared. "This is Air Traffic Control. Unidentified hover-craft, please acknowledge."

Lexus toggled the mic, "This is unidentified hover craft, we're friendlies, repeat friend-lies."

The voice echoed around the bridge, "Unidentified hover-craft, what are your call letters or your point of origin?"

Jamis grabbed the comm, "Look, mister Air Traffic Control. My name is Jamis and I've been flying this hunk of junk from the other side of the planet. Our population center came under attack and we are the only survivors." His voice cracked with emotion.

A moment of static wafted through the system before the calm, steady voice of the Air Traffic Command. "Alright son, simmer down and breathe slowly. I'm here. I'll talk you in."

Jamis flexed his fingers and rubbed his neck. "I'm listening."

Exactly thirty minutes later, his hover-craft skimmed along the thin atmosphere on a direct flight path for the Providence Central Hover Port.

Providence, one of many growing megopolises scattered throughout the earth, was located along the eastern seaboard of what once was North America. It sprawled in every direction and like her sister cities, she was a city of cities covering hundreds of square kilometers.

"Just look at the horizon," sighed Emma. "There are literally thousands of space scrapers."

"Yeah, and each one is taller than the last. They are so tall they punctured the uppermost limits of earth's exosphere."

Emma sat wide-eyed as they passed the towering giants of crystalline and steel, glittering in the defused light of the sun. "It's a perfect example of the genius and creativity of Emperor King Jesus."

Shaking his head, Jamis said, "Don't forget who did the

hard work of driving stabilizers deep into the earth's core to keep the tectonic plates from collapsing. It was us Eonians," he added with a smug grin.

"Yes, and the Eonians are the ones moving out of the population centers into the unoccupied territories and are rebuilding forbidden cities. Against God's explicit command, I might add."

Jamis shrugged his shoulders, "Hey, it's not their fault they outgrew the population quota. I think it's pretty cool that the names of such renowned cities as Gog, Magog and Babylon reemerge. They were once magnificent cities in their day, and a little competition would be good for the economy."

Emma threw her hands up in frustration. "Jamis, you're impossible. How could you say such a thing? Here, everyone works; we have no poverty, no slums, no crime, and everyone is happy, except for you. And of course, those rogue nations that have established their own system of government. From what I understand, those kingdoms are fighting like they always have. The last hundred years of the Golden age is beginning to look like the last century of the previous age, the Age of Man, if you ask me."

Jamis craned his neck and stared out the window at the forty foot high, fifteen feet thick wall surrounding Providence.

"I wonder why they built such imposing walls around the city."

Emma uncrossed her arms and peered down, "Not only Providence, all the cities built walls that big or bigger."

"Yes, but why? What are they afraid of?"

A wry smile curled Emma's lips, "Possibly Gog, Magog and your all-time top favorite city…Babylon."

Chapter 5

The Newton's Home

A light wind rustled the tops of the trees while Emma's parents packed the family hover-craft. Leaves tumbled across the tarmac in summer-salts, with a dust-devil giving chase. It had been one month since the attack on the remote population center of Celebration, and no further action had been reported. With her return from Edenica School of Higher Learning, she was looking forward to the fall break. Her father Michael had been planning for their pilgrimage to Jerusalem for months. Now they were hours away from departure.

"Do you think your friend Jamis will get here in time?" asked her mother Joanna, a stately woman of 89 years young.

Emma shook her head, letting a few strands of her golden hair fall across her eyes. She brushed them aside without a thought. "I'm not sure. He's so non-committal," Doubt filling her voice. "If I've asked him once, I've asked him a quadrillion times to join us and all he says is, 'I don't want to promise.'"

Joanna nodded her head knowingly, "Sounds familiar."

Emma cocked her head and started to ask a question, when Joy, her younger sister, came running up. She scooped her in her arms and tickled her ribs. "Well at least you're coming, that I can count on," she said amidst a bevy of giggles.

"Girls, don't forget your sandals. Once we get to Jerusalem, we'll have to park in the hover garage and hike the rest of the way in, and you're not allowed to carry hover boards."

Disappointed, the two stared at each other. "Don't worry Joy, I'll carry you on my shoulders."

"What if you get tired, can I ride on Jamis' shoulders?"

Emma caught a twinkle in Joy's eyes.

"Don't get your hopes too high. At the rate he's going, we'll be long gone before he gets here. If he doesn't arrive soon he's going to get left behind."

"Is Miss Xhu coming with us?" her voice full of expectancy.

Emma shook her head, "I don't think so. At least not at this time, she still has a few classes to finish teaching."

Joy's lower lip pooched.

"I understand. I wish she were coming with us too, but she'll be here when we get back, you'll see," Emma said as she set her down.

A moment later a supercharged hover-craft whizzed past them inches above the treetops. The sleek craft made a tight circle, banked hard on its side and came racing back. Pulling its nose up, the engines reversed its thrusters and eased to the ground. The domed cockpit cover popped open and out jumped Jamis. He pulled his flight helmet from his head and shook his thick head of dark hair loose.

"I'm here, are you ready to go?" he asked, looking around.

Joy ran to his outstretched arms, "Can I ride with you?"

Jamis stepped closer to the Newton's hover-craft, glanced over his shoulder and let out a chuckle. "That thing? It only gets a thousand kilometers per uranium charge. That wouldn't make it halfway there before I'd have to ditch it in the ocean. Besides, it's on loan."

Emma eyed the sleek lines of the aircraft. She stepped closer and ran her fingers along the curved shell. "And who'd you go borrowing this from anyways?"

"It's from the dealership. My parents are thinking about buying it for my twenty-third birthday, and I went by to check it out. Cool, aye?"

Jamis, who'd always prided himself as being older and wiser than Emma, was all of six months her senior, but was quick to make that distinction.

Michael and Timothy, her brother, gathered around the hover craft oohing and awing over it.

"That's some set of cool jets you've got there, son. Are you planning on keeping it?"

Jamis shrugged, "I'm not sure, depends who's paying the insurance and fuel. Right now, I'm too young to get a real job and ..."

"And with your record of stealing an intergalactic hover-craft, I doubt you'll qualify for a hover-board," Emma said with a twinkle in her eye.

Michael raised an eyebrow. "How did you get those charges dropped anyway?"

Jamis' dropped his eyes, "Well sir, were it not for Miss Xhu speaking on my behalf, I'd be in some penal colony on Alpha Centauri."

Emma chuckled and patted him on the shoulder. "Maybe in time and with good behavior, you will be allowed to fly that thing without a homing device."

Michael cleared his throat, "Well, if we're going to leave before the peak of day, you had better shake a leg. Get your stuff stowed in the luggage compartment."

Emma scratched her head, trying to imagine what her dad's last statement meant.

"Mr. Newton, if you don't mind, I really need to return this before we leave. Could you wait? I'll be an hour, tops."

Michael took a quick glance at his timepiece and let out a breath slowly. He knew the caravan would be leaving at any minute and how dangerous it would be to get caught out in the open without the protection of numbers. Since no one's hovercraft came equipped with a weapon, it was better not to leave, then to be shot down over no-man's-land, or worse the open ocean.

"Uh, Mr. Newton, I'll hurry. I'll be back before you know it." Jamis pleaded.

Emma slipped her arm around her daddy. She wanted him to go more than anything. She fixed her eyes on her father, and he melted.

"Okay, but hurry. I'll have to break all the speed limits to catch up to the caravan as it is."

Two hours later, the sun began its slow descent and no Jamis.

Mr. Newton paced the floor of their palatial home; the cat had been fed, the automatic cleaning and watering system programmed, and the environmental maintenance set. All they were waiting on was Jamis, and he was late.

"He probably changed his mind," suggested Joanna in a motherly tone.

"Nope, won't happen."

"Oh? What makes you so confident Emma?" she asked.

A triumphant smile brightened her face, "He left his Nexcom X and ear buds. He wouldn't go anywhere without his music."

Just then a taxi-craft glided to a halt, sputtered, and coughed a cloud of fusion gas.

Jamis popped the hatch and jumped out, "Sorry I'm late, there was a huge pile up at the corner of Technology Boulevard and Satellite Way. Traffic was backed up from Substation K407 to the cooling tubes," he said, palms held in surrender.

Michael pulled his hands from his pockets, scuffed at

the wind-swept launch pad.

"Well we're burning daylight, let's get a move on."

Emma could hardly contain herself. Her cheeks pinked every time Jamis glanced in her direction, yet his cavalier approach to other people's schedules drove her insane. After a brief prayer, they set off on their journey. It was late in the day, and the sun was low on the horizon. Ominous clouds gathered to their north. It was no time to be out, alone, over uncharted land.

Chapter 6

The Journey to Jerusalem

After hours of pushing his hover-craft to the limit, Michael caught a few blips on his radarscope. He breathed a sigh of relief.

"There," he pointed to the specter screen. "I think we're starting to pick up on a few of the stragglers from the caravan."

Jamis, who'd been riding in the co-pilot's seat, watched Michael's every move. He too had noticed the blips, "I'm not so sure they're stragglers, Mr. Newton."

Michael tapped the screen and squinted.

"Those blips were moving toward us."

"On second thought Jamis, you're right. They may not be stragglers; they're moving too fast. They could be poachers, hoping to catch a loner by surprise."

Jamis pointed to a large cumulus cloud formation, "Why don't you try to get up to that cloud?"

Michael adjusted his sun-shades, eased the joystick in the direction of the cloud and gunned the jets. "I hope we can make it. I feel very vulnerable out here. Without the protection of numbers, we are defenseless."

Despite his best effort, the family hover-craft wasn't up to the task. An attack craft appeared high above him and swooped down, firing wildly. Photon shells stitched a line across his bow.

"We're hit. I'm losing control." Mr. Newton said as he grappled with the control yoke.

Another armed hover-craft appeared behind them, firing

its weapons. The Newton's craft vibrated as the bullets peppered the outer shell. Smoke filled the cabin. Joanna moaned and slumped over. Michael gripped his chest. "I'm hit, take over," he coughed.

Jamis grabbed the control yoke and yanked.

Nothing.

"We're going down," he said through clenched teeth. "Everybody hold on."

The hover-craft screamed downward and struck the ground with deadly force. Rocks and debris flew into the air and came raining back down upon them. What damage the bullets didn't do, the impact, rocks and debris did. Michael lay slumped to the side, blood dripping from the corner of his mouth. Jamis felt his pulse, there was none.

"Everybody out!" Jamis barked.

Timothy kicked at the shattered canopy until it fell to the side. He grabbed Joy and carried her out while Emma and Jamis struggled to unharness her mother. She was bleeding badly from a wound to the abdomen. Her ashen face confirmed Emma's worst fears.

"I think we're losing her, Jamis."

He swiped a bloody hand across his forehead.

"Jamis, are you alright?" Emma's breath came in short gasps.

He shook his head. "It isn't my blood M, your dad; he didn't make it."

She took a step toward the smoldering aircraft when a spark ignited the fuel tanks. The explosion knocked her off her feet. A thick cloud of smoke and burning metal signaled their crash site.

"Timothy, Joy, are you guys okay?" Jamis asked, looking around, their faces smudged with soot, their togas stained with blood and dirt.

Timothy and his sister, sat, huddled together over their mother's body. "She's gone Emma. Mother is gone."

Emma buried her face in Jamis' chest. His arms enfolded her. "Emma, I'm so sorry I caused this to happen. I was late, and now your parents are dead," his throat closed with emotion.

All he could do was hold her close and repeat the words, "Sorry."

She pulled away, tears streaking down her cheeks. She wanted to pound her fists against his chest, yet she knew it wouldn't bring her parents back. Maybe it was his fault…maybe it wasn't. Her mind fluttered like a moth to a light, trying to make sense of it. She couldn't.

Timothy stood, and marched straight legged toward Jamis, fists clenched. One swing and Jamis was on his backside. Timothy, though the smaller of the two, was quick, quicker than Jamis thought possible. Timothy jumped on him and began punching him. One blow cracked his jaw; the other caught the upper cheekbone.

Emma was on him, in a moment.

"Get off him Timothy, stop! You're hurting him."

She grabbed one arm giving Jamis the moment he needed. His fist came up and caught Timothy in the gut. He doubled over, knocking Emma to the ground.

Joy jumped to her feet and ran to where Emma laid, hands on her hips. "Will you boys stop fighting? You are acting like a couple of kindergartners fighting over a toy."

The sight of this little girl, lording over the three older young people, her pudgy hands on her hips, made Emma stop and stare. She wanted to laugh and cry at the same time.

Timothy clambered to his feet, face red, the veins of his neck bulging. "It's his fault our parents are dead." He shouted.

"Well, beating him to a pulp wouldn't bring them

back," Emma said, standing up and brushing dirt from her knees.

"Neither will saying sorry." Timothy said, walking in a circle. He kicked a loose stone, sending it flying to the side. "I don't understand. I just don't understand," he said through clenched teeth. "We prayed for safety and still this happened. Why would God let this happen?"

Emma stepped to his side, took his hands in hers and held them close. She looked into his eyes and spoke, barely above a whisper. "I don't know Timothy. We may never know, but God does." She laid her head on his shoulder and released a volley of tears.

"The first thing I'm going to do when I see Jesus is to ask him why he let my parents die," Joy said, bitterness tinged her young voice.

"This is hard, so hard, but we can't get bitter at God," Emma said through her tears, "He has always been good to us. He wouldn't arbitrarily punish us."

Timothy put his arms around his sister's waist and breathed into her ear, "I hold Jamis responsible for our parent's deaths, and one day he's going to pay." Tears streamed down his cheeks unabated.

"No Timothy, you can't say such things, and you can't get mad at God either. Remember, God has a plan," Emma said with as much confidence as she could muster, "He will bring something good out of this."

Timothy released her and stomped the ground. "What possible good can come out of losing our parents?" he shouted, his mouth gaping open.

Emma wrapped her arms around her waist, wiped the tears from her eyes and glanced between Jamis and Timothy, the two most important people in her life, and they hated each other.

Jamis looked so pitiful, so vulnerable, so broken.

"I don't know, maybe it's to teach us how to forgive," she said.

He stood a moment, and let his eyes search the ground. "I have no idea what you're talking about, M."

She shook her head, letting a few strands of hair fall forward. Without thinking, she tucked it behind her ear, and she realized she had a gash on her forehead. She looked at her bloody fingers. Her knees buckled, and she swayed.

A moment later, Jamis was at her side, easing her to a mossy stump. Joy took her hand and held it tightly, her forehead a mesh of concern.

Glassy-eyed and pale, Emma let out a shallow breath. "I feel light-headed," she said through chalk white lips.

She leaned on Joy's slight frame for support while Jamis tore a strip of cloth from his toga, wetting it from Joy's proffered water bottle.

"Here, let me get you cleaned up."

He wet the cloth and dabbed her wound. Having him this close, she felt his breath against her skin, the heat of his body on hers. At first, she recoiled, then surrendered to his touch.

"I don't fully understand the meaning of forgiveness either Jamis, but I forgive you, and I don't blame you for what happened," her eyes following his every move.

"It's not that bad. I think you'll live," he said in an attempt to cheer her up. "Do you think because I'm not a believer, God let this happen?" His eyes searched hers.

She returned his gaze, unblinking. "No Jamis, that's not the kind of God I serve. He is too good and too kind to treat people that way." They sat a moment, looking into each other's eyes. Emma squirmed, and looked down.

"Well let's at least give your parents a decent burial and

then try to find our way out of here. It won't be long before those poachers come looking for us," Jamis said, eyeing the column of smoke.

Timothy stood frozen, intransigent, his heart a stone.

Chapter 7

Restricted District K29DC

The sun hung low on the horizon, and the shadows of two homemade crosses stretched across the graves of Michael and Joanna. Emma threw the last stone on one of the two small mounds; it landed and rolled to the side.

In the distance, the low rumple of earth bound vehicles echoed off the hillside. Jamis cupped his ear.

"We've got company and I don't think they're the rescue squad. Let's get out of here," he said, helping Joy with her back pack. He took her by the hand and headed for cover.

Emma wished it were her hand he grabbed but smiled, picked up the bottle of water and ran after him with Timothy at her heels.

Like a herd of deer, they crashed through the undergrowth. They ducked behind a stand of trees, panting heavily. Jamis led the way to a narrow pass which took them deeper into a secluded valley. The further they ran, the more the temperature dropped. Under the heavy foliage, the air was close and held its moisture. Emma rubbed her arm with her hand to chase away the chills while small puffs of condensation escaped her lips. The soft rippling of water over moss-covered rocks gave pause to their flight as narrow rivulets bubbled over rounded stones. They splashed through the stream and stopped on the other side, panting.

"Jamis, stop. I can't go any further," Emma called.

She stood, hands on her knees trying to catch her

breath.

"We must be near the Outer Zone," Jamis said, looking around.

The moon poked its head out from behind a cloud, bathing the creek bank in golden light. Timothy splashed his face with the cool water, and took a sip. "They say carnivorous animals have returned. It would be nice to have a weapon about now," he said pointing to a tall skinny tree.

"Why don't we make spears like in the olden days," Emma said.

"Yeah right, are we a couple of cave people? What good would a spear and a club be against those giant lizards," Jamis chided.

Emma cocked her head, "Probably not much, but I'd rather have something in my hand, even if it were a rock tied to a stone."

Across the valley, a creature of the night snorted. Jamis' eyes widened, and he reached into the brook and pulled out a fist-sized stone.

Within a half hour, each of them had a spear, primitive tomahawk or short stick which they'd sharpened to a point on a nearby rock.

"Do you think we should make a fire and rest here?" Emma asked, rubbing her feet.

Jamis smirked, "And how do you suppose we start a fire, by rubbing two sticks together?"

Motion caught Emma's attention as Timothy jumped up from the bolder he'd been sitting on, his eyes red, nostrils flared. He stomped across the clearing.

"Hey, you don't be making fun of my sister. She was making a joke."

Emma sidled up next to Jamis. "That's alright Tim," pushing him back. "I can handle Jamis. I know when he's kidding and when he's not." She elbowed him in the ribs. Jamis took a step back. "Okay, okay." Hands held in surrender. "I was just kidding. Come to think of it, as cold as it's getting, it might be a good idea."

"Yeah but, out here in the wild ... I don't think so," Emma added, the whites of her eyes peering through the darkness.

"What?" asked Jamis, his hands outstretched.

"Say you're sorry." An impish grin parted her lips.

He pawed the ground with his foot. "Sorry, I was kidding," he said in a low tone. "Seriously, even if we could start a fire, it would probably draw unwanted attention. Let's rest here a while, and move on at first light."

Timothy relaxed his stance, backed away and slumped down on the bedrock. Looking around, he didn't see his sister. "Where's Joy?"

The three spread out scouring the area whispering her name. After searching for several minutes in the waning light, Emma stumbled over a leg. "Hey guys, she's over here."

Joy lay in a tight ball under a large elephant leaf, asleep.

"Looks like she's got the idea," Jamis said. Within minutes, they followed her example.

The sky grew brighter, and a flock of birds stirred in the tree tops. Wild monkeys leaped limb to limb, while on the ground, four-legged creatures scavenged for food. A light rain had fallen overnight, and the air hung heavy with condensation. Joy awoke needing to relieve herself. As she stood, her shadow crossed Emma causing her to jolt to life.

"Oh, you scared me," she said in a whisper, hand on her chest.

"Sorry, I got to go to the bathroom."

Emma glanced at the sleeping guys. "Me too, let's go." She grabbed her spear and led her sister ten paces deeper in the woods. The damp leaves stroked against her toga, soaking her skin and sending a wet chill over her body. When they returned, they found the guys awake and looking around.

"M, where'd you two go?" Jamis asked.

Without speaking, Emma narrowed her eyes.

"Oh," he said, scuffing the ground, "I get it," and shrank away.

"Emma, I'm hungry," Joy said, holding her stomach.

She smiled, "Me too. Let's see what we have by way of groceries," and began to root through her hand bag.

Triumphantly, she withdrew a couple of protein bars and a bottle of water.

"This will have to last us until we find a Safe Zone," she said, then broke off a piece and handed one to Joy. "Too bad this isn't the two loaves of bread and five little fishes, or we'd have a feast."

Jamis knelt and laced on his sandals. With a quizzical look he said, "And I suppose you still believe in miracles?"

Out of nowhere a humming bird appeared and dipped its beak into a sagging sunflower. It hovered a moment taking in a supply of nectar, then buzzed away. Emma smiled and tossed him the last piece of an energy bar with a half-smile. "Well yeah, we survived our first night in the outer zone. That's a miracle in itself."

He caught it, and took a bite, "Which, by the way, we don't know if there even is a Safe Zone in this area," he said smacking his lips.

Emma turned up the water bottle and gulped, then wiped her chin. "There has got to be. Let's travel north. With God's help and blessing, we should get to New Birth."

"We sure didn't have God's blessings so far," Jamis said, without thinking.

"We're still alive aren't we?" Timothy chimed in.

Joy crinkled her nose and glanced up at Emma. "I wonder if we will run across one of those giant lizards?"

In the distance, a large brontosaurus lifted its head and roared. They grabbed their weapons and scampered deeper into the forest as fast as their legs could carry them.

Jamis led, climbing over fallen logs and fighting his way through the thick underbrush. Vines and sticker bushes reached out like unwanted arms pulling at him, resisting his every step. He chopped at them with his club as if it were a machete until his arm ached. Scratched and exhausted, he slumped to the ground in a clearing.

"Hey," Timothy said. "We're walking on an old highway." Taking his spear, he pounded the gnarled pavement.

Jamis tugged at the matted roots. "You're right, I wonder where it leads?"

The road was covered with vines. Oak trees grew where vehicles used to pass, cracking the concrete with their roots. Further ahead was a bridge overpass which had been claimed by the jungle.

"We need to be very quiet and avoid those as much as possible." Jamis said, looking warily ahead. "They seem like great places for poachers to hide."

"How about I take the point for a while," Timothy volunteered.

With a nod, Jamis stood and bowed. "Knock yourself out."

The narrow path turned north and followed the remains of the old highway. With every attempt to penetrate the forest's secret passages, biting insects and ancient thorn bushes tore at their flesh. Soon their thin togas were shredded, and they were covered in lacerations.

Timothy stopped at what use to be a crossroad, and pulled a thorny branch from his hair. "Man, I hate those things," and wiped a trickle of blood from his brow. "You guys look beat, why don't we spend the night here?"

The weary travelers gathered in a circle amid fleeting rays of daylight.

"Do you think this is safe?" Jamis asked, scanning the area.

"It's about as safe as anywhere," Timothy answered. Jamis searched the sky. Dark clouds united, threatening to drench them with another volley of icy rain. "Well, let's at least build a shelter."

"Good idea," Emma said and began scouring around for something soft to lay on.

Jamis bent a small tree over to form a hut, while the others covered it with stacks of palm branches and lined it with pine needles and elephant ear leaves. By nightfall, the shadows had grown long, and the transition was complete. They sat in a thick blanket of darkness surrounded by unfamiliar sounds.

"Psst, Timothy, are you awake?" Jamis whispered.

"Me and everybody else. Who can sleep with all these weird noises?"

To his left, Emma and Joy lay huddled together . . . snoring.

Chapter 8

The Providence School of Higher Learning

The afternoon sunlight filtered through the tutorium windows, casting a soft yellow glow across the empty room. Miss Xhu had just concluded her class and began the laborious task of grading papers. Out of habit, she flipped on her receiver and tuned into the local classical music station.

"Ladies and gentlemen, we interrupt our usual programing to bring you a live broadcast of Professor Christos' address to the United Council of Religions."

Miss Xhu sat, listening. her arms wrapped tightly around her waist, and she was livid. Before the pod-cast was over, she pushed herself up and pranced to the Head Master's office.

"Enter," came a voice from within.

Miss Xhu pushed the door release, and it silently slid to the side.

"Greetings in the name of King Jesus," Nguyen said with a bowed head.

"In the name of King Jesus, I greet you," said Prince Bartholomew, the Head Master.

She pushed further into his office. Though modern in its appointments, his office maintained a quaint atmosphere. The yellowed manuscripts lay strewn across his desk, curling with age. The old ink-well with an antique fountain pen added to the ambiance. A thick candle stood, the lone sentinel of light on his desk. Hot wax coursed in tiny rivulets through fissions, pooling around its base like a miniature volcano. Nguyen inhaled the musty air and longed for simpler days. She stood fingering the hem of her robe. "Sir, have you heard the latest pod-cast from Professor Christos?"

Prince Bartholomew, an immortal saint, came from the fourth century. His faithful service even unto death afforded him a position of great authority. He rose to his feet, smoothed out his robe and stepped from behind his desk. His grizzled hands gripped the staff which had been his companion from the past, long forgotten. "Yes I have."

"Do you think he's the one?" she said, a slight tremble in her voice.

Bartholomew padded across his palatial office, stroked his long white beard and stared through the palladium window.

Outside, the teeming city of Providence throbbed with life. Space-scrapers dotted the horizon. Hover-crafts carrying a myriad of wares whizzed past his office with urgency and direction.

He sighed heavily. "I have been studying the ancient writings with the greatest care, looking to see what the prophets said."

"And what have you learned?"

"Sadly, I have discovered in this book," he heaved a large volume to his desk and thumbed through the crinkled pages. His weathered finger skimmed the lines until it found its place. "Ah, here it is," he cleared his throat and summarized. It states when the thousand years end, the Evil One will be set free from his prison. He will go out to deceive the nations in the four corners of the earth—Gog and Magog—to gather them together whose number is as the sand on the seashore, for one final battle."

For the first time in her immortal life, Nguyen felt fear. "So do you believe he's the Evil One?"

He knit his fingers behind his back. "If not, then he is the forerunner, of him who is to come."

"Either way, we must report the news to King Jesus," Miss Xhu said, taking her place next to Bartholomew.

"Believe me, he knows, Miss Xhu. He knows."

She shifted her weight and looked at the head master, "I know I have only been here a few months, but the pilgrimages have begun. It is my desire to go up to the mountain of the Lord and celebrate the Feast of Tabernacles. This may be our last."

The head master kept his keen eyes straight, "Most certainly, Miss Xhu. Is there anything else you desire?"

"Yes, by lord. Since her departure, I've not heard from Emma, and it's not like her. I've tried her sat comm and haven't been able to reach her. I understand that Jamis accompanied her this year. However, with his parents in incommunicado, I need your permission to contact them."

Bartholomew stroked his long white beard and rocked back on his heels. "This is an unusual request indeed, Miss Xhu. Damien and Jolie are in quarantine because of their subversive and independent rhetoric. They were even contemplating leaving Providence and moving into the outlaw cities, however, under the circumstances, I will consent to your request. Be advised, though, these people cannot be trusted. They have spoken out against our Lord."

The news of Jamis' parents struck Nguyen like a bolt of lightning. "Oh, I had no idea. He told me they were involved in some secret scientific experiment."

"Indeed, that is only partially true, the nature of which I am not at liberty to disclose. Even so, be aware of this, the apple doesn't fall far from the tree."

Miss Xhu stepped from her hover-craft, smoothed out her robe and walked to the front door of Holding Facility PPC #10. She pressed the button on the keypad and waited. A soft snap sounded, and the door popped open. The single sheet of paper bearing Prince Bartholomew's name granted her admission and access to detainees 952477 and 952378, Damien and Jolie.

Guided by a uniformed guard, Miss Xhu was led down a long, wide corridor. The soles of her sandals slapped lightly on the tile floor, with each step. As she passed iron doors of countless inmates, she couldn't help but notice the various poses they took: some stood; others paced like caged animals, still other sat, head in hands staring blankly. The air inside was dank with sweat and fear. One man reached through the bars in a futile attempt to grab her. She pressed closer to her guide and quickened her pace. After passing several locked doors, the guard stopped, punched in a code, which only a few knew. He swung the door open to the visitor's center.

She stepped into the room and noticed the plasma energy field which separated the two sides. On one side of an invisible energy wall sat two detainees flanked by two guards. On the other was an empty chair.

Miss Xhu took a seat and tried to calm her shallow breathing.

"Hello Damien, Jolie, sorry we have to meet under these circumstances."

Damien put his elbows on his knees, "I hope you're not here to tell us our son flunked out of Providence School of Higher Learning."

Miss Xhu shook her head, "Oh no. That's not it at all … fact is, Jamis is one of my best students."

"So why are you here? Is he in some kind of trouble?" Jolie asked.

Nguyen allowed her eyes to search the room. Within the confined space, the four bare walls offered no comfort; the thick glass windows discouraged any light, which might try to penetrate them, and the tile floor felt cold through her sandals.

She licked her lips, "Well, yes and no. He decided to accompany the family of Emma Newton to Jerusalem to celebrate the Feast of Tabernacles and—"

"And what? They eloped?" Damien spat.

"No, it's not like that at all, I think—"

"You think," Jolie interrupted, "don't you know. He was entrusted to your care, and you don't know where he and some girl are?" her voice tensed.

"I, I was hoping he'd called you."

"Miss Xhu, it's obvious you don't understand the whole picture. You see, we are here, doing highly sensitive research for the government. We have not talked to Jamis in over six months. So what makes you think he's contacted us?"

Miss Xhu shifted uncomfortably. She looked at her guide who shook his head slightly.

"Oh, I thought you were here for other reasons."

Damien started to stand when a hand came down on his shoulder. He sneered at the guard.

"Other reasons? What other reason could there be? You don't believe that drivel about us speaking out against the government now do you? That we were planning on leaving the population center and moving to the Outer Zone?"

"Mr. Damien, I assure you. I only have your son's best interest at heart, I—"

"Then you had better find our son, Miss Xhu, or we'll have your job." Jolie said, her finger jabbing like a hot poker at Miss Xhu.

Nguyen left, no closer to her quest than before.

Chapter 9

Restricted District K29DC

Emma paused long enough to take a sip of water from their only supply. She wiped the sweat from her eyes and wondered if they were ever going to get out of the jungle. The thick, lush undergrowth made walking difficult. Her feet ached, and her stomach growled yet she pressed on. The constant buzzing of the saccade bugs had given her a headache, and she was covered with red welts from swatting hungry flies and mosquitoes. The searing heat and humidity made her journey all the more difficult, but it was the constant threat of being eaten alive which drove her forward in search of the Safe Zone.

After wandering through the tangled undergrowth for hours, they broke into a clearing. A flock of sparrows dipped and swooped through the open air in a constant game of chase. To their west rose a volcano spewing black ash and cinders like an ancient fiery furnace. The trees throughout the valley lay twisted from the pyroclastic blast. The stench of rotting animal flesh and burnt wood hung thick in the air.

"I feel as if we've stepped back in time, like we've discovered a lost world of some sort," Jamis said.

Timothy stood, hand blocking the glare of the sun. "Jamis," he pointed, "to our north. Is that buildings?"

He squinted and shaded his eyes. "Yes, and by the looks of it, many of them have collapsed."

Heavy boots on pebbles crunched behind her. Emma whirled about. "Watch out!" She screamed.

49

A band of armed men rushed from the underbrush, weapons leveled. Jamis swung his spear, knocking one man's weapon to the side. It discharged, sending a flash of energy toward an unsuspecting tree, setting it ablaze.

Jamis pivoted and jabbed one man in the chest with his spear. He fell backward, blood seeping between his fingers. Timothy lunged, swinging his tomahawk. It struck another man on the head. He staggered and fell quivering.

"Run!" Jamis hollered over his shoulder, and the four paired off in two different directions.

Timothy grabbed Joy by the arm and dove for cover behind a large tree. He tumbled and fell but was on his feet in a second with Joy in tow.

A couple of soldiers chased Timothy and Joy into a ravine. Kudzu vines grabbed at their legs, slowing their escape. Joy lost her footing and fell. Landing twenty feet deeper, she became ensnared in vines like an insect caught in a spider's web. "Help Timmy, I'm stuck." Her pitiful cry cut into his heart.

He leapt after her, hoping to find a soft landing. Hitting the ground, he rolled, coming to a stop next to a stump. Still as a wooden Indian, he held his position, listening. The only sound he heard was his heart pounding like a jack-hammer. Peering up through the underbrush, he wondered why the soldiers broke off the pursuit so easily. The forest around him fell deathly silent, as if it knew the answer. He waited, counting the minutes.

Standing on the rim of the ravine, two heavily armed men peered into the shadows. One soldier started down the sloop but the other grabbed him and yanked him back.

"You really don't want to do that Jimmy," he said, the lines in his face deepening, his voice filled with caution.

Jimmy jerked his head up, "And why not? Those two kids are our ticket outta here."

"Not by my reckoning," the other man snarled. "You go down there at your own peril, buddy." Then he pointed with his forehead to the other end of the ravine.

Something large moved.

"Things have a tendency of growing out of control in these parts. Creatures, the size of a dog, grow to enormous proportions, and so do their appetites."

Putting his finger to his lips, they backed away from the edge.

Timothy looked at Joy, her face pale and smudged. "Can you move?" he whispered.

Wide eyed, she shook her head as she began to tremble.

With care, Timothy pulled back the vines enough for her to shinny out.

"Let's go," he said keeping his voice low. Then scooped her in his arms and ran, the whites of his eyes straining over his shoulder. He couldn't see it, but whatever it was, he was sure had claws and teeth and was hungry.

Jamis took off running, followed closely by Emma. He scampered over vine-covered rocks and tree stumps with the agility of a playful squirrel on steroids. Bolts of energy from the soldier's impulse weapons shattered limbs overhead, sending clouds of shredded foliage through the musty air. Thorny vines scratched at his flesh and toga like the paws of a rabid cat.

After fifteen minutes, the soldier's aimless shots ceased, and he pulled Emma behind a large oak tree. She leaned against the rough bark, panting, eyes wild. He poked his head from around the corner enough to see four men fanning out in hot pursuit. He ducked low and zigzagged through the uncharted forest. A limb reached its thorny finger out and slashed at his face. He felt warmth and touched his cheek. Crimson blood seeped from the fresh laceration. He wiped it away with the back of his hand and bulled through the forbidding mesh. With every pounding step, he could hear Emma's heavy breathing. He longed to stop, but knew it would mean certain capture.

With a sickening thud, Emma disappeared in a heap of tangled vines.

"Jamis wait," she called. "I've twisted my ankle."

He slowed his pace, and came to her side, breathing hard.

Emma grimaced and bit her lower lip as pain shot up her leg. "I think I stepped in a pothole."

Jamis looked around to see if they were still being followed. The voices, in the distance, told him that the chase wasn't over.

"Here, let me help you up. Let's get in this tree and hide."

Locking his fingers together for a foothold, he raise her enough to reach the first limb and climbed up behind her. Emma fought to control her breathing as the soldiers brushed past their position. The men wore camouflage uniforms similar to those worn in the twenty-first century and moved with precision. These were no ordinary poachers.

"What do we do now Jamis?" she whispered once they disappeared. "We're lost and separated from Timothy and Joy. How will we ever find them?"

"I don't know M. Things have gotten really complicated."

"We could try to go back the way we came," she suggested without conviction.

"What! And run into those army guys with the impulse guns again? No thanks. Let's keep walking and maybe we will come across a road or something that can take us outta here."

Jamis climbed down and helped Emma to the ground. "Can you walk?"

She flexed her foot and grimaced when she put weight on it. "I'll be okay, so long as I don't have to run," putting on a brave front.

"Okay, but stay close, I'll try to help you as much as I can."

She nodded and tried to still her heart.

Chapter 10

Providence School of Higher Learning

Nguyen stepped from her tutorium after a long day of instruction. To her, history was more than just a series of events documenting the course of time. It was a study of the workings of God in the affairs of mankind over the past seven thousand years of the Age of Man, a testimony to the infinite wisdom and power of God to affect his choice creation without effecting man's freedom to choose.

The golden sun set low on the horizon, its blistering heat a distant memory. In its place was God's presence within the eternal city, giving light far greater than the blazing orb in the sky. She sighed heavily, knowing most of her students weren't accepting her teaching. They were, however, eagerly absorbing the messages taught by Professor Christos. Old feelings long forgotten stirred within her breast. *Lord, I know you're in control, but I hate what Christos is saying, and more than that, I hate what he's doing to your kingdom. If there is any way of stopping him, please do it before it's too late.*

She neared her hover-craft and noticed an oily substance dripping from its undercarriage. *Oh brother, not again. This is the third time I've had this thing in the shop, each time for something different. I'm going to have to rent one if I'm going to make it to Jerusalem and back.* She pulled out her sat-comm and dialed a number.

"Yes, I need a lift. Could you pick me up and take me to the Rental Exchange?"

The man on the other end, an Eonian, admitted he was new on the job but assured her he would do all he could to get her the assistance she needed. She gave him her location, shut her sat-comm and leaned against the craft and waited. Within a few minutes, a sleek hover-craft with its dome darkened glided to a stop next to her.

"Dispatch said you needed a lift, hop in," said a voice from inside.

Giving it no thought, she slid in and the hatch closed. A moment later, she knew she was in trouble. The man behind the control yoke sat holding a phaser. Before she could react, he pulled the trigger, stunning her temporarily. He hit the thrusters and sped away.

Gradually, Nguyen's senses returned. Her head throbbed and every nerve screamed in angry protest. As awareness crept into her mind, she cracked her eyes opened. An array of orange and yellow stung her sight with every movement. Outside the domed window, the world blurred past her. She was seeing parts of Providence, she'd never seen before. "Who are you and where are you taking me?" she demanded gripping the hatch release.

"Not to worry, Miss Xhu, we're just going for a little ride. Now sit back and enjoy the view." His voice turned cold.

She crossed her arms and stared at the phaser lying on the man's lap. The pilot pulled the yoke toward his chest, and the hover-craft lurched skyward speeding past the massive wall surrounding the city.

"What are you doing? It is forbidden to leave the city limits without permission," her eyes wide.

"Now, now, don't go getting all legal on me. I'm just the driver. You'll have to take that up with my boss," he said with a smirk.

Nguyen's mouth gaped. Who is this guy working for?

Her fingers dug into the fabric as she tried to control her emotions, her breath coming in short gulps. *Whoever is behind this is going to pay.*

The hover-craft dipped, slowed and cruised to a stop in front of an abandoned building. Spanish moss grew from the eves and swayed gently in the breeze. Its front door hung by a hinge, roof sagged with the weight of time and neglect. What windows weren't boarded up were broken out.

The auto lock popped and the hatch silently swung open. "We're here, get out," he demanded with the wave of his weapon.

Nguyen released her harness and stepped out. The air was dank and musty, a sign they were outside of the 'Blessed Zone.' It was here evil men resorted to get away from the ever watchful eyes of God. She felt alone, vulnerable, naked.

A light drizzle fell leaving the ground soggy and uneven. A nudge of his weapon in her ribs told her to move forward. With care, she stepped on the warped board leading to the porch, it groaned yet held. She climbed the rest of the steps fearing at any moment she'd fall through.

"Go ahead inside. I'll wait out here," said her captor a crooked grin on his face.

She pushed the cobwebs aside, stepped in and stood waiting for her eyes to adjust. Dust particles drifted through the air. A mouse scurried across the warped flooring and dove into a hole.

"Step closer Miss Xhu."

I know that voice. Where have I heard it?

Sweat beaded on her upper lip. The palms of her hands slicked, and her pulse quickened. *It couldn't be. He died over a thousand years ago. I know it ... I killed him.*

The sudden realization struck her in the gut.

"President Randall?"

Chapter 11

The Outer Zone

Timothy and Joy stumbled headlong through the undergrowth until their legs could carry them no further. Whatever was following them had long since given up the chase, but he was taking no chances. They slowed their pace yet kept a wary eye behind them. In the fading light, a soft rain began to fall making it difficult to climb the hills. Exhausted, muddy and slick with sweat, they found a hollowed out cedar tree and climbed in.

Gathering a pile of pine needles and leaves together and using a large elephant leaf for a covering, Timothy made a pallet for his sister. "Here Joy," Timothy said, still breathing hard. "Lie down on this and try to sleep, while I keep watch."

"Shoo, you smell," she said rubbing her nose.

"And you don't? We both could use a good old-fashioned bath."

"I'm going to sleep dreaming of my big bathing pool filled with bubbles and swirling with hot water." She gave him a weary smile, leaned against him and was asleep within a minute.

Timothy sat rubbing his fingers through her hair and fought the urge to sleep. His body ached. His stomach growled, and he wished he'd gotten his backpack out of the wreckage. *Why is this happening?* He questioned. A wave of grief and guilt washed over him. *Was there anything I could have done to have saved mom?* A soft whimper escaped his throat. Tears

59

scalded his cheeks. After a few moments, he took a ragged breath and let it out slowly. I must be strong for Joy's sake. He swiped his face with the hem of his toga, and laid his head back. I'll just close my eyes for a minute.

Shafts of sun rays jabbed through the canopy of the rain forest like javelins. Songbirds, the chatter of monkeys and unfamiliar grunts of strange creatures brought Timothy to an upright position.

"Where is Joy?" he mumbled, looking around the empty tree trunk.

Panicking, he jumped to his feet, grabbed his spear and charged out.

"Joy!" he hollered.

A step later, he stumbled over her sending him sprawling. He looked up, pealing moss and leaves from his face. She was bent over, picking berries, and eating them. She smiled at him; her teeth and lips smeared blue from the juice.

"Here Timmy, try some, they're delicious," her pudgy hand outstretched with a dozen plump berries.

His stomach growled, and he scooped them up and tossed them in his mouth. For the next half hour, they consumed all they could and pocketed the rest.

Timothy leaned against the tree. "I think I ate too many berries," he said, rubbing his belly. He laid his head back and inhaled. "I love the smell of the air after a rain, don't you Joy?"

She swallowed the last berry on the shrub, wiped her mouth with a grungy hand and smiled. "Yes, but now I'm thirsty."

Reaching for an elephant leaf, Timothy caught a stream of rain water flowing down from the limbs overhead.

"Here, cup your hands."

She did so and drank deeply.

"Now it's my turn."

After sucking down as much as he could, he filled her water bottle, twisted the lid and placed it in her knapsack.

"That should hold us for a while."

"Timmy, I'm cold," she said with a slight chill.

"Yeah, me too, this toga isn't made for running through the woods."

"Neither are these sandals," she said looking at a broken thong. "I'm going to go barefoot from now on."

Timothy lifted his blistered foot and inspected it. Between the briers, sharp stones and roots, his feet had taken a beating. He massaged them and longed for relief.

"Come on Joy, we need to find Emma and Jamis," he said, though not convinced.

With each step, his bare feet complained, and he winched as he stumbled over a root outcropping.

Why is it I have the distinct feeling we are being watched, or followed, or both? He peered over his shoulder warily.

Shaking his head, he trudged on, feet heavy with mud. Ahead, water gurgled over rounded rocks made slick with age. Moss formed swirling pools that shimmered like liquid silver. The air was cooler than the surrounding forest causing him to rub his arms to chase away the chill.

"Look Timmy, a creek, I'm so thirsty."

"You have your water bottle, drink from it."

Joy wrinkled her nose, "I can't, I drank it all."

Before he could stop her, she splashed into the brook and scooped up a hand full and guzzled it down.

"Oh Timmy, this is so cold," she said, her blue lips shivering.

Keeping his eyes on his surroundings, he knelt and scooped a handful and lapped it up.

"Just look at you, Joy, you're soaking wet," he chided. "Let's get out and dry off. I can't have you getting a cold, now can I?"

She pooched her lip and clamored out of the creek.

"Here, sit on that rock in the sun and dry off, while I scout around."

Timothy climbed a pile of rocks and scanned the horizon. He groaned, "Trees, for as far as I can see."

"Heeelp!" Joy screamed. A giant Goliath Tarantella crawled from its hole.

Keeping his eyes on the creature, he bounded down the slope. Joy tried to back away, but the furry legged creature sprang, nearly landing on her. She turned to run but it leaped on her backpack and sunk its yellowed fangs into the canvas. Losing her balance, she fell into the creek, smacking her head on a rock. Blood seeped from the wound and trickled down her face. "Timmy, help me!"

He landed flat-footed to the ground, grabbed his spear and plunged it into the creature's abdomen. Legs flailing wildly, it struggled to break free. Timothy took a step back, caught his foot on a rock and stumbled. The spider was on him in a heartbeat. As if in slow-motion, Timothy stared as it climbed up his leg, eyes red, its fangs dripping with poison. Joy regained her footing, grabbed a rock and smacked it in the head. The spider fell into the water twitching. Timothy was on his feet in an instant. He jabbed the creature with his spear until it stopped moving. Grabbing Joy, he carried her from the bloody creek and collapsed on the ground.

Chapter 12

Restricted District K29DC

Like a flock of bald eagles, Michael the archangel led his platoon in lazy circles high above the earth. With his gilded wings extended, he rode the thermals in ever ascending circles. From his vantage point, he scanned the forest looking, probing, and searching.

His keen eyes caught the movement of two figures struggling through the underbrush. It was his two charges. They were alive and heading in the right direction. Satisfied, he gave a quick nod to Orifiel the angel of the Forest.

"See that they make it safely to their destination. I have other errands to attend to."

Orifiel saluted his commander, assembled his squad and swooped down. Keeping their distance, they formed a protective barrier around Emma and Jamis and waited.

"Look Jamis, a town," she said pointing to a few ramshackled buildings.

He crouched low behind a young pine tree and peered ahead. "I don't know, M. I wish there was another way, but as thick as this forest is, I'm afraid that's it," he pointed to Main Street."

Emma placed her hand on his shoulder, swallowed hard, and nodded.

"Stay behind me and don't talk."

Emma glared at him. They'd been walking for hours without speaking, and she was dying to ask him about his parents, his hobbies, favorite food, anything. The urge to talk was overwhelming, and she broke her silence. "This place gives me the creeps," she said clinging to his side.

He shrugged her fingers from his arm, not being the clingy type. "It reminds me of one of those ghost-towns from the wild-wild-west days."

An armadillo scurried across the road, Emma jumped. "That scared me to death," she said, between gasps.

Jamis let out a nervous chuckle, "I sure hope we don't run into a modern-day gun slinger toting an impulse weapon. Let's hurry up and get out of here."

With cautious steps they plodded down the once thriving thoroughfare. Rusted hulks of what used to be vehicles sat along the road, their ancient skeletons a silent witness to a by-gone era. With each breeze, the ghostly remains of homes whispered of happier days, while a massive willow tree draped its swaying branches to the ground as if it covered its face in shame.

As they neared the outskirts of the town, Jamis noticed an old decaying mansion. Its wrap-around porch was mostly intact, albeit, covered with overgrowth, vines hung down like witch's hair. Over the centuries, most of the structure had collapsed leaving four tall chimneys standing as sentinels of the past.

Jamis knelt down and inspected the muddy ground.

"What is it Jamis?"

"I'm not sure, but I think someone has been here recently."

She squatted next to him. "It's a foot print. Do you think it belongs to Timothy?" her voice rising with excitement.

"Don't get your hopes too high; it's not big enough to

be his foot, and it's too large for Joy's, but one thing is for sure ... we aren't alone."

The front steps leading up to the porch still remained intact, and a couple of solid oak rocking-chairs survived the passing of time.

"M," he pointed with his nose, "that porch is inviting, and get a load of those old rocking chairs. I sure could use a rest.

"Yeah, and the minute you sit in one, you'll be on the floor," she said with a dare in her eyes.

"Race you," he took off in a full run.

Emma charged after him and sprang up the steps. She tripped on the last one and fell into the closest one. It held, and she leaned back just as Jamis reached the other.

"Crack"

His rocker collapsed beneath his weight, and he tumbled to the porch. "They don't make 'em like they used to," picking himself up, his ego only slightly tarnished.

Emma sat, hand to mouth, giggling.

"Stop laughing," he said, dusting off his toga. "Why don't we take a break and rest for a little while."

"Splendid idea," she said in her best British accent. "I just hope the folks that own this place don't come home."

"Very funny, M, very funny."

The belly of the clouds raked the treetops and began to weep great droplets of rain. The steady, rhythmic drumming against the tin roof hypnotized them, and soon they were asleep, Emma on the rocking chair and Jamis leaning against the crumbling wall.

Hours later, Jamis' eyes cracked open. His mouth felt like he'd eaten gravel, he was disoriented and hungry. Pushing himself up, he teetered a moment, then took a generous yawn. He stretched out the kink in his back and started from the porch.

A rotten plank groaned and Emma's eyes popped open.

"Sorry, I woke myself up dreaming I was eating a juicy steak," Jamis said.

Emma forced a smile. "Don't even mention food; I'm so hungry I could eat anything." She stood and grabbed a large leaf which hung from a nearby bush and bit into it.

"Mm, this thing is good. You should try one Jamis. It tastes like a slice of watermelon."

Jamis shook his head. "You've got to be kidding me. Stop, you're going to make yourself sick eating that thing."

"I don't think so. Remember in Bio-Class, they taught us that God changed the natural world to provide all of mankind's needs, even making formerly poisonous plants, edible?"

Jamis scuffed the wooden porch, hands in his pockets. "Yeah, well, I kinda slept through that class."

She shook her head in a womanly fashion, yanked off two leaves and handed him one.

"Here, didn't your mother tell you to eat your greens?"

Emma finished one leaf and reached up for another when a creeping vine stretched out its tentacles, wrapped itself around her ankle and pulled. She fell and tried to crawl, but the plant seemed to have a mind of its own.

"Jamis, help." She screamed, trying to pull herself away from the gaping mouth of a large flesh eating flower.

Reaching down, Jamis grabbed a shard of broken glass and sliced the stalk in two. Its heavy head plopped onto the muddy ground and rolled.

"We're not the only ones who are hungry around here," he said as he helped her to her feet.

She looked up at him. "Suddenly I lost my appetite for leafy things."

Chapter 13

An Abandoned Building

Nguyen stood, staring into the eyes of President Randall. Her pulse quickened, sweat slicked the palms of her hands and her mind raced. How he'd gotten to be the president of the United States was a mystery to her; how he'd been resurrected was even more puzzling.

"I thought a lot about you over the last thousand years, Miss Xhu," Randall said, his acrid voice crackled. "I hold you personally responsible for wrecking my plan. If you had not killed me, that charade perpetrated by Chase Newton would have fallen apart. Were you two working together?"

Nguyen's mouth filled with cotton. She tried to speak but her tongue stuck, all she could scratch out was a feeble, "No."

Randall stood, adjusted his tie, and began pacing. "Well no matter. I'll deal with the offspring of Mr. Newton in time. Now you're going to pay for your interference."

A light suddenly went off in Nguyen's mind, followed by panic. Chase Newton ... Emma Newton. Her breathing shallowed into cold, short breaths.

"Ah, I see you have connected the dots. "I've had a long time to think about him. I plan on personally dealing with his grandchildren before this is all over.

The room began to tilt as Nguyen tried to comprehend what he'd said. Her knees buckled, and she fell to the floor with a thud. Overhead, a light rain beat an uneven rhythm on the tin roof. Drips of water fell around her, forming a puddle, quickening her spirit. *This place is outside the safety zone of God's blessing. Lord, I need your grace, right now.* A surge of energy coursed through Nguyen, which she'd not known since she received her new body. Boldness swelled within her chest, and she pushed up from the floor.

"Look President Randall, or whoever you are. You can't kill me I'm— He cut her off with a wave. "My name is not important. But just so you know, over the centuries I've gone by many names. Before I became the President Randall, they called me Pastor T.J. Richards, and now I am masquerading as Professor Adoniram Christos, catchy name, aye? Lord Christ?"

While he spoke a metamorphous began to take place. First, the face of Randall changed to Pastor T.J., then to Professor Christos. The ground shook, rattling windows and sending dust in the musty air. Nguyen tried to swallow but couldn't. Her bulged eyes, unblinking, while the professor's skin cracked open and peeled back. Like a mammoth butterfly emerging from its cocoon, the grotesque form of a dragon squeezed out and grew in proportion. Discarding the empty shell, he stretched his leathery wings to full extension, raised his head to the heavens and bellowed. Nguyen backed into a corner and pulled her knees to her chest, barely able to control her bladder. He leered at her with two narrow snake-eyes.

"Miss Xhu, apparently you fail to comprehend the one with whom you're dealing. I am Lucifer, son of the morning, the anointed cherub, master and lord of the earth. And I have returned to claim what is mine."

Nguyen buried her face in her hands. *Oh Lord, help me,* she eked out a prayer.

"I may not be able to kill you, but I can make you suffer." He thrust his hand toward her, palm up.

An unseen force brought her to a standing position and

lifted her into the air. Nguyen hung, suspended in space, her feet dangling. He spun her around until she lost her equilibrium, laughing wickedly. Then the hardwood slats pulled apart, revealing a bottomless hole, filled with blackness.

Lucifer released his grip and she fell, headlong into the abyss. The light faded until it became a pin dot, and then disappeared. The wind screamed in her ears; bile crept up her throat. *Oh Lord, help me.*

A distant memory percolated to the surface of her mind. Once, during her college days she went sky-diving. Remembering her lessons, she spread her arms and legs out like a flying squirrel and assumed a guided free-fall. A verse from the ancient writings echoed in her ears, "He shall give his angels charge over you, and in their hands, they shall bear you up, so that you don't break your foot against a stone."

The wind tore at her clothes. Her skin prickled with a cold chill as the air scraped past. How far she fell remained a mystery. All she knew was that she was in trouble.

In the distance, a light appeared, and approached at a break-neck speed. She closed her eyes, fearing the worst. In the darkness, she felt the soft touch of angels gently holding her, keeping her from smacking her head on the hard surface. Her speed slowed, and she glided to a stance on the floor that moments earlier had opened beneath her.

Nguyen stood, shaking, heart racing. *What just happened?* She wondered. The room, now dim, was empty and cold. Outside, the rain beat a rhythmic cadence on the roof. Large drops of water dripped on her forehead, ran down her chin, and joined the growing puddle around her. She wiped her eyes with the back of her hand, and blinked. *Thank you Lord.*

Looking around, she saw no one and wondered, *where is the president or Professor Christos or whatever his name is?*

Voices on the wings of a light breeze, wafted through

the broken windows.
    She stepped to the door and peered out.

Chapter 14

The Outer Zone

    The sun dipped low over the horizon sending horizontal rays of muted light through the foliage. Long shadows grew, and wisps of condensation formed above an ancient brook like lost spirits. The lonely howl of a wolf crept through the forest, chilling the night air. For a moment, the forest held its breath as two wandering souls emerged into a clearing in search of a place to rest.
    Timothy plopped down upon a mossy rock and let the cool water swirl around his blistered feet, Joy did the same. Within a few minutes, the scene transformed into an enchanted forest as the last vestiges of the day died and nocturnal creatures found resurrection. Evening calls echoed throughout the trees and grew in intensity into the night.
    "I wonder where we are." Joy said, looking around.
    Timothy lifted his foot and inspected the damage. "I don't know but this place looks strangely familiar."
    He heard Joy take a sharp breath, and glanced up. Joy sat up straight, her hand covering her gaping mouth. "It should be. We've been here before," she said, pointing to the dead spider bobbing against a moss-covered rock.
    In the distance, something bellowed; its cry reverberated through the trees.
    "What was that?" she asked, fear in her voice.
    Timothy cocked an ear. "What was what? I didn't hear anything," he said, half smiling.

"You can't fool me. You heard it too, I can tell."
He raised his hands, palms up.
"I just didn't want to worry you."
"Too late Timmy, I'm already scared spitless.'"
"Roarrrr!"
"There it goes again. Let's get out of here before that thing thinks we're its next meal." She yelled over her shoulder, running downstream. Timothy swung his spear in a circle, turned and followed, close on her heels. They splashed along the shallow stream until they stumbled upon a well-worn path.

"This way," called Timothy, springing up the embankment and deeper into the forest. Limbs reached out like tentacles grabbing at his arms and legs, yet he slammed through a brier bush with reckless abandonment.

As the roaring faded, so did the adrenaline, and Joy stopped, hands on her knees, panting. "I can't go any further. If they eat me, they won't get much," she said between gulps.

"If they ate you, they'd get a belly ache," Timothy kidded, breathing heavily. "Let's walk a while and see where this leads."

"I hope you've got better eyes than me, 'cause, I can't see my hand in front of my face." Her voice echoed through the darkness.

A shaft of moonlight stabbed the path ahead, and Timothy found a clearing. He quickly threw together a makeshift lean-to, covered it with pine boughs and pulled Joy inside.

"Let's rest here until morning."

She snuggled next to him and soon nodded off to sleep while he kept a tenuous vigil.

Timothy, who'd drifted off and on throughout the night, woke to a cool, red dawn. Small drops of dew scurried down the leafy roof, and shimmered in the morning light. Not wanting to awaken Joy, he slipped out of their shelter and stretched. Wondering if his growling stomach would disturb her, he began to forage from a blackberry bush while Joy slept. After filling a couple of elephant leaves, he returned to find Joy still snoring.

"Wake up sleepy head, I've got breakfast."

She roused, and formed two fists which she screwed into her eye sockets. After an ample yawn, she perched on the corner of a tree stump and sighed. "Thanks, these are delicious," she said, taking the offered leaf.

Timothy popped one into his mouth. "You're welcome, they are."

The two munched in silence until they finished.

"What's that sound in the distance?" Joy asked.

Timothy cupped his ear. "I've been listening to it all night. I think it's a waterfall. Do you want to investigate?"

She smiled and jumped to the ground, "Let's go. I sure would like to wash my hands, they're sticky," she said, looking at her purple fingers.

The path meandered through the forest and ended at a waterfall. Timothy stopped short and peered over the ledge. That sure is a long way down, he thought.

Snarling quickened his senses and he twisted at the waist. A pack of creatures resembling Wolverines, emerged from the thicket, their teeth bared, claws extended.

"What are they?" Joy asked, as she backed closer to the precipice.

"I don't know, and I don't want to find out." He swung his spear scattering them temporarily. "Watch out, these things are aggressive."

"And hungry."

"Run!" Timothy screamed. They splashed across the creek, and back into the forest, the angry creatures, close behind.

Without warning, a volley of arrows whizzed overhead striking the animals, and pinning them to the ground. They lay kicking wildly. Another wave of arrows fell, killing the rest of them. As suddenly as it started, it ended ... all was quiet ... nothing moved.

"What happened to them?" Joy asked in a small voice. Her arms wrapped tightly around Timothy's leg.

He held his breath and knelt down next to her. "I'm not sure, but I think we're about to find out."

A shadow moved and an archer wearing green leather clothing emerged from behind a tree, then another and another. He pointed his arrow at Timothy's head. Joy ducked behind him.

"Out of the frying pan into the fire," Timothy muttered through pinched lips.

"Intah um jah majah?" The leader spoke in a questioning tone.

"I think he's asking you a question," Joy said, poking her face around her brother.

"Yeah, but I have no clue what he asked."

"Intah um jah majah?" he repeated with more intensity.

Timothy lifted his hands in surrender. "I don't understand."

Another archer stepped up next to the leader and spoke. "We have not heard your language for many years. Most of my people have forgotten it," he said looking around at the dead creatures. He kicked one. "Are you alright?"

"Yes, thank you. What were they anyway?" Timothy asked."

"Oh those, we call them 'rauckucha', means, meat pickers. They can pick the meat off of your bones before you're dead."

He leaned over and whispered to his leader in muted

tones. He lowered his arrow and returned it to his quiver.

"Now, who are you and why are you wandering through our forest without permission?"

Timothy shifted his eyes from side to side. "Your forest? I thought we were in the outer zone."

The man swung his arm in an arc. "It is and yet it is our home. Now tell us who you are."

"My name is Timothy Newton, and this is my sister Joy. We're sorry for intruding into your forest. The hover-craft we were traveling in got shot down, our parents were killed. We survived, but were attacked by a band of armed men who tried to kill us. My other sister and her friend ran one way, and we ran the other. We've been wandering around in these woods for days looking for them."

The archer adjusted his belt and drew closer. "I know, my hunting party, along with every man-eating beast in this forest, has been following you."

"I knew it," Timothy said, looking at Joy. "I knew we were being watched."

"I saw him once," Joy said pointing at their leader.

Their interpreter lifted an eyebrow and cocked his head up at his leader and repeated her statement. A sheepish grin appeared then faded.

"Why didn't you say something Joy?"

She shrugged her shoulders, "I didn't want to make you worry."

She smiled, at the spokesmen, "Mister, what's your name and where are we?"

He knelt upon one knee and gave her a reassuring smile. "My name is Andorra, and you are in the Royal Forest of Marlborough, it has been our home for centuries. We are the Forest Saints. The Good King granted us leave to dwell in these woods to keep and to tend to them as our ancestors did."

"Sorry mister, please forgive us," Joy said, her eyes searching the ground.

"We must take you to our chief. He is an immortal saint, with great wisdom and authority. He will know what to do with you. But you must not learn the location of our camp." Reaching into his pouch, he pulled out two silken hoods. "Here, put these on."

The archers guided Timothy and Joy through the forest in silence. Timothy could tell his guide chose the best path as he only occasionally stumbled over a loose rock or root outcropping.

After walking for several miles, the forest sounds gave way to the laughter of children. Hearing Joy giggle made him wonder if she were not receiving the same treatment as he. With every step, little hands rubbed against his flesh. Somebody pinched his backside and he swatted at a hand. Who are these people? Haven't they ever seen a white man before?

The parade stopped, and someone yanked the hoods from their heads. They stood in the center of a host of tall, tan-skinned people dressed in rugged buck-skins. Their long dark hair braided or held back with a leather thong. A mixture of young and old gathered, pointing and jabbering.

Andorra, the leader of the hunting party stepped up to Timothy and pointed with his nose. "I am taking you into the meeting tent. This is where our tribe gathers to worship the King of Heaven, and it is where our leader, Nicholas the Wise, sits. You would do well to show him honor."

Timothy nodded, not knowing what to say.

"First, however, you must leave your spears and tomahawks with us."

Timothy swallowed and looked up. His primitive weapons would have been no match anyway. He shrugged and handed over his spear and tomahawk. Joy did the same. Then they followed Andorra to the center of the camp. Timothy raised his eyebrows at the sight of a large tent, covered in animal skins.

They neared the tent door, and the two armed guards crossed their spears, barring the entrance. The copper-toned men towered over Timothy by at least a foot. Each one stood, muscles taut, ready to strike.

Andorra saluted them and the two guards resumed their stance, eyes straight ahead. He pulled the flap back and nodded for them to go in. They stepped in and stood, waiting for their eyes to adjust. The yellowed light from old-fashioned oil lamps mingled with a thin haze from a small campfire, gave the interior a mystical appearance. Timothy took a deep breath and let it out slowly. The sweet scent of pine and hickory smoke filled the air. His eyes wandered as he trod upon the pelt covered floor. Located in small groupings were homemade wooden chairs and tables surrounded by pots of green foliage. It appeared that every attempt had been made to make the inside of the tent look as much like the outside as possible. "I feel like I've stepped back in time." Joy spoke in a low voice.

"Yeah, something from the 'Lord of the Rings,' or 'Narnia.'"

Chapter 15

Restricted District K29DC

Jamis guided Emma down the steps into the muddy road. He stopped and listened.

Pin-drop silence. "What's wrong?" Emma asked.

"Nothing, I thought I heard footsteps coming from inside that house." He held his position, his ear cocked. "There it goes again," he said as a foot crunched broken glass. He swirled around, spear at the ready. His mouth fell open and he dropped the spear in the mud. "Miss Xhu?" His voice cracked.

Emma took a quick gasp, turned, and ran up the steps. "Miss Xhu, how did you get here?" She sputtered.

Nguyen, too shocked to answer, caught herself on the door frame. Placing a hand on her forehead, she muttered, "I, I don't know. My hover-craft sprang a leak, and I called for a lift. This guy picked me up in his craft. He phased me and the next thing I knew, I was here. I can't believe it. I was standing in front of…" she let her voice trail off.

Emma, seeing her teacher teetering, caught her before her knees completely buckled. "Jamis, help me."

In an instant, he was by her side. "Here, take a seat," he said guiding her to the rocking chair. He found a large leaf, shaped it into a cup, brimming with rain water and offered it to her. "Here Miss Xhu, drink this," he said.

The cool water, mixed with the nutrients of the leaf revived her and within a few minutes, she sat up straight.

"You wouldn't believe what I've been through, even if I

told you." She blinked, her mind still not clear. "What are you two doing out here? I thought you, and your family, were going to Jerusalem," her eyes dancing between Emma and Jamis.

Tears welled up in Emma's eyes and cut rivulets through her smudged face. She'd been so busy trying to stay alive, she'd not had time to grieve the loss of her parents. She cupped her hands and buried her face, sobbing.

Jamis placed his hand on her shoulder and gave her a light squeeze. "That's all true," he paused, guilt, and grief pressing in on his heart. "But I was late, and we missed the caravan, and ..."

Nguyen's hand covered her mouth. "And you got caught in the open. What happened, did you get shot down?"

His eyes searched the floor. All he could do was nod; a tear scalded his cheek.

"Emma, where are your parents and brother and sister?" her voice rose with concern.

Jamis jammed his hands in his pockets. His head hung and spoke barely above a whisper. "Mr. and Mrs. Newton didn't make it. Their wounds were too serious. Timothy and Joy did, but we got separated when some men attacked us." His throat closed, and he pinched the tears from his eyes. "I blame myself for being late," he croaked.

Emma lifted her head, tears streamed down her cheeks. She swiped them from her swollen eyes and spoke softly, "Jamis, I already told you, you're forgiven."

"Yes, but I don't feel forgiven."

Something crashed deep within the forest, making Nguyen jump. "What was that?"

Emma took a ragged breath and gave her a weak smile, "Oh that, it's just some carnivorous creature hunting its next meal. You'll get used to it," she said as she stepped from the porch.

Overhead, strands of sunlight penetrated the canopy of trees. An assortment of birds called to one another and answered in a cacophony of sounds while insects buzzed through the air as if on some urgent mission.

"Maybe we should move before that thing thinks we're its dinner," she said, picking up her spear.

Jamis helped Nguyen to her feet. Emma tossed him his weapon and moved down the lane, without making a sound.

The road they'd been traveling soon narrowed as vines and bushes reclaimed their property. Once again, they were hacking through uncharted territory.

"I had no idea how much this place has changed," Nguyen said, eyes wide. "Look at the size of that pin-oak," she paused and craned her neck.

Emma caught her by the arm and kept moving. "If you think the trees are big, you should see the flesh eating plants."

"Yeah, not to mention the lizards that grew into monsters with voracious appetites," Jamis added.

Something snorted in the distance and they ducked into the underbrush.

"What are you giggling about M?"

She took a halting breath and covered her mouth. "For a moment, I thought it was you, Jamis."

"Me? I don't snore."

Emma resumed a measured pace, "Well if you don't, I'm a monkey's uncle, uh, aunt."

Jamis scratched his head thinking of a pithy come-back, but none came.

Miss Xhu watched them banter. "Don't tell me you two have been sleep…"

A chorus of 'No's' broke the humid air as both Emma and Jamis recoiled at the suggestion.

"Miss Xhu! How could you think such a thing, let alone

suggest it? I've made a commitment to the Lord to remain pure until marriage," Emma said, jaw resolute.

"Me too," Jamis chimed in.

Although Jamis liked her, and enjoyed her company he had never thought of Emma in that way. "You need to understand, Miss Xhu, we've been wandering around in this place for days. We're hungry, dirty, sweaty, and frankly, getting on each other's nerves," suppressing a light chuckle.

Emma's jaw dropped, "Oh really. I thought we were getting along quite nicely," she said, crossing her arms in mock offense.

"Yes, I can see you two have absolutely no interest in each other. I'm certainly glad we got that cleared up."

"You're right about one thing, Jamis."

"What's that?"

"I'm hungry … again."

"Come to think of it, so am I. Any hope of you sharing part of your energy bar?"

Emma cocked her head. "No way, if I'm so sweaty and dirty and getting on your nerves, why should I want to do that? Besides, we ate my only energy bar days ago."

Jamis' shoulders slumped, "Sorry, I meant nothing by it."

"You're forgiven, but you're right about another thing."

Jamis' eyes darted between the two women. "Oh? And that is?"

Emma grinned, "Your being sweaty. Stay behind us ladies." She turned and marched ahead.

They fought through the tangled jungle battling vines and swatting at hungry insects until they reached a clearing. Breathing heavily, Jamis flopped to the ground. "My feet are raw," he said looking at a freshly ripped blister.

Miss Xhu knelt down and found a small plant poking its head from under the leafy canopy. She snapped off a branch and handed it to Jamis. "Here, if that's what I think it is, it will get rid of the infection and sooth the wound."

He followed her instructions. "Wow, what is that? The pain is gone, and the redness is too."

"Aloe Vera, you can purchase it at any pharmacy," she said with a smile.

Jamis wrapped his foot in a large leaf and stood smiling, "feels like new."

A light wind blew and a piece of fruit fell, nearly hitting him on the head. He picked it up and inspected it. "Look M, there's fruit on this tree." He snatched another golden ball from a branch, peeled back its outer skin and bit. "Man, that's good. You should try one."

"Okay, but I don't want to bite into a worm or something."

Emma pulled off one, handed it to Miss Xhu, then sank her teeth into hers. Her eyes flooded, and she began sputtering.

"Jamis, this is as bitter as a persimmon."

He slapped his knee, laughing. Emma threw the half-eaten fruit at him, barely missing. He ducked and took off in a run. Emma close on his heels, calling his name.

He dashed through the underbrush, leaping over stumps and weaving around thorn bushes. A moment later, he stopped, arms swinging wildly to keep his balance. Emma, not seeing him stop, bowled him over, and they tumbled down a grassy slope. Miss Xhu, hearing her screams, climbed to the edge and peered down.

Emma lay. Her legs tangled in his, "Jamis, why did you stop?"

"Just before you ran me over, I thought I saw a city or something."

Emma jumped to her feet and scampered back up the

hill. Nguyen stood, scanning the horizon, hand over her eyebrows.

"What is it? Do you think it's a population center?" excitement filled her voice.

"No, but it does look like a city or town up ahead," Miss Xhu said, "but don't get your hopes too high, it could be one of the Forbidden Cities the authorities warned us about."

Jamis stood, brushed off his backside, came up and peered in the direction of their gaze. "It's at least a day's journey. But I'd like to check it out."

"I sure hope we don't run into anymore of those soldiers."

Miss Xhu's eyes widened. "Soldiers?"

"I'll tell you about it on the way," Emma said over her shoulder.

By night fall they'd passed the outer limits of the city. Jamis stopped, his shoulders slumped.

"This is not just any Forbidden City."

Chapter 16

The Meeting Tent

Andorra stepped into the Meeting Tent and approached the throne upon which Nicholas the Wise rested. The carved structure was a study in simplicity and beauty. He crossed his right hand over his chest, fist closed and bowed on one knee. "My lord, we have ... visitors," he said looking over his shoulder.

The chief lifted his gaze. Two grey eyes stabbed Timothy, searching, probing, questioning. His white hair parted in the middle, hung past his shoulders. With each breath, the muscles of his bare chest rippled in rhythmic motion. A large scar, still visible on his immortal body, glowed pink from where he'd entered the realm of the eternal. As a member of the ruling class, he once lived in the third century. Now, for the last ten centuries, he'd governed the Forest Saints, guarding the domain allotted him and his people. To enter his forest without his permission was to do so at their peril. A gold-domed staff stood constant vigil, resting comfortably in his right hand. He lifted it and motioned for his guest to approach. "Who is this that dares violate our sacred lands and thinks to discover our resting places?" His voice firm yet played on his lips like a winsome spirit. "Come, stand in the light."

Andorra stood, moved to the side, a small device in his hand.

Timothy looked at Joy, not sure what to do. She took him by the hand, "It's okay Timmy, he reminds me of great, great Grandpa Newton."

She stepped forward and did a quick curtsy. "Sorry mister for cutting through your woods, but we had no choice," her pudgy hands outstretched. "We were being chased by some men with guns and then by hungry animals."

A half smile crinkled the old chief's weathered face.

Timothy knelt, every muscle quivering.

"Not since the days of my sojourn have I seen such garments. I had no idea they would come back into style," he said, scanning the two youths. "Although yours look a little worse for wear," he gestured, "Now rise to your feet and speak, for you are guilty of crimes again the Kingdom."

Timothy repeated his sister's reasons for entering the forest. Nicholas listened attentively.

"So you say your parents died in the crash, and you were chased by men with weapons. How many men were there?"

Timothy did some quick calculations, "I counted about ten in the hunting party. Two of them chased my sister and me. The others chased the rest of my family," he replied.

"How many of your family survived the crash?"

"Four sir, my two sisters, and a young man named Jamis. My older sister's name is Emma, and this is Joy, We have not seen the other two since we got separated several days ago."

Nicolas stroked his chin, "Our scouts have been tracking a couple fitting your description, but they have not violated our forest. If they do, we will have to deal with them as we have you."

Andorra stepped up beside Timothy. "May I speak, my lord?"

The elderly chief shifted his gaze. "Yes Andorra, you may."

"As you were questioning our guests, I did some research in the archives of the ancient books of families. I found the name Newton is an honorable one that dates back before the millennium began. If my research is correct, their septillion grandfather was responsible for the defeat of the great enemy."

The chief's burly white eyebrows knit into a question, "Is this so? Are you the great great-grandchildren of Chase Newton?"

He took a quick breath. "Yes sir, we are, and we are also followers of the Lamb," he answered, his chest swelling with pride.

The lines in the old chief's face softened. "Well then, that is good news indeed. You are our honored guests. This calls for a celebration." He clapped his hands and called for his minister.

"Arthures, please see to it that our new friends have everything they need, provide them with new garments, food, clean water and a place to rest. Tomorrow we will have a great banquet and toast Mr. Timothy and Miss Joy."

The two young people looked at each other, eyes wide with excitement. Arthures took his place next to Timothy. "This way."

They stepped from the meeting tent, into the greenish light of the forest. As he followed Arthures, he couldn't help but notice all the people going about their daily routine. Women knelt around small fires, stirring pots of aromatic stew, hunting parties stalking through the camp, some coming in, and others going back, children playing kick-ball, while the older young people tossed a ball and struck at it with a heavy club.

An elderly woman approached them baring a tray. Steam rose from two bowls of aromatic stew like welcoming spirits. She set the tray on a hand-hewn table. With a quick nod from Arthures, she bowed and disappeared into the shadows.

"I trust this will hold you until morning," he said.

The aroma of the still boiling stew mingled with the

night air, made Timothy's stomach growl. Arthures smiled.

"I trust you will find these accommodations to your liking," he said pulling back the tent flap. "Now get some rest. If you need anything, let me know. I have also left you with a change of clothes." Scanning their tattered garments, he added, "Those togas didn't hold up very well in the forest. These will be much more appropriate to wear on your quest," he said.

Timothy bowed his head and said a quick prayer. "I was hoping I'd get something to eat before going to bed," Joy said, a smudge of dark broth dripped from her chin. Timothy wiped it off with his thumb, and smiled. "You'd better slow down or you'll be wanting mine," eying her nearly empty bowl. "This is the best bread I've ever had," she said between bites. Timothy nodded and allowed the warm liquid to warm his insides. "I think we'll sleep a lot better now that we've had a decent meal."

One single ray penetrated a small opening in the tent where Timothy lay sleeping, and struck him in the eyes. He groaned and pulled the heavy woolen blanket over his head. A ball struck the side of his tent followed by childish giggling, and he knew his night's sleep was over. He threw the covers off, sat up and looked around. Joy's bed roll was empty. By the sound of her laughter, he knew where she was…playing. "Man am I hungry, what is it that smells so good?"

He quickly dressed and stepped from his tent into the defused light of the forest. The crisp morning air mingled with hickory smoke and greeted his first breath. He ran his hand over his arm to brush away the goose-bumps. Returning, he grabbed a blanket and threw it over his shoulders. *Now to find the source of that aroma.* He thought.

The camp was a bustle of activity. All around were

small fires tended by women in long leather skirts. Columns of smoke arose and gathered among the trees above as others prepared for the feast. Loaves of hot bread steamed in the morning air while bacon simmered on iron skillets and formed a delightful offering for his palette. A group of men assembled in the center of camp and began hoisting ropes and propping up the side of a large colorful canopy. Others brought in tables and chairs. Musicians with stringed instruments assembled and began tuning. Soon the camp was ringing with music and laughter.

"Good morning, Mr. Newton," Arthures said. He handed Timothy a mug of black coffee and a slice of bread.

"We have butter, honey, and an assortment of jellies over there," he nodded in the direction of a large table. "Come with me, I'll show you around."

Timothy tore a piece off and popped it into his mouth. "Man, this is wonderful. I could eat a ton of that."

He took a swig of the hot brew and washed it down. The heat radiated through his body and warmed him to the core. They reached the center of camp and found a buffet table filled with a variety of fruits, berries and meats.

Timothy scanned the table eager to satisfy his gnawing stomach. "Thanks, but you shouldn't have done this for just me."

Arthures smiled and picked up a slice of ham. "You're welcome. We didn't. This is what we do every morning. The good Lord supplies us with all the best food in the forest. All we need to do is gather it in. We all share his blessings."

Timothy was taken aback; this would make any chef proud. He spent the morning eating and talking with the few who remembered the English language. By mid-afternoon he had a group of children at his feet teaching them. The children eagerly picked up on it, and soon he was surrounded by a gaggle of youngsters all trying their new skills on him.

Later, a blast from a ram's horn signaled the start of the festivities. Chief Nickolas, the Wise, gathered people in the center of camp, lifted his arms to the air and said, "Blessed art thou, O, Lord, ruler of Heaven and Earth, who giveth us the good things of the earth and sky to enjoy. Blessed is your kingdom and those you gladly serve you. May the knowledge of your glorious majesty fill the earth. Bless this feast from whose hand we have received it, in the name of our great king Jesus Christ, amen."

The assembly joined in a song of praise, which ended in, "Amen."

"Mr. Timothy, would you and Miss Joy sit with me at my table?" the chief asked, his hand beckoning.

Timothy's pulse quickened at such a request. He'd never eaten with anyone of such importance. The eyes of those sitting around the table pressed in upon him. Sheepishly, he nodded much to the delight of the chief.

As they sat and ate, Chief Nickolas leaned his elbows on the table and drew Timothy into his confidence. "Tell me Mr. Timothy, is it true? Is the millennium coming to an end?"

Timothy's mind raced for a cogent thought. "I, I don't know sir. I haven't been paying much attention to the political scene."

The chief sat back and rubbed his chin.

"I have. My scouts inform me of an evil shadow covering the earth."

Timothy sat up straight and looked into the chief's eyes. They were tender, inviting. "One thing is happening, which might be of interest to you, sir."

"Yes, my son. What is this new thing, you speak of?"

Timothy cleared his throat, hoping he could deliver on the expectation he engendered.

"The Solar-link, it's a way for us to communicate and broadcast messages throughout our galaxy."

The wise, old chief nodded, following his every word with keen eyes.

"Well, there is a man."

"A man?" he repeated.

"Yes, his name is Professor Christos; he went on the Solar-link a few weeks ago and was saying the most outrageous things."

"Oh? How so?" stroking his chin.

"Yes sir. He spoke against the Kingdom and called for a universal work stoppage. He said he wanted the people of the earth to unite and take dominion of the earth, which he claims belongs to us in the first place."

Chief Nicholas sat back, his eyes on a distant object. "It is as the ancient writing said. The end of days is upon us."

The chief arose and motioned for his councilors to assemble in the meeting tent. "We will speak no more of these things," he said, the lines of his face deepening.

After the meal, Timothy found Arthures sitting around a blazing fire, in animated conversation. "Arthures, I am worried about our family, is there any word as to their whereabouts?"

Arthures took a swig of coffee from a clay mug and wiped his mouth. "Our scouts followed them as far as the Forbidden City. We are prohibited from going anywhere near that evil place. Once they entered the city limits our scouts returned."

Timothy placed his hand on his forearm, "Sir, we must find them and return to Providence Population Center; that's where we came from," he pleaded.

"You are safe as long as you stay here, you are welcome to remain with us as long as you like. Why would you want to risk your lives searching for those who are lost within the Forbidden City? There are things living in that place which are too evil to speak of, they won't last a day."

Timothy kicked an unsuspecting twig into the fire and swallowed the lump in his throat, "Sir, they are our family. If there is any way to help them, we must try. You would do no less for yours. Will you guide us?"

Arthures mused for a moment, then returned his gaze with a slow nod, "I will ask Nicholas, the Wise. If he agrees, we will prepare you for the journey. However, we can only guide you as far as the outer limit of the forest and no further. Even there it is risking our safety."

The feast continued throughout the night as the music and dancing occupied their attention. Joy laughed and clapped her hand with glee as she watched other children parade the center area dressed in colorful feather covered costumes. Following the parade, they cleared tables and the music changed. Couples began pairing off and dancing.

Timothy stood, tapping his foot to the rhythm of the drum, watching the festivities when someone tapped him on the shoulder.

"Would you join me for the next dance?"

A portly, round faced girl stood waiting for his answer. Timothy knew he had no choice but to acquiesce. He nodded, and she led him to the center of the dance floor.

Dust swirled as his feet scuffed the ground, while the young lady daftly took him through a routine she'd known since childhood. Joy giggled watching her brother's clumsy attempt at dancing.

"I'm sorry for stepping on your feet, miss?" He said with a sheepish grin.

She smiled and glanced down at the top of her foot, now smudged with dirt. "That's okay. You may call me Rose. I am Andorra's daughter." She paused and bit her lip. "I wish you to stay."

Timothy got the picture pretty quick. *Yeah, and marry you and live happily ever after,* he thought.

"Look miss, I think you're nice and all, but my sister is lost in the Forbidden City. I must find her."

Rose's face clouded, "You are very brave, you will make a good husband."

Yes, but not yours, his mind raced.

"Uh, Miss Rose, it's getting late. Would you excuse me? I must check on my sister."

Reluctantly, she released her grip on his shoulder, and he disappeared into the crowd. After searching, he found Joy curled up in a circle on one of the women's laps.

"She's had a long day. I found her asleep under the table." The motherly woman said, her fingers stroking Joy's golden hair. The woman leaned her head up, a question shaped her face. "Sir, I'd like to ask a favor of you?"

Timothy's eyes widened with interest. "Yes? What is it?"

The woman lowered her eyes and searched the ground. "May I have a few strands of her hair?"

Taken aback by the unusual request, Timothy inhaled, and exhaled slowly. "I, I guess it would be alright." He answered, with caution.

The woman smiled and lifted her hand. Clinging to each finger were dozens of golden strands. She gathered them together and tied them with a ribbon which she'd laid aside for such an occasion.

"I will cherish this and pray for you every time I see them."

Grateful for the prayer support, Timothy thanked the motherly woman, gathered his sister in his arms and trudged to their tent. His mind locked with concern.

What is it about Professor Christos that upset the chief so much?

Chapter 17

The Forbidden City

In the distance, a dying beast moaned, while high above in the cloudless sky circled a flock of vultures, waiting. The constant drift of acrid smoke from the volcano filled the air, bathing splintered trees and broken rocks in an unholy layer of grey ash.

"I feel like we've just stepped back in time," Jamis said.

Emma and Miss Xhu climbed up next to him and stared at the jagged landscape.

"What is this place?" asked Emma, dread building in her voice.

"This is the Cursed City called Washington D.C. It is a dangerous place," he explained.

Emma shaded her eyes, following his gaze. "Why? Jamis, what makes it so dangerous?"

At her raised eyebrows and obvious curiosity, he bit back a grin.

"They say that the spirits of politicians still roam the halls of Congress trying to raise taxes."

Emma gasped, her hand over her mouth.

Jamis burst out in laughter as he watched Emma's face.

She punched him in the shoulder. "Very funny, Jamis, very funny. I think you should run for office," she said.

Nguyen grinned at Jamis' pun. "Maybe we should find a safe place around here to sleep tonight. I wouldn't want to set foot in there after dark," she said, eying the jagged horizon.

Emma nodded, "I'd rather not go there at all, if you ask me."

A moment past as a stray cloud drifted over the broken city, giving it an ominous appearance. "If my geography is correct, that city lies directly between us and New Birth. In order to reach our destination, we'll need to get through it," Miss Xhu observed.

Jamis scouted around and found the remains of a block building. A light wind whistled through the broken panes and a loose piece of siding beat an uneven cadence. Vines shrouded the doorway like a beaded curtain. Jamis parted them and stepped out of sight. Within the crumbling structure, lay a menagerie of rotting and smashed furniture. Each step brought a new chorus of crunching glass and scraping metal as Jamis pushed in deeper. Above him, cobwebs rocked back and forth by an unseen hand like tattered sails on an old pirate ship. The pungent smell of mold attacked his nostrils causing him to sneeze. *I hate the smell of mold,* he thought.

Sheepishly, Emma and Miss Xhu crept in. "Do you think it's safe?" quizzeled Emma, eying the sagging ceiling.

Jamis glanced over his shoulder. "It's way safer than out there," he nodded to the door.

After clearing a space in the center of the room, he scooped up a hand full of twigs and piled them in the shape of a tee-pee.

"How are you going to start a fire, Jamis?" Emma asked, doubt tingeing her voice.

Lifting his head, he cocked an eyebrow. "If I strike these two rocks against each other, I think I can get a fire started," he pushed a weak smile past his frustration.

The air scintillated with tension as each attempt failed. Jamis let out a mumbled curse and tried once more. With a crack, a spark shot from the blow and landed on a thin twig.

Jamis shielded the infant flame with the palms of his hands like a hen guarding her brood. The spark leapt from leaf to leaf.

Whoosh!

The flame spread throughout the kindling. Within minutes the three gathered around a roaring fire. Jamis stood back, arms crossed, a smug look on his face.

"Don't gloat," Emma chided.

"What?"

Amid dancing shadows and unearthly sounds, the three prepared for the night. Emma and Miss Xhu made a pile out of pine needles, leaned against each other and fell asleep. Jamis tossed another log on the fire, sending embers in the air like resurrected souls. He settled down on a bed of leaves and watched the cool, deep, star-lit sky pass in review.

After a long night's vigil, Jamis breathed a sigh of relief when the first hues of sunlight streaked across the sky. An hour later, the sun broke through the trees sending shafts of light through the decaying roof. He stood and stretched stifling a yawning, then stepped into the morning air. Outside, the unfamiliar terrain looked far different from the shaded woods of the previous night. Columns of condensation appeared and dissipated with every breath as he took a brief walk in search of food.

Finding a blackberry bush, he gathered as many as he dared and returned with his bounty. He found Emma and Miss Xhu standing, picking pine needles from their hair. A large red spot glowed on Emma's cheek, marking the place where her head rested on her elbow.

"Morning," Jamis grunted, and poured the berries on a large elephant leaf.

Emma rubbed the sleep from her eyes, "What's so good about it?"

He blew a few more times, and a flame jumped to life, he added a hand full of twigs and cocked an eye. "I didn't say good morning, I just said 'morning.'"

Mindlessly, she stared into the young fire, "My mouth feels like it's full of rocks."

Miss Xhu picked up a few sticks and tossed them on the fire. "What I'd do for a steaming hot shower."

Jamis stood, "I understand they have rooms available at the Waverly." A wry smile tugged at the corners of his lips.

The women returned a blank look, not knowing if he was kidding or not.

After a scant breakfast of berries and leaves, the three set out on their journey. They approached a narrow bridge, covered with thick vines. Part of it had collapsed and the only way across was to crawl over a network of tangled vines.

"How about I go first," volunteered Nguyen, being the lighter of the three.

Nimble as a cat, she traversed the dangerous gap while Emma held her breath. Still breathing hard, Miss Xhu stood and waved Emma across. "Okay, I made it, but you must be extremely careful in the center," she said in a cautious tone.

Emma followed her teacher's instructions, and carefully picked her way across.

Snap! A vine broke and Emma disappeared.

"Help!" she cried, her feet kicking wildly.

"M, hold still, I'm coming." Like a man walking a tightrope, Jamis scaled the mesh bridge and found Emma hanging by a thin vine.

"Hurry, I don't know how much longer I can hold on."

A moment later, the vine stretched, sending her another foot down. White knuckled, she clung on, her cries for help being drowned out by the thundering rapids, which cascaded over jagged rocks.

Jamis laid down and distributed his weight as evenly as possible. Locking one leg through a thick vine for support, he reached down. The spray from the rapids slicked his arms and face, partially blinding him. Cautiously, he willed himself forward as far as he dared. Like a vice-grip, his hand closed around her thin wrist and held. Every muscle screamed in pain as he strained to lift her up. The sickening sound of tearing quickened his already pounding heart. With one final surge of energy, he pulled.

"Hold still," he said, through clenched teeth. Grabbing hold of a stout vine, he hoisted her through the hole. Then placed her on his shoulders like a sack of potatoes and carried her to the other side. He set her down and collapsed, exhausted.

Miss Xhu rushed to her side. "Honey, are you alright?" her forehead, a mesh of concern.

Emma blinked and wiped the moisture from her face. "I, I think so." Her words came between gulps. Her body began to tremble as the rush of adrenalin surged through her veins. Miss Xhu enfolded her until the tremors subsided.

A few minutes passed in silence while the three caught their breath. Finally, Emma sat up, tears of joy and gratitude glistened down her cheeks. She brushed herself off, with a smile. "Jamis, I don't know how to thank you," her voice soft as the whispered breeze.

He leaned on his elbow; a grin parted his lips, exposing a set of perfectly white teeth. "Well, I could suggest a few." His dimpled chin moved with expectation.

Emma rolled her eyes and stood, "Men," she said, glancing at Miss Xhu. "I was speaking metaphorically."

In a fit of laugher, Jamis sat upright holding his stomach. "I was just kidding."

She eyed him in mock disgust, "Yeah, right. But thanks anyway." Looking into the abyss, she paused thoughtfully, "I think I dropped my spear."

Jamis shrugged his shoulders, "So did I. I certainly hope we don't run into anyone, or we're in big trouble."

Miss Xhu eyed them, a smile parting her lips.

"What?" Emma asked.

"Oh, nothing."

To Jamis, the passage of time was not in minutes or days, but in seasons. He eyed the riddled buildings in the near distance. They offered no comfort, no relief, no hope to the weary trio.

Standing over him, Emma stretched her hand out. Jamis accepted the proffered help and stood to his feet.

Clutching her hand, they climbed up the embankment and entered the city.

"This place gives me the creeps," offered Emma, clinging close to Jamis.

Miss Xhu paused, "You think it's scary now, just imagine what it must have been like when it was populated with unregenerate people bearing the mark of the beast."

"It is no wonder why God dealt so severely with this city. I'm surprised there's even one building standing at all," Emma said.

They neared a domed structure covered with overgrowth. Inside the column lined building sat the statue of a man. So thorough was the covering of vines that he appeared to Emma as a high priest or pope robed in full regalia.

"If I didn't know better, I'd have thought he was some sort of green ghost," Jamis said pointing at the sleeping giant.

"Look at how thick the vines are covering the steps leading all the way up to this man. Who is he anyway?" Jamis asked.

"I don't know, do you Miss Xhu?"

Nguyen stepped up next to them. "Yes, I do. This is a monument to one of the greatest men of the nineteenth century. His name is Abraham Lincoln."

Emma crossed her arms around her waist. "Why is it that I have a strange feeling I've been here before?"

Nguyen's eyes narrowed and cut to her left, her breath caught in her throat.

Minutes passed in silence as they gazed at the gentle giant. Finally, Emma broke the spell, "Why was he honored?"

Miss Xhu placed her hands behind her back and rocked on her heels, "Mr. Lincoln was a very godly man during a very godless time."

"Why, what was happening?" Jamis asked.

Clearing her throat, Miss Xhu continued her impromptu lesson. "The nation was engaged in a great struggle. Brother fought against brother; thousands of people died over the right of one man to own another," she explained.

"Who won?" Jamis asked.

"The nation was divided, north against the south. Mr. Lincoln was a praying man. God heard his prayers and gave the north the victory. He preserved the union and set the slaves free." She smiled at Emma. "He's my favorite historical figure of all time."

Jamis lifted a hand, "Uh, Miss Xhu, is this going to be on the exam?"

A gentle laugh bubbled up and she smiled. "Yes, Jamis, since you mentioned it. I think I'll include our little excursion into Washington D.C. on the exam."

Emma rolled her eyes and punched Jamis in the ribs.

101

"Oh brother, why'd you have to ask?"

He lifted his palms in surrender. "What?"

They pressed in deeper past the Washington Memorial. Long ago, it had toppled into the reflection pool. All that remained was a pool of sludge.

Turning left, they approached a wide area which appeared to be the cross-roads of two highways. Large oak trees violated the concrete, pushing their upper limbs heavenward. A flock of birds taking refuge in branches ceased their conversations at the entrance of the visitors.

"Where are we anyway?" asked Emma, eyes wide with wonder.

Nguyen knelt and lifted a rusted sign. "This is Constitution Avenue; over there is the Capitol building, or at least, what's left of it." Her legs straightened and she pointed to a few broken columns. "That use to be the Congress building."

High above them, circled a flock of winged creatures. Orifiel and his platoon of angels kept a constant vigil over their charges. With a quick, nod he dispatched a squad to investigate a cloud of dust which rose in the distance.

Emma scanned the scene. "It looks like something you'd expect to see in Rome or Greece."

Nguyen nodded. "Yes, only the destruction was much worse.'"

"Why's that, Miss Xhu?" asked Jamis.

Nguyen took a breath and let it out slowly. "The ancient writing tells us, "To whom much is given, from him much is required and to whom much had been committed, of him, they ask even more. America was the greatest nation on the face of the earth, yet she fell into decadence and greed. She got proud thinking she didn't need God. Remember what I said, 'I was there.'"

Jamis stepped into the clearing and scanned the scene.

"I'm beginning to get the picture."

For the next hour, they climbed over a menagerie of obstacles, stopping occasionally to listen for any intruders. Finally, exhausted, and needing water, they paused to take a break.

"What's that building?" asked Jamis, looking at a long row of structures.

Miss Xhu climbed to top of a pile of rubble, squinted in thought. "It was the Smithsonian Institute."

Joining her, Jamis shaded his eyes. "I remember studying about them. Weren't they a series of buildings housing the important inventions and discoveries from the past?"

Nguyen nodded. "You're right. They had every kind of marvel categorized and identified. Now it's all gone. What wasn't looted was burnt, and what was left was picked clean by the relic hunters."

A glint of sunlight reflected catching Jamis' attention. He jumped on a vine covered hump. "Look, I think I see a—"

Thud!

He disappeared. Like a giant spider web, vines encased him in the shell of an abandoned taxi. He cursed himself for being so stupid. He hated to embarrass himself in front of women, especially one. Grabbing a stout vine, he pulled himself out. Like some unearthly creature, he emerged from his tomb, covered with a new layer of scratches, rust, and cobwebs.

Reclaiming his position, he pointed, "M, Miss Xhu, over there. I think I see an old hover-craft."

He reached out and helped Miss Xhu up next to him. She clung to his arm trying to get a better look. Emma glanced at the two of them, clearly irritated.

He jumped to the ground and fought his way closer. "By the look of it, this thing's been here for some time."

"Yeah, vines are all over it. Do you think it is in flying

condition?" Nguyen said, unaware of Emma's cold stare.

"I don't know. Someone must have come here and never left." Miss Xhu spoke with renewed animation.

Feeling left out, Emma threw her hands in the air and pressed closer. "I thought it was against the law to come to the Forbidden Cities and search for relics."

Nguyen leaped to the ground and caught up to Jamis. "It is, but in the last few years, people started doing what they pleased and disregarded the authorities."

They neared the craft and began inspecting it. Jamis pulled off a hand full of vines and wiped away a layer of dirt from its surface.

"Woe, would you get a load of this," he exclaimed, rubbing his hands along the Cobalt Zircon skin.

"Well, it doesn't seem like whoever came here is coming back. Let's say we borrow it," Emma said, looking at Jamis. "It's not like you've never done that before." Her voice carried an edge.

Jamis' face darkened. "Don't remind me. If Nguyen uh, Miss Xhu had not gone to bat for me, I'd be on some chain gang on Alpha Centauri cracking rocks."

"It would have served you right," Emma half kidded.

Jamis' hands rose in mock surrender. "Hey, I saved you from being incinerated, didn't I?"

She shrugged and returned his smile. She couldn't stay mad at Jamis for very long. "Yeah, I suppose you're right. I can't imagine you swinging a sledge hammer anyway."

The two women gawked at each other, giggling.

"Don't laugh, it's not funny. I have a mark on my record for being a hover-craft thief."

Crunch! A heavy boot crushed gravel.

"What was th—" his statement was cut off with a wave.

"Shush." Nguyen held her hand up. "I think I heard something."

The three crouched behind the leafy hover-craft.

Jamis peeked up and caught a glimpse of movement followed by voices.

"What was it?" Emma asked in a whisper.

"I'm not sure, and I certainly don't want to find out, let's get a move on," Jamis said. With urgency, he began pulling off the vines.

The voices drew closer.

"I don't think they're the welcome committee," he whispered. "Get in."

"But we're not finished," Nguyen said, fear etching her voice.

"If we don't get out of here in a minute, we'll all be finished. Now help M get in." His voice carried authority.

They quickly climbed in, and Emma slapped the button to close the door. Jamis skipped through the pre-flight steps, as the engines whined to a start.

The team of para-military soldiers began running in their direction.

"Hurry Jamis, they're coming," Emma said, eyes wide with fear.

"Please select your destina—" the automated voice commanded.

"Jamis, hit the lift button," Nguyen screamed.

He did so and the jets roared to life.

"Please wait for maximum thrust capability," again the computer warned.

"She's not lifting," Jamis said, fighting with the controls.

"Hit the jet infuser," Emma hollered, pointing at a green button."

Jamis' fingers trembled as he reached for the button. An instant later the hover-craft rocked to its side. "I think we've been hit."

"Nope, the impulse round missed by inches. But they won't miss the next time." Emma said.

Seeing Jamis struggling, she reached up and punched the infuser button. The hover-craft lurched forward, jets screaming. Vines snapped, and it shot from its cocoon before the men could fire again.

Jamis sat, white knuckled, holding the manual override directional fork. He yanked back and zigzagged as a red hot missile whizzed past within feet.

"That was close," he said over the roar of the jets.

"Too close," the women agreed in unison.

Emma hung on to the hand grips as Jamis accelerated into the thinning atmosphere. Within a minute, they were out of danger, and she relaxed her grip slightly.

"Please select a destination," again the computer prompted.

Jamis smiled, "Providence Population Center."

Emma stared down at Washington D.C. as its crater pocked landscape disappeared in the background. Its images seared into her memory.

Chapter 18

The Forest Saint's Camp

    Timothy knelt down on the pelt covered floor of their tent and laid Joy in bed. She stirred.
    "Oh, I'm sorry sweetie, go back to sleep." He pulled the covers up and tucked them around her. Then leaned over and placed a kiss on her forehead. Suddenly, the image of his father flooded his mind. Memories long banished scraped at his memory with claw-like tenacity. The impact of the moment struck him like a kick to the gut. His lungs constricted, and a wall of emotions broke. Burying his face in his hands, he wept bitterly. "Oh, God, why did you let this happen?" He listened for an answer. None came to salve his shredded spirit.
    All he heard was the rhythmic breathing of his sister.
    Outside, someone cleared their throat. He pushed himself from the ground, brushed the tears aside and opened the flap.
    "You have many burdens to bear my friend, some too heavy for one man," said Arthures, eyes warm with concern.
    Timothy shrugged, not wanting to make eye contact. "I'd rather not talk about it." He took a halting breath and looked up. "Any word about finding my family?"
    With a slow nod, Arthures stepped back, and let the tent flap close. "Yes, I have a message from Andorra."
    Seeing his concern, Timothy braced himself. "I'm listening."
    "We can escort you and your sister as far as the outer

limits of the forest, but no further. After that, you're on your own. However, if you are interested, we have some ancient weapons left from the latter years. We have no use for such, but if you think you could use them, then they are yours."

Timothy left his sister sleeping under the watchful care of the motherly woman and followed his friend to a cave. Overgrown with vines that hung like witch's hair, the entrance to the cave was obscured from all passers-by. Arthures pulled the curtain aside and slipped from sight. Immediately, the temperature adjusted to a moderate sixty degrees, yet the chilled air chased Timothy's body heat away. With a small candle as the only illumination, Arthures lit a torch and led Timothy deeper into the passage. At intervals of twenty paces, he stopped to ignite a row of torches until the corridor was bathed in amber tones. As they descended into the bowels of the earth, his warm breath came in short wisps like wanton spirits. The cold air bit through Timothy's exposed flesh sending chills rippling across his skin.

The musty, stagnant air assaulted Timothy's olfactory glands, and he sneezed. "What is that smell?" Timothy asked wiping his eyes.

Arthures sniffed the air. "I don't smell anything."

Timothy shook his head in unbelief.

Their measured pace ceased, and they faced a door embedded in rock ... its only defense, were layers of cob-webs. Arthures brushed them aside revealing a shiny metallic surface which glittered in the flickering torch light.

"Here, hold this," he said handing Timothy his torch.

With spider like movements, his fingers punched in a series of numbers into a panel. Timothy heard a soft snap, and the door popped open. He pulled the handle, and a swirl of dust rose in protest as the door swung silently in a wide arch. They stepped into the blackness, triggering an unseen sensor. The silent darkness yielded to the growing light, and soon the room glowed with a soft florescence.

Lining the rock walls from the ceiling to the smooth hand-hewn floor were glass cases containing weapons dating back to the twentieth and twenty-first centuries.

"This place is amazing!" Timothy said, his eyes wide with excitement. He felt like a kid in a candy shop, as he roamed the vault. Leaving steaming finger prints on the glass enclosures, he admired the weapons with interest. Many of them lay in rusted repose, the result of time and moisture, still others held out offerings of hope.

"Could I take a closer look at that one?" he asked as if he were in a gun shop and Arthures, a salesman. As a younger boy, Timothy was quite intrigued with the guns from the past and had a working knowledge of many of them.

He picked up an AK47 and checked its action. The simplicity of its construction and the durability of the weapon amazed him.

"Does this gun come with any ammo?"

"What is ammo?" Arthures asked.

"Ammo is ... um ..." He paused to think of the right word. "Ammo is like the tips of your arrows, only they don't have the wooden shafts and feathers."

Arthures nodded absently. "I think we have what you seek. Follow me." He lifted the torch and stepped into another room. Lying scattered throughout the vault was a cache of crates marked 'Ammunition.'

Timothy rooted around until he found the one he was looking for. "Would it be permissible with Nickolas the Wise if I shot the weapons to see it they work?"

A knowing smile parted Arthures' lips and he patted Timothy on the shoulder. "Our leader anticipated your question, and knew you would want to try them out. He has granted me, and a small hunting party, permission to take you to where we teach our young men the art of archery."

On the way out, Timothy grabbed a Rugar 9mm, a shoulder holster and several magazines.

They re-emerged from the cave, and Timothy straightened his back. "Could we meet after the morning meal and try them out?" Timothy asked, anxious as a kid on Christmas Eve.

Arthures glanced through the barren limbs. Reflected light for the sentinel of the night shimmered through the trees. "I'll see you at first light."

As Timothy turned, Arthures placed a calloused hand on his forearm. "I saw you dancing with Rose," a wry smile played on his lips.

"Yes, is that important?"

"Andorra is a very powerful man. You would do well to consider that."

Like a child waiting for Christmas morning, Timothy spent the night counting the hours. Between Joy's rhythmic breathing, the constant dripping of condensation off the sides of the tent and his dreams of squeezing the trigger, the notion of sleep eluded him. Finally, he threw off the covers, dressed and stepped from the tent. The crisp night air pricked his lungs like a thousand needles as steam ascended from his warm body.

An eerie silence shrouded the campsite, filling his soul with a sense of loneliness. He missed Emma; he missed his parents, and though he still was angry at Jamis, in some twisted way, he missed him too. Pairs of guards moved stealthily around the perimeter, while a couple of men warmed themselves at a blazing fire. Timothy gathered his cloak tighter around his body and stepped into its amber glow.

"Couldn't sleep?" inquired one guard, a tall lanky man with deep-set eyes.

Without speaking, Timothy gave a slow nod and stretched his hands toward the fire. Flames licked at each log like a dog licking on a bone. Beneath the blaze, a bed of embers breathed orange and pulsated with demonic cadence.

The uncounted moments passed, and suddenly, Arthures emerged from the darkness as silent as death. Handing him a ceramic mug of steaming coffee, he gave Timothy a wry smile.

Timothy received the proffered mug, took a swig and let its warmth radiate throughout his inner being. "Couldn't sleep either?"

He shrugged his shoulders and returned a sheepish grin. "It is like this before every great hunt."

"Where did you get this?" Timothy asked after gulping down the last of the brew. "This is better than anything I've ever had?"

Arthures took another sip and looked over the rim of his mug. "We grow it."

A pleasant moment passed as each man fell silent, lost to their thoughts.

By the time they finished their second mug, the tips of the trees played catch with the earliest rays of golden sunlight.

The shadowed forms of women began moving throughout the camp as if by some unheard signal. Soon the camp was abuzz with preparations for the morning meal. The aroma of baking bread mingled with sizzling bacon and frying eggs. Timothy's stomach gnawed at him while he waited. His patience was rewarded by Rose as she emerged through the haze with a large tray of pastry, eggs, grits and an assortment of fruit.

"I make it specially for you." An eager smile played on her lips.

Timothy's heart palpitated, but not for the reasons the gawking onlookers thought.

He swallowed hard and eked out a shaky, "thank you."

She bowed slightly and backed away, keeping an affectionate eye on him. He felt as if he were eating the Last Supper. Reluctantly, he set the tray on his lap and scarfed down the steaming breakfast.

He cut his eyes in Arthures' direction. He stood, arms crossed, chuckling.

"What are you laughing at?" Timothy said with chagrin.

Arthures wiped the smile from his face, and laid aside his plate. "After you," he said, and led Timothy and a small hunting party away from the warmth of Rose and the fire.

A well-worn path led out of camp and took a circuitous route through a wooded valley and into an abandoned canyon. The young men set up a number of targets on distant logs, returned and waited. Timothy slapped the magazine into the Rugar, charged the weapon and extended his arms. With steady pressure, he squeezed off several rounds, and turned to Arthures, ears ringing.

"Good shooting, we could use another sharp-shooter."

Timothy ground his teeth. A dozen thoughts converged in his mind, but he resisted the urge to speak. He holstered the hand gun and picked up the AK47.

"This is going to get loud, so cover your ears."

Lying in the prone position, he fired three shots in rapid succession. In the distance, three pumpkins exploded sending chunks of orange shell in every direction.

"Sweet! This is great," he said climbing to his feet.

Arthures stood staring at him, a blank look painted his face.

"I told you to cover your ears."

His friend leaned closer, "What did you say?"

Timothy smiled, and shook his head. "Do you want to try?" he hollered, offering him the weapon.

Arthures pushed the gun backed. "No, we have no need for such primitive weapons."

Glancing at the bow and arrows, he grinned at his host, "and you call this primitive?" He shouldered his weapon and prepared to leave.

The hunting party re-emerged from behind the trees and gathered around Timothy.

"We should be getting back to camp," Arthures announced. "You have a long journey ahead of you."

When they arrived, he found Joy encircled by a group of ladies making the final adjustments to her newly sown outfit. Her legs were covered in a greenish felt-like material. The top covered her chest and arms past the waist. A belt of leather girded her mid-section, and she wore two buck-skin boots.

"Look at me, Timmy," she raised her arms did a quick pirouette, "They made me an official member of the tribe."

He stepped into the circle, smiling. "You're as pretty as a pixy."

"More like an elf if you ask me," she said with a grin.

Andorra moved closer to Timothy. "Rose made you a special outfit as well." He handed him a stack of folded clothes. Timothy swallowed hard, a knot formed in his stomach. *I'll bet she'll have me looking like Peter Pan when she gets done*, he thought.

Timothy gave Andorra a crooked smile and headed for the tent. He had no choice but to wear it.

Much to his chagrin, the new garments fit him to a tee. *I guess all that dancing gave Rose an opportunity to size me up ... literally.*

By mid-day Timothy and Joy were ready to say their good-byes.

"Here, my friends," Nickolas the Wise said as he handed each of them a back-pack. "We have filled these with fruit and bread enough to last you several days. Take them on your journey and may God's speed go with you. May his Spirit guide you and keep you. If you face danger, which I believe you will, take courage, knowing that the prayers of Nickolas the Wise are with you."

Timothy took the proffered hand and gave him a firm squeeze. Then Nickolas turned to Andorra and gave him a quick nod.

Andorra stepped forward. "Take this," he handed Timothy a globe with a tiny arrow floating in a pool of green liquid. If ever you need to return here, follow the arrow. It will point the way."

He knelt on one knee, looking Joy in the eyes, "And to you, young lady, we give you this. He handed her a jar of lightning bugs. Just shake it and they will light your way wherever you are."

Joy's eyes lit with delight, "Oh thank you," her voice crackled with a mixture of happiness and grief.

Timothy and Joy knelt before the wise chief, and he placed his hands on them and prayed, "May the Lord bless you and keep you, may He make his face to shine upon you and give you peace. May he instruct you and teach you in the way that you should go and guide you with the skillfulness of his eye." He paused, looking down. "Now rise and go in the strength of the Lord."

"I can't thank you enough for all you and your people have done for us. We will remember you as long as we live," Timothy said.

The chief smiled, "Then I will pray that you will live a

long time. If, however, my study of the ancient writings is accurate, none of us have much longer to wait before the end of the age. Until then," he lifted his hand, "'live long and prosper,' to quote from your noted, Mr. Spock." A wry smile parted his lips.

Timothy chuckled, "Yes, thank you." Then he slipped on his back pack and helped Joy with hers.

Arthures handed them their hoods, and the hunting party guided them from the camp.

As the voices of the Forest Saints receded in the distance, a lump of guilt formed in Timothy's throat for not showing enough gratitude to Rose. They traversed the rugged terrain for what seemed an hour until the air grew warmer. Timothy knew they neared the edge of the forest. They paused and the hoods were removed. "That should be much better. Follow me, but you must remain quiet."

When they reached the clearing, marking the end of the domain of Nicholas the Wise, Arthures turned, stuck his hand out. The two men clasped each other in a warm embrace.

"I must bid you farewell, my friends. Follow that path and it will lead you to a creek. Stay on the north side, and it will take you to the Forbidden City. Hopefully there, you will find your loved ones. If you fail to find them, however, you may return the way you came. Build a fire here, where we now stand. We will come and get you. Nevertheless, you should know this, if you return, you must remain with us and become part of our tribe until the end of time. This is the will of Nickolas the Wise." He leaned down and kissed Joy on the forehead.

Timothy swallowed hard. The thought of marrying Rose was enough for him to keep going. He felt a tug on his sleeve. Looking down he saw Joy's tears well in her eyes and streamed down her cheeks. It was clear what she wanted.

"Thank you, my friend. With God's help and the prayer

of the good chief, I am confident we will find our sister and her friend.

Arthures bowed and quietly receded into the shadows of the forest, leaving Timothy vulnerable, exposed, alone.

The sun crested over the horizon when they reached a small creek. Its cool waters bubbled over the rocky shoals.

"Look Timmy, there's the path Arthures talked about," she said, her voice filled with hope.

Despite the friendly call of birds and the constant buzzing of bees, Timothy took the path, wishing he'd never left the camp. Already he missed the safety of his friends but knew what staying longer meant. They followed the path as it wound along the creek. The forest behind them lay in regal shadows punctuated with unblinking eyes. A chill ran the length of Timothy's spine yet he pressed on. The path turned to the right and ascended a small hill.

"Who made this path any way, Timmy?"

He paused and studied the footprints in the dirt. "I'm not sure, but whoever did had large paws and a wide gait," he said glancing over his shoulder. He took his weapon from his shoulder and held it at the ready.

They crested a hill and stopped, his heart pounding.

"Timothy! the Forbidden City. I wonder if Emma and Jamis are still there."

The jagged teeth of the skyline revealed only a portion of the destruction the city had endured. One nuclear explosion after another rocked the city. Multiple meteors pounded what was left until nearly every building lay in ruins. Then, after a thousand years of decay, all that remained of the once great metropolis was a pile of toxic rubble.

"I don't see how anyone could live in that God forsaken place for very long."

Joy's eyes misted, and a single tear slid from the corner

of her eye. She wiped it away and took a halting breath. "First, we lose mom and dad...we can't lose Emma and Jamis, we can't." Her lower lip trembled.

Timothy bit back his tears, trying to be brave. "Maybe it's not too late."

Chapter 19

Escape from the Forbidden City...

The hover-craft vibrated under the strain of the g-force as Jamis pushed it to its limits. They raced across the open sky, scattering a flock of unsuspecting birds in their wake. Ahead, clouds like cotton dinosaurs roamed the heavens. Jamis aimed his craft toward them and plunged in. Tiny droplets of moisture pelted the windshield, making it impossible to see beyond the white fog. Then, to his relief, they broke through to a dazzling sight. Looking down, Jamis watched a field of snow drifts unfold beneath his feet. He relaxed his grip and leveled off.

Beep! Beep! Beep! An alarm sounded.

A flashing green light beat out an inane cadence.

"Uh oh, we have a problem." Jamis' tone was ominous. Light-headed, he glanced at Emma; she sat rigid, back straight, her eyes unblinking. "What is it Jamis?" What's wrong?"

"We've penetrated the upper atmosphere, and I failed to engage the bio-support system. The cockpit is filling with carbon monoxide. If I can't find the evacuation valve, we'll be dead within a few minutes," he said as he frantically searched the confusing panel of gages and monitor displays.

"Speak to the command and control unit, maybe she can override the system," Miss Xhu called from the back, her words coming in with staccato deliberateness, punctuating every word.

An array of information scrolled on a monitor screen.

"Hold on a second," he reached up and pushed a button. A moment later a soft swish sounded followed by a whiff of fresh air. "That's much better. However, this thing isn't equipped to fly at this altitude," he said after a wide yawn. "I'm going to have to bring it down to about twelve thousand feet."

He eased forward on the yoke, and the craft eagerly responded. The alarm fell silent when they reached a safe cruising altitude.

"Okay, let's set a course for Providence Population Center," he said.

A monitor blinked to life and a series of navigational maps appeared.

"Providence Population Center, please allow for course adjustment," said the mechanical voice.

Jamis took his hands off the yoke while the air-craft made the corrections.

"There, we should be there in a few hours," he said, crossing his arms.

"Your flight time is exactly two hours fifty-five minutes," corrected the computer. "Please do not make any more adjustments to the flight controls."

A broad smile occupied Emma's face and lingered while Jamis pouted.

The minutes wore on and finally Emma broke the silence. "I don't like flying this high." Emma said, pointing at the open sky. "Those poachers are still out there, and this thing would be no match for them. I, for one, don't want to get shot down again."

Jamis rubbed his chin and considered his options. He could either continue to fly at this altitude and run the risk of being seen, or lower his altitude and hope for the best. He chose the latter. Pushing the control stick forward, the hover-craft responded and skimmed just above the tree tops. The backwash of its jets swirled the upper limbs and sent birds scurrying to safety. "How's that?"

Emma gave him a satisfied smile and patted him on the arm. "Good, now I hope we don't run across a battery of anti-aircraft missiles."

Suddenly, a knot formed in Jamis' gut. Sweat slicked his palms, and his mouth filled with sand.

Orifiel and his angelic warriors formed a barrier between the earth and the hover-craft as it raced across the sky.

A sudden rush of motion drew his attention. "Uriel, in coming," cried Orifiel.

In a flash, the winged angel shot into position and held up his golden shield. A soldier on the ground heard the hover-craft coming and fired his weapon. The impulse charge struck his shield, and veered off in the other direction.

"Attack," commanded Orifiel to the forces under his command. Immediately, his angels swarmed the para-military soldiers like killer bees. The men flailed at the unseen enemy, firing their weapons wildly. Several soldiers fell to the ground, a pool of blood forming around their lifeless bodies.

Glancing over his shoulder, Orifiel saw his charges had escaped the immediate danger. He stretched out his hand and struck the remaining men with blindness. Then he gathered his squad together and raced to catch up. Moments later, they formed a shield, keeping the hover-craft from unwanted eyes.

A light breeze carried shards of ash across the winding path on which Timothy and Joy tread. To his left, a distant volcano belched out the remains of its ancient fury. Ahead lay a barren plain, painted in a deathly pallor. Courageous stalks of grass gathered in clomps and fought against the onslaught. Broken rocks littered the uneven ground like tombstones. Timothy stopped at the southern border and sighed heavily. Time lingered as if the world ground to a halt.

"Here Joy, drink this," he handed her a hand-made jug filled with water from a brook. She took a sip. "Ah, that reminds me of my friends back in the forest."

"Yeah, me too, I'd much rather be with them now than to go across that." He pointed to the range in front of them. A lonely breeze stirred the rugged terrain.

"This is going to be the most dangerous part of our whole journey," he said. "Stay low and let's go from one boulder to the next as quickly as possible."

She nodded, not speaking.

Timothy took a deep breath and plunged down the narrow path and headed across the field. Claw-like briers threatened every step, loose gravel yielded beneath their feet, making progress painfully slow. They kept a low profile, neither spoke.

The trickle of water from an unseen brook quickened Timothy's spirit.

"I think we've made it about half way," he said, scanning the field ahead. He led Joy down the bank and into a ravine. The cool damp air stung his nose. Joy pushed aside a few reeds, and plopped down on a flat rock. Placing her feet in the water, she let the cool liquid dance over her swollen feet.

"Timmy, I'm tired." Her voice wavered.

He looked at his time-piece. With two hours remaining before nightfall, he didn't want to be stranded on the open plain.

"I know honey, but we need to get across this field before nightfall or we'll be fair game for any predator."

She sniffed back a tear and smiled bravely.

Still breathing hard, he filled their empty water bottles and climbed up the bank. Cautiously, he took a few paces, and stopped.

"Look Joy, a dirt road."

Fresh tire tracks told him all he needed to know.

Half-way across, Timothy stopped, ears alert. "Someone's coming."

A truck filled with para-military soldiers bounced along a rutted dirt road. The gunner tapped the driver on the shoulder and pointed. He cut his wheels and jammed it into high gear.

Timothy grabbed Joy by the hand and stumbled headlong through the underbrush. They broke into a clearing and took off in a full sprint, zigzagging between outcropping rocks and the tall weeds. Loose gravel kicked up with every pace, thorny vines like barbed wire grabbed at his legs. Shots rang out. Bullets whizzed past them, striking the ground, kicking up small explosions of rock and dirk.

A fallen tree offered little protection. Timothy jumped over it followed by Joy. She landed on him, knocking him on his back. He scrambled to his knees, heart slamming against his ribs like a prisoner in a burning prison. They lay behind the rotting tree, panting.

Hearing the approaching truck, he poked his head up. The truck bore down upon them. He laid the barrel of the AK47 on the log and squeezed off three quick shots. The gunner slumped to the side, and the truck swerved into a stump. The soldier next to him kicked him out of the truck. He backed it up, cut the wheels and kept coming. More shots ripped through the air, like angry hornets.

With his limited ammunition, Timothy knew it would only be a matter of time before they would be caught or killed.

"Sweetie, I need you to run as fast as you can, for as long as you can. Do you understand me?"

She nodded, unblinking. "Where will you be?" her question cut to the heart.

He swallowed back a tear. Hating to lie, he knew she'd never leave him if he told her the truth. "I'll be right behind you. Don't stop running and don't look back. Oh and here," he fished in his pocket, drew out a few matches Arthures had given him and handed them to her. "You might need these."

She smiled, tears streaming down her smudged face. Her slender arms clung around his neck and squeezed. "Okay honey, I love you too, now go." He tore her from his neck, kissed her on the forehead and gave a shove. "Now run!"

She jumped up and made a bee-line for the next boulder.

Timothy turned and fired until he'd emptied one magazine. Another man fell only to be replaced by another. He switched the magazines and continued firing. He glanced over his shoulder, *keep running honey another hundred feet.* With only his hand gun left, he stood and fired until it was empty, then dropped the spent magazine, replaced it and dashed after his sister.

Thirty yards, twenty-five, twenty, she'd reached the boulder, but he still had half the field to run. His legs burned and his lungs screamed for oxygen, yet he willed himself forward. A stubborn vine caught his foot, sending him sprawling. He rolled to a stop, striking his knee on a rock. Something popped, and fire shot up his leg. Struggling to his feet, he tried to move, but his leg refused to obey. Knowing the chase was over, he turned and faced the approaching vehicle. He extended his arms and fired. The jeep lurched to the left as the front tire exploded. Sparks flew and metal crunched as the truck ground to a halt.

Five men jumped from the wounded truck and raced toward him. With only three rounds left, he fired twice and tried to run. A searing pain shot up his leg like he'd stepped on a live electrical wire. He fell and struck his head on a rock, then blackness.

With effort, he cracked his eyes open. A shaft of light stabbed his brain, and he winched in pain. The throbbing knot on his head accentuated his misery. His ears rang with every beat of his heart and fire shot up his leg. The sudden realization struck him, that his hands were tied and his mouth was gagged. He struggled to cock his head enough to inspect his leg. Relieved at seeing only a gaping hole in his pant-leg, he tried to relax. The buckskin must have kept the bullet from passing through his leg.

Blinking the pain from his eyes, he looked through the flickering campfire. Joy sat, eyes wide as a man stroked her head, her body quivering. A wave of rage surged through him, and he struggled to break free.

The man stood, walked over and kicked him in the stomach. Bile filled his mouth. The last thing he remembered hearing, was Joy's pitiful voice … then nothing.

Awareness of movement brought Timothy near the realm of the living when a bucket of cold water splashed on him. He jolted to life.

"Well, well, well. What have we here?" asked the man who'd been stroking his sister's head. "It's about time you woke up, you lazy piece of trash."

His pocked face and rumpled uniform told Timothy that he was a man who was comfortable with causing other people pain. He tried to speak but all he could do was let out a muffled curse.

The man laughed.

Joy looked at the man, her eyes pleading. "Don't hurt him mister. We're only kids."

The innocent comment made the man laugh even louder.

Suddenly, two other equally unkempt men stepped into the clearing carrying weapons and talking about the deer they'd killed. The three men dragged the carcass of an emaciated buck to a stubby tree and began to field dress it.

Timothy got Joy's attention and nodded for her to come near. She helped him to a sitting position, and loosened his gag. Movement in the tall grass brought him to attention. "Get behind me, something's coming," he whispered. The hair on the back of his neck bristled.

Joy took a sharp breath and obeyed.

"Squat down and untie my hands, sweetie." His voice calm, sweat beading on his forehead.

Her little fingers tickled his wrists but within a few minutes, his hands were free.

"Now back up," he said as he scooted further from the camp-site. Thorns cut into his legs and gravel crunched but his captors were too engrossed to notice.

A moment later, a wild scream broke the morning air as a pack of wolves leapt from their hiding places. They encircled the men and began to draw closer. One man reached for his gun but was met with snarling teeth. He backed away and stumbled. The wolf pounced on him, sinking its teeth into the man's throat. It shook him violently, snapping his neck. Timothy watched in horror as the other men flailed and kicked at the encircling pack of wolves.

A twinge of guilt pricked his conscience as he eyed one of the soldier's weapons. He quickly ruled out the notion of a rescue. Grabbing Joy by the hand, he backed further away. Screams of pain, anger and terror, echoed through the morning air, then faded.

"Let's go before those wolves pick up on our trail."

She wobbled to her feet and began running. Timothy

stood and limped as quickly as he could. In the distance, the sound of another heavy vehicle thundered across the open field.

Emma watched the barren terrain whiz by as the hover-craft clung low to the ground. "Hey Jamis, look down there. I see two people, running." Her head whipped back trying to catch a better glimpse.

Jamis and Nguyen craned their necks, at the fleeing figures.

Jamis swung the craft around to get a better look. They passed them a second time, and he sat up straight. "That's Timothy and Joy, and someone is chasing them."

Another group of soldiers on patrol had seen them and were cutting across the field in hot pursuit.

"And they're gaining on them too," Nguyen said with tension building in her voice.

Jamis spun the hover-craft around and nosed it in their direction.

"I wish this thing had some sort of weapons," he said absently.

The on-board screen lit up and a female voice said, "Weapons System On."

Jamis jumped at the sound of her voice, but quickly gained control of his racing heart.

"Weapons Display," he said.

The screen scrolled and listed the weapons ordinance.

"Arm impulse gun," he ordered.

The computer repeated the order.

He flipped off the safety cover and squeezed the trigger. A burst of energy shot out and scorched the ground.

"Wow! Look at that! This thing is great," Jamis cried

out as a kid with a new toy.

"Be careful. You don't want to shoot the wrong people," Miss Xhu warned.

"Engage Cloaking System," he said, pointing to the third line on the screen

"Did it work?" Emma asked, looking at the screen.

"I'm not sure, let's try touching that yellow blinking light."

Nothing.

He shrugged his shoulders, "Maybe it doesn't work. After all, this thing has been sitting around for a long time."

Seeing Timothy suddenly brought a flood of memories. He didn't like him, and he'd often dreamed of ways of getting even. His heart pounded and streaks of heat, like fingers crawled up his neck. Pushing aside his feelings he sighed and yanked the yoke to his left. "Okay, let's get in between Timothy and the hunting party."

He handled the hover-craft with ease and came down to within inches above the ground.

"Acquire firing solution," Jamis commanded.

"Firing Solution acquired," repeated the computer.

As the vehicle crested a ridge, Jamis squeezed the trigger. The blast of white energy shot out and struck the approaching truck with blinding force. It exploded sending body parts and pieces of metal in all directions. When the smoke cleared, the attackers were gone.

"Okay, let's get Timothy and Joy before any more of those guys show up," Jamis said inadvertently pushing the yellow button a second time.

Timothy caught his breath as a bolt of white energy shot

out of nowhere. It hit the truck with blinding force. A moment later, all that remained were smoldering hulks of bodies and twisted metal. Ducking behind a boulder, he shielded Joy for the flying debris. He blinked and covered his eyes as a shining hover-craft appeared, its jet engines screaming. Joy grabbed him by the shirt and pulled him down.

"Get down. Do you want them to see you?" she whispered through pinched lips.

From behind the rock, he peered, hoping to get a better look. Gun in hand, he knew he'd have to make it count. Four small legs protruded from the hover-craft's undercarriage and the engines wound down to a low purr. With a swish, the hatch popped open.

Timothy flinched and pointed his gun.

"Don't shoot, it's me," Emma said, jumping out, arms extended.

Joy poked her head around the boulder and ran.

Timothy's heart raced at seeing Jamis. He knew it was sin for him to harbor an unforgiving spirit toward Jamis. Grateful to God for sending help, he lowered his head, *Lord, forgive me for hating Jamis. Help me to forgive him and somehow bring him into the family of faith. Amen.*

He stood and steadied himself against the rock. "Man, am I glad to see you," his voice shaky. "Where did you come from and where did you get that?"

Jamis jumped out of the hover-craft and cautiously approached Timothy. He shoved his hands in his pockets and glanced over his shoulder. "I've taken up the art of stealing hover-crafts these days."

Emma punched him in the ribs with her elbow. "I don't think so."

Timothy kicked an unsuspecting stone and stuck his hand out. "I'm sorry for beating you up the other day. I've been on the receiving end of that for the last day or so and I know what it's like. Would you forgive me?"

Jamis staggered back. He'd never been in the position of forgiving someone. He held Timothy's gaze and swallowed. His throat felt like a dry creek-bed. "I, I forgive you…I guess."

Emma smiled, "you're forgiven. Now let's get out of here."

Miss Xhu poked her head up.

Timothy's eyes glanced between her and Emma, "Miss Xhu? How? Where?"

"Climb in," Emma said, "I'll explain it on the way back to Providence Population Center."

Suddenly, a bolt of energy flashed through the air and struck Timothy in the leg. He fell to the ground writhing in pain. Jamis picked up the handgun, fumbled with it a moment, took aim and fired. The soldier slumped to the ground. A puddle of blood grew in a widening circle.

Timothy lay gripping his leg, muttering through clenched teeth.

"M, help me get him in and let's get out of here before any more of those guys show up," Jamis said.

They lifted him in and got him buckled. As the hatch closed another bolt of energy flared, grazing the side of the craft.

"We're not out of the woods yet," Jamis said and spun the craft around.

Another armored personnel carrier, lumbered toward them, its fifty caliber machine gun blazing.

"Acquire firing solution," he repeated.

The computer made the calculation and a light blinked.

Jamis squeezed the trigger. The bolt of energy found its mark, and the firing ceased.

"Man, that was close," Miss Xhu said as the craft lifted off.

Joy leaned against Jamis, eyes wide. "I didn't even see you when you shot that truck."

Emma sat up straight. "It worked. This thing really does have cloaking capability."

Moments stretched into an uncomfortable silence as Jamis considered her last statement. He rubbed his chin and glanced at Emma, "I sure would like to know how that technology works."

The image of his father's face appeared. *Why was my father and mother arrested? Was it something to do with cloaking?*

Chapter 20

Restricted District K29DC

"Now where is that little snit," Professor Christos asked, peering into the black hole. "I leave her hanging for only a few hours and poof, she disappears. Bad enough I have to do everything myself now days. Now I can't even depend on people staying where I put them without them wandering off," he seethed.

He inhaled, then let it out slowly, and he began a measured pace. "No matter, I'll find her and when I do, no more Mr. Nice guy. In the meantime, there is a world to corrupt and an army to raise."

General Hakeem, the pilot of the black hover-craft, stood at attention, listening to his commander rant in silence.

"General, how are our plans coming along?"

Hakeem's hands shook. His fear ridden features brought a smile to the General's face. He smiled with slavish glee as the man pulled from his attaché a sheet of paper.

His voice trembled, "Sir, we've got the masses of Eonians leaving the Population Centers, gathering in the mini-nations. The problem is keeping them from fighting each other. It will be a miracle if they don't destroy themselves before D-Day."

Hum, imagine that, me doing miracles. Christos thought.

"We've got them cranking out weapons of mass destruction by the thousands. New hover-crafts are rolling off the assembly line every day. And they are equipped with the latest technology in cloaking. They'll never see us coming, sir."

Christos' face wrinkled into a wicked grin.

"I have signed a directive, requiring millions of soldiers to begin the most rigorous training. Soon we will be ready. We await your order,"

Hum, the Order, I've always liked that multi-national conglomerate. It worked well for me until Chase Newton came along and messed up my plans. He and that Miss Xhu will pay. I'll get them for that if it's the last thing I do. Now where was I ... Christos thought.

"As per your orders, my commanders will encircle the Population Centers of Providence and New Birth and unleash their fury. Once we've completed phase one, we will move to phase two and attack Jerusalem."

"Not until I'm ready will you attack the unholy city," Christos shouted. "You will do nothing, I repeat, nothing, until I give the order."

"Yes sir," the man answered in a whisper.

"I will wait for the right time, when the Feast of Tabernacles is at its peak. Then, we'll attack. With each soldier wearing a personal cloaking device (PCD), they won't even see us coming. We'll have the element of surprise on our side," Christos mused.

Victory was so close he could taste it. Nothing stood in his way. Jerusalem had no standing army, no air force, no military. He had an army numbering as the sand of the sea. Soon he would mount the final assault against the God of Heaven.

"Sir, we do have one small glitch," Hakeem's face blanched as he spoke.

Christos' yellowed eyes glowed. "Glitch? What is glitch?"

He cleared his dry throat, tongue sticking to the roof of his mouth. "Your guy Jamis…he stole a hover-craft."

"So, what's the problem, stealing and lying come natural to him, he's a child of the devil like you."

Despite the cold, Hakeem, mopped his brow with his sleeve. "Yes, but he is beginning to ask questions—"

"Questions?!" What kind of questions?"

"Questions about…the cloaking device, sir. And about his parents."

Chapter 21

Providence Population Center

"Navigation System," Jamis commanded.

"Navigation System On," the computerized voice responded.

"Plot course to Providence," he stated.

The screen flashed and a set of numbers appeared.

He read the coordinates and the hover-craft righted its course and ascended to the upper atmosphere.

Suddenly, the hover-craft began to shake. Jamis sat white knuckled staring at the console of blinking amber and green lights.

"I think the last impulse shot must have done more damage than I realized," Jamis said, the yoke shaking violently in his hand.

An alarm sounded, smoke began seeping into the bridge. Jamis coughed, and wiped his eyes.

"Hit the internal ventilation switch," he hollered through a raspy throat.

Emma squinted, searching for the correct blinking light. She pushed one, and the craft dipped.

"No, not that one, that disengages the gyroscope," he muttered in disgust. He pushed the reset, and reached across her and punched a red button. He released a frustrated breath.

The air cleared, and Emma sat rigid, wiping her eyes, fighting back a sniffle.

"What's wrong?"

She bit her lip, not wanting to admit she was seeing a different side of Jamis, one that she didn't like. He'd always picked on her, but in a kidding way. *He doesn't respect me. He thinks I'm dumb.* She took a halting breath and shook her head. A few strands of golden hair fell across her face. She swept them aside. "Oh nothing," her voice shaky, cold.

Jamis worked the controls attempting to correct his trim and stop the vibration. Nothing worked.

"This thing is a far cry from the one we stole from Edenica," Jamis said, breaking the silence which invaded the bridge.

Emma crossed her arms, head straight. "We stole?" She asked, eyebrows rising, "I'm not the one with the record."

Heat crept up his neck, and he wondered if she could hear the ringing in his ears. "You could be walking, you know."

Emma bit her lip to keep from sounding ungrateful. "I suppose you're going to keep it?" The hover-craft I mean?"

He sat a moment, gripping the yoke. The palms of his hands slicked and his heart palpitated. Something in her voice told him she was ticked. He shrugged. "Well yeah, to the victor, goes the spoil. Anyway, I'd like to stick my head under the hood and get a look at its cloaking system. There's something about it that's got me puzzled."

The sat-comm transponder crackled to life as central air command sent out an inquiry. Emma reached up and flicked it off. "I don't want to talk to anyone right now." She released the harness, stood and walked from the bridge, leaving Jamis to wonder what just happened.

Emma took a seat further back. The cushioned seat, though coarse and a bit dusty, offered her the relief her body craved. Staring out the porthole, she watched the terrain change from forests to fields and then to suburban sprawl. The magnificent population center of Providence spread beneath her feet. Its towering crystalline space-scrapers gleamed like sheets of diamonds in the night sky. Massive cooling tubes snaked through the city. Hover-crafts crowded space highways which weaved between buildings. The contrast couldn't have been more stark between here and the forbidden city, yet she wondered what it would take for all this to come crashing down. *I'm sure the people of that day, never thought their city would lie in ruins for millennium.*

Her thoughts turned to her mom and dad. They were godly people. As far back as she could remember, her family called upon God. Now it was up to her, Timothy, and Joy to carry on the legacy. She roused and looked at Timothy. "We should have a memorial service for our mom and dad."

Joy lifted her head from Nguyen's lap and sat up, "M, that's a great idea."

Emma recoiled. "Hey, since when did you start calling me M? That's Jamis' nickname for me."

Her slight shoulders rose and fell, as she searched the floor, "Oh, I don't know, I kinda like it too. Can I call you M, M?"

Taking a deep breath, she closed her eyes, not wanting to admit her deepest fears. *He doesn't even think of me as a person...just a letter. I don't know about this. Maybe when we get back I'll end it. Anyway, he's not a believer and probably never will be.*

"Joy, you'll need to talk with Jamis about that since it's his nickname."

Joy scampered to the bridge, and cuddled next to him, "Mr. Jamis, can I call M, M?" She asked, her nose wrinkling, and her voice painted in plaintive tones.

Jamis cocked an eyebrow, a broad grin stretched his cleft chin. "Who could resist those big blue eyes…specially when asked by such a cute girl. You can call M, M, but just don't tell her I told you so."

She clasped her hands under her chin, and ran back, her face beaming, "M, he said I can call you M," her eyes danced with glee.

"That's great 'J,' why don't we all start calling each other by our first letter and make things simpler," her voice crackled.

Timothy, who hadn't been paying attention, leaned forward, "I'll contact the Head of the Sanctuary of the Truth and have him prepare a proper eulogy for mom and dad. He is an immortal saint. His life dates back before the millennium began. He probably knows all of our kin-folks and will have some real nice things to say."

Emma nodded her head in agreement. "Let's invite everyone to our estate. It can be a great reunion and celebration."

"I just thought of something," Joy's eyes filled with expectation. "Since mom and dad died and went to Heaven, do you think we will see them if we go to Jerusalem?"

Emma paused and looked at Nguyen. She shook her head and brushed the hair from Joy's smiling face. "I'm afraid Jerusalem isn't Heaven, sweetie, but still it shouldn't be long before we see them again," Nguyen said.

"If Nickolas the Wise is correct in his calculations, the end of the age is very near," Timothy said.

The hover-craft bumped to a shaky landing and Jamis pushed himself out of his seat, stretched and walked back to the seating area. He felt Emma's cold glare, and shifted uncomfortably.

"Maybe then I can apologize to your parents for causing

their deaths," he said.

Emma's hand shot up, her finger jabbed the air like a hot branding iron. "That won't happen if you don't trust Jesus as your Savior and soon." Her words fell like chunks of ice. She folded her arms across her chest and sat back. Miss Xhu gaped at Emma, she'd never heard her speak so sharply to Jamis.

Miss Xhu released her harness and helped Timothy to his feet. "Here, let me take you to a Healing Center before that infection gets any worse."

He stood, shaken but able to limp. Joy held his hand and the three of them stepped into the night air. Above them shone a velvety sky dotted with sparkling diamonds. Timothy looked up. "It sure is good to be home."

"M, I can understand you being ticked at me, but how can you be so forgiving? Your parents are dead, we nearly got killed on several occasions, your brother and sister were being shot at when we found them. Aren't you just a little angry at God for letting this happen?"

Emma bit back her emotions. "Well, Jamis, I know how much God loves me and has forgiven me. As far as being bitter, well, bitterness only consumes the vessel holding it. I can't be bitter at God. He has always been so good to me." Her hands moved in small circles. "As far as being cheerful" She paused and looked down at her fingers. "Right now, I'm not!"

A curtain of silence hung between them, keeping them locked in their pain. Finally Jamis broke the tension. "To be honest with you M, I'm sort of mad at God."

She sat up straight, her mouth fell open. "Mad at God! Why?"

Rubbing the back of his neck, he squeezed his eyes shut. "For killing my ancient ancestors. There, I said it. I've been mad at God for a long time."

"Jamis, God didn't kill them, they died because they

were mortals, and rejected God's plan of salvation. Don't blame it on God," frustration seeped through her voice. She pushed herself up and started for the exit.

Jamis wiped his forehead with his sleeve and let out a terse breath.

Timothy poked his head back inside. "How about we give it a rest, and get some sleep. Tomorrow we'll meet at the Sanctuary and plan a memorial service. Okay?"

Jamis shifted his weight and looked at Timothy, "Do you think I could be a part of the service, I feel so, responsible?"

Timothy bristled at the suggestion. He cut his eyes at Emma. She stood, unblinking.

"Did I say something wrong? I mean, all I wanted to do is buy flowers or something. It's not like I wanted to speak or anything." His stomach knotted.

Hearing the pain in his voice, Emma took a ragged breath. A tear coursed down her cheek.

"Sure Jamis, meet us at the Sanctuary tomorrow at noon, and this time…don't be late," she said with an edge to her voice.

Chapter 22

The Sanctuary of the Truth

An air of excitement filled the Sanctuary of the Truth as friends gathered to celebrate the home-going of Michael and Joanna Newton. The aroma of Orchids and Roses, Plume-aria and Sunflowers mingled together and drifted across the spacious hall as if on angel's wings. Butterflies, the symbol of rebirth fluttered from stamen to flower, occasionally lighting on the head of a well-wisher, much to the delight of onlookers.

Rather than disturb the solemnity of the occasion, Emma chose the traditional ground transportation. The Newton family gathered on the grounds of their estate and loaded into anti-g limousines. From there, the long procession snaked through the city to the Sanctuary of the Truth. The lead carriage paused momentarily to allow Emma, Timothy, and Joy to disembark. Each carried a white rose. Behind them gathered Titus and Andre Newton, now in their late three hundreds, Paul and Victoria Newton, well into their six hundreds, and Jeremiah and his wife of six hundred years, Grace, both over seven hundred. The processional of kin-folk stretched for nearly a mile. Providence held its breath at the spectacle.

Emma's silken slippers lightly touched the lush carpet, as with measured pace she proceeded down the aisle. Looking from side to side, she couldn't help but notice the grandeur of the Sanctuary of the Truth. It was not often she attended services there. Her local assembly was much smaller, the building not large enough for such a gathering. The Sanctuary, with its spires ascended hundreds of feet in the air. The arches on the exterior walls, reminded her of the old Notre Dame of centuries earlier. Her heart thrilled as she passed a pedestal upholding Stephen, one of the churches first martyrs. His posture was as one railing at the darkness. Other pedestals held notable preachers and evangelists; all poised in an evangelistic fervor. One statue held her gaze, it was of an unknown prayer warrior, knees bent, head bowed, fingers locked in fervent, effectual prayer. Emma inhaled and took strength, knowing her Savior's tuned ear heard her most sacred thoughts.

A rainbow of dazzling light filtered through large stained glass windows. Like treading the pages of the ancient manuscripts, she scanned the major events recorded in the ancient writings; Daniel in the Lion's Den, David fighting Goliath, the Crucifixion, Resurrection and Ascension. On the ceiling of the Sanctuary were paintings of the War Angels and Peace Angels, Children's Angels and Messenger Angels. Her heart resonated with the warm glow cast into the sanctuary from the outside.

The procession moved with dignity until it reached the area reserved for the family. The cushioned seats invited them to sit and ponder the moment. Emma took her place next to Timothy and Joy. Each held the other's hands giving warmth and strength.

In the center of the Sanctuary of the Truth, on a raised platform, stood the Head of the Sanctuary, Saint Vincent, his long flowing white robes gathered at his feet, like drifts of snow. A golden crown rested lightly on the dome of his head. Long white hair fell loosely to his shoulders, joining his beard in one continuous display of honor and dignity. Two embers glowed out from under a hedgerow with compassion and radiated with the likeness of the Lord he served.

He lifted his arms to heaven. "Greetings in the name of

King Jesus," his voice reverberated throughout the sanctuary, warm and filled with love.

"In the name of King Jesus we greet you." The congregants replied.

"My friends, we are gathered here today to remember our loved ones Michael and Joanna Newton, who finished their race and have won the victory. We do not grieve for them. If we grieve, it is for us that we cannot be with them," his Irish accent lending an air of kingly dignity to every word.

He stepped aside, allowing the grand pipe organ to play one of Michael's favorite pieces, "It Is Well with My Soul." After the last tone faded in the distance, Saint Vincent stood, and knit his fingers in front of his mid-section.

"They cannot come to us, but we can go to them. You ask how can I prepare for the day when I am to cross over. It's the way all of us have taken, since time in memorial. By simply putting your faith in the finished work of Christ. That's what I did many years ago; that's what Michael and Joanna did. I should know; I was there when it happened. I told them the old, old story of Jesus and His love, and they responded with childlike faith and were gloriously transformed from children of darkness into children of light. Nothing would bring Michael and Joanna more joy than to know their death opened the door for you to come to Christ. Let me invite you to pray this simple prayer." He bowed his head. "Lord Jesus, I now place my trust in you alone for forgiveness and salvation. In Jesus' name amen!"

Looking over the crowd of mourners, he spoke with tenderness. "If you made that decision, share the good news with us and let us rejoice with you. I know there is joy in Heaven in the presence of the angels over one sinner who comes home."

His hands fell loosely to his sides as he descended the

steps. Then with kingly gate, he proceeded down the aisle, followed by the immediate family. Jamis slipped from his pew and sidled next to Emma. He tried to take her hand, but she crossed her arms and continued walking out of the Sanctuary.

"Were you listening?" her voice tense.

"Yes, why?"

"Because it is important that you make the right decision."

Jamis kept pace with Emma. "I don't get it, why can't we be friends or even more than friends without religion getting in the way?"

She let out an exasperated sigh and sped up. "Because it is!" she said over her shoulder.

Jamis stopped mid-stride and gazed at her as she disappeared back into the sleek black limo.

Frustrated and confused, Jamis headed back to his apartment. He quickly changed and went to the hover deck with a bag of tools. He tried to brush aside his thoughts of Emma, but their curt meeting, touched a nerve. Putting on his headphones, he cranked up the volume until nothing registered.

"What is it about the cloaking device that's so intriguing? And what's it got to do with dad?" he muttered to himself over the din.

Father was always secretive about his work. Although his skills were in research and development, it wasn't clear where he worked. He assumed it had to do with the Kingdom industry, but now he wondered.

Lifting the hood, he took a flashlight and began to inspect the various components. The jet infusion sequencer, the navigational connections, the gyroscope all checked out. He opened another panel, one he'd overlooked earlier. Inside, a crystal studded panel, decked with diodes of silicone, sat at the junction of a nest of lead wires. The color-coded wires connected to the panel with the outer shell of the hover-craft. Jamis yanked off his headphones. *Hmm, I wonder.*

Reaching into the cock-pit, he fired up the engines and threw the cloaking switch. A moment later, he was standing, touching the cold Cobalt Zircon skin of his hover-craft but saw nothing. He flicked it off, and it reappeared. *So this is the cloaking device.* He carefully unscrewed the panel and detached the wires. A voice echoed from deep within his consciousness to keep digging, probing, searching for its secret. With trembling fingers, he gently lifted the panel and looked at the underside. His breath caught as he stared, unblinking. His mind refused to accept what the panel proclaimed...CD2176.6-Damien.

So that's it. I've got to speak with my father.

Chapter 23

The Newton's Estate

Jamis streaked through the air-ways of Providence, trying to make up lost time. His newly acquired hover-craft, had been washed and given a complete tune-up. Its sleek form sliced easily through the air. As he approached his destination, he peered down. Beneath him, spread the pristine landscape of the Newton estate. Lined with prim hedges, its rolling hills, like emerald waves held back by golden sun light, stood in stark contrast to the barren wasteland he and the others passed through. Behind the manor house, lay an ornate labyrinth of Boxwoods encircling a large goldfish pond with a fountain. Gatherings of people met in small clusters along the gravel paths leading to one of the many gardens.

He set his hover-craft down on the private landing pad and climbed out. Pulling off his flight-helmet, he shook loose a flock of curly hair, and entered the fray. The reception was well under way with people laughing and enjoying getting reacquainted. He pushed through one gaggle of well-wishers only to be pushed back by another. Frustrated, he took a secluded path enshrouded by Bougainvillea.

He emerged and found Emma in the middle of a tight circle. Her shoulders sagged as yet another well-wisher offered her hand in sympathy. With trembling lips, she returned a weak smile and tried to remember everyone's name.

"Oh, hello, Mrs. Spencer, uh, Ms. Schneider, so glad you came."

The elderly woman muttered a few platitudes and moved on to the serving line.

"Boo!" Jamis said, sneaking up from behind.

Emma jumped, catching her breath. "Jamis! Don't do that, I'm jumpy enough without you scaring me half to death."

She smiled at the next well-wisher, hoping he'd leave.

Taking his place next to her, Jamis gave a weak smile to the next greeter. "Nice party. You look gorgeous, by the way," he whispered between tight lips.

She blushed slightly and scanned the floor, "It's not a party, but I'm glad you made it. What took you so long?"

He scanned the grassy turf, and scuffed. "Uh, I had a few things to take care of, sorry."

You haven't changed much have you Jamis? She thought.

Reaching into a small hand bag, she reapplied her lipstick and rolled her lips together. They glistened like moist apples. "Have you ever seen so many people in one place?" she asked, scanning the crowd.

"Nope, but I'll bet a lot of big shots are here just to be seen."

Suddenly, a photographer brushed past them trying to get a better angle.

"Somehow, I feel like this all happened before," she said absently.

Grabbing Jamis by the hand, she said, "Let's walk."

She led him out into the rose garden. The fragrant air from trellised roses wafted on a gentle breeze. The variegated flowers smiled at Emma and Jamis, hoping to lift their spirits.

"What's wrong, M?" noticing her sudden change of demeanor.

She shrugged, "I don't know. I guess the realization that all this," she waved her arm around like a wand, "all this property is my responsibility; the manor house, the guest houses, the grounds, acres and acres of vast farmland. I feel so overwhelmed." Her throat closed, and a single tear coursed down her cheek.

Jamis opened his mouth, but she held up her hand. The path curved and an elderly couple nearly collided with them, their features dark as if in somber conversation.

"Oh, hi grandpa," Emma said, turning to Jamis. "Jamis, this is my grandparents Charles and Andrea Newton, they recently celebrated their two hundred and fiftieth wedding anniversary."

Jamis stuck his hand out, "Congratulations. That's quite an accomplishment."

The elderly gentlemen leaned on his walking stick. "Oh 'twas nothing, we Newtons tend to be rather committed to long marriages," he said with a wry smile. His eyes danced with interest.

"By the way, young man, what are your intentions with my granddaughter?"

"Oh Charles," Andrea said with a nudge to the ribs.

He turned, his face awash with innocence. "What?"

Emma's cheeks pinked, and she led Jamis back into the main hall where most of the family had gathered. "Over there by the punch bowl is Great Grandma and Pop Pop Newton. Their names are Paul and Victoria. He is the son of Jeremiah Newton, the famous Time Traveler. He discovered by projecting yourself back into the 'known past,' you could actually go there."

Jamis raised a finger, "Does it work the same way for the future?"

She shook her head, letting a few hairs fall. She brushed them aside. "No, because we don't know what the future holds, but the past is a different thing. Have I mentioned that all the men on my father's side have names taken from the ancient writings?"

He paused and glanced around the room. "No M, I hadn't noticed, until you mentioned it. Interesting, I don't think any of my family are named after anyone in the ancient writings."

"Interesting, I wonder why? Emma said thoughtfully.

"I'm not sure. I'm afraid I don't know much about my ancestors. Especially since ..." he let his voice fade.

Silence, like a fog settled between the two. Each seemed to sense the other's thoughts, and pain.

"So you said your great, great-grandfather was an inventor?" he asked in an attempt to restart the conversation.

"Yes, his name is Jeremiah New—"

"You know, I just discovered my dad invented—"

Frustrated at his interruption, she jutted her chin and narrowed her eyes, "Oh Jamis, you're always bragging about your dad, comparing him to some great inventor," she huffed, chest heaving. "I've never seen anything he's *supposed* to have invented. Why don't you admit it, your family and my family are ... different."

Jamis stood, stunned. His mind raced as her words assaulted him like fiery darts. "It's true, my father really did invent something..."

Emma stomped her foot; unstoppable tears glistened on her cheeks. "Would you get off it, Jamis? If you're trying to impress me, forget it, I'm not."

"Okay, I'll prove it. I just need to look it up in the book of family records."

She wiped her eyes and blew her nose in a colorful napkin. "I can't believe this. Here I am still grieving over the loss of my parents and all you think about is proving you're right."

Jamis gulped.

"If you really want to prove your point, there's only one place to go."

Jamis folded his arms and rocked back. "Okay, where," he paused squeezing his temples.

Without missing a beat, she lifted her chin, her eyes held him in rapt attention. "They are kept in Jerusalem, which I might add, where *you* need to go."

"And how do you suppo'..."

Miss Xhu stepped up and offered her a warm hug, "I am so sorry for your loss."

Emma nodded mid-sentence. "Thank you, Miss Xhu, I miss them so much." Her voice escaped her throat, soft and low.

Jamis hadn't seen her so broken, so vulnerable. He yearned to do something to take away her pain, but everything he tried…backfired.

"I know sweetie, I know," Miss Xhu said, letting a moment pass.

Jamis took his cue and headed for the refreshment table.

"One other thing Emma, this might not be the best time to mention this, but while it is on my mind, I thought I'd tell you. According to Kingdom Law, it is unlawful for orphans to go without a guardianship."

"Yes?" Emma asked, wondering where she was going with this line of thought.

"Well, since you three are, unfortunately, orphans, I've asked the Head Master if I might become your God- mother … you know, just until you become of age."

Emma lifted her head; a bright smile tugged the corners of her lips. She lunged forward, throwing her arms around Miss Xhu and burying her head on her shoulder. "My God-mother!" She said between gulps of air. "I don't know what to say."

Nguyen stepped back and held her two hands, "Well,

don't say anything until you've consulted with your grandparents. I'm sure Timothy and Joy would want to be included in the decision."

Emma clutched her hands under her chin. "I'll let you know as soon as possible. When do you need an answer?"

"I'm planning to make the annual pilgrimage to Jerusalem this year after all, and I'll be leaving with the next caravan."

Emma pranced with delight, "I'll talk with Tim and Joy and Grandpa Newton tonight."

Her teacher bowed slightly and receded into the crowd.

A moment later, Jamis returned with two cups of punch and some cookies.

"M, did I hear Miss Xhu say, she'd like to be your God-mother?"

She took a frustrated breath. Hearing Jamis call her M, instead of her name, grated against her spirit.

"Now you and your family won't lose 'Standing' among the citizens of Providence. I was worried about that," he said, between bites.

She stood, unblinking, "Whatever does that have to do with anything?" she spat.

He shrugged. "You know, your position within the social order. Someone with 'standing' has all the rights and privileges of citizenship. Someone without it is, uh, limited."

"So." Her voice cut cold through the air.

Jamis was taken aback. He struggled for a cogent thought. "Uh, for example, someone without 'standing' could only marry someone without 'standing.'"

Emma cocked her head, "And why is that important. I'm not thinking about marrying anyone." She let her eyes search the floor.

Jamis jammed his hands in his pockets. "I don't know,

you just look like you should be a person with standing. That's all I'm saying."

A sparrow landed nearby and pecked at an unsuspecting worm, then fluttered away.

Emma took a quick glance at him, his eyebrows knit into deep furrows.

"Well, if we accept Miss Xhu's offer, the law states we must leave our home and move into our guardian's home."

He took a sip of punch, "Does that bother you, M?"

Like fingers, streaks of hives crept up her neck. She'd had it with him calling her a letter. She set her cup on the table. Her eyes burned like two embers. "Would you stop calling me M. My name is Emma, and if that's not good enough for you, then fine. Find another letter and marry it!" Wheeling around, she stomped off.

Chapter 24

Restricted District K27DC

"Are all the members of the World Congress assembled?"

Colonel Hakeem straightened, "Yes sir, shall we go?"

He nodded and stepped through the doorway followed by his underling. They rode the elevator to the upper floor and exited. Moments later Christos and his general entered a large room, filled with delegates from around the world. A hush stilled the low conversations as Supreme Commander Adoniram Christos stepped to the microphone.

An air of anticipation wafted through the assembly as they awaited his opening comments.

"May the Knights of The Order stand to attention."

The assembly stood and recited their pledge of allegiance to the United Nations of the World, then took their seats.

"Ladies and gentlemen, Knights and members of the Order, we are about to embark on our most ambitious endeavor; to pull down the Kingdom of God. As you know, I have been gone for quite some time."

Like leaves stirred by a breeze, laughter swirled in the air, then settled. He continued, "but as you can see, I am back, and I am ready to take my rightful place at the head of the table."

He paused while the room erupted in celebratory applause, then quelled at his raised palm. "

157

"The last time I sat in that chair, Mr. Chase Newton disrupted our little enclave, and I had to, uh, disappear for a while. I fear, since I didn't destroy him when I had the chance, I would have to face him yet again. Those fears were realized on the steps of the Supreme Court. Now his offspring dog my heels, and threaten my undoing."

A rustle of low conversations spread like winter across the grass-lands of Kansas.

"Not to worry, I have plans to wipe his seed from the earth. Meanwhile, I will be making my usual broadcasts on the solar-net, and expanding my outreach by visiting Gog and Magog. Together we will force the nations of the world to sign the Declaration of Independence from the Kingdom of God and declare war upon it."

The enraptured assembly jumped to their feet in thunderous applaud.

"And to show my power, allow me to demonstrate." He pointed to the representative of Ethiopia. "You there, stand." The shaken man stood, hands outstretched. "Please sir, I tried to convince my nation to sign the Declaration of…"

Christos' arm extended, his open palm closed and the frightened men fell to the floor struggling to breath. His hands fought the unseen grip which enclosed around his throat. His eyes bulged, and tongue protruded. His kicking feet slowed until all movement ceased.

Christos dropped his arm, tugged his coat sleeve, straightened his tie and smiled. "I hated to have to do that, but I needed to make him an example. You will convince your nations to sign the document or suffer a more severe punishment."

He turned to his assistant. "I am now ready to review my army."

Hakeem, staggered uncomprehendingly to his feet and

led his commander to the double-case door. Mechanically, he flung it open. Commander Christos stepped through the passage and onto the portico, and scanned the landscape.

Crimson wisps of clouds drifted across a cobalt sky under a blazing sun. From one end of the horizon to the other, stood soldiers, and machines of war, awaiting his command.

No military had ever been more unified; more determined, more blood-thirsty than the one he stood before. To the man, all swore allegiance to the cause. All were willing to go to the ends of the earth for this one cause, all were willing to pay the ultimate price to accomplish one goal; to dethrone the God of Heaven.

Christos crossed his arms over his vesture, and narrowed his gray eyes. "We must maintain the element of surprise. Do you understand? I have installed a cloaking device in all our weapons, and our position cannot be compromised. They won't know what hit them until it's too late."

A shadow of fear crept into his eyes. "Yes, my Lord. However, Jamis knows too much. What if he escapes, and lets the authorities know…" Christos cut him off with the wave of his hand.

"I want you to destroy Providence. Then I'll be rid of that nuisance once and for all. Pound them from the sky, tear down their walls, march straight in and wipe them out." He commanded.

Of all the great battle cries, from "Dieu et mon driot," "God and my right" to "Climb Mount Sarabachi" and "Tora, Tora, Tora," none shook the earth as did, "Conquer the Throne!"

The chant echoed from one end of the valley to the other.

Chapter 25

Miss Xhu's Home

"Pack for at least two weeks," Miss Xhu said to Emma.

In a flurry of activity, Emma emerged from her bedroom dragging an oversize suitcase. She puffed a stray hair from her eyes and dropped it with a thud. "What will we do the first week?" Emma asked, barely able to contain her excitement.

Nguyen arched an eyebrow at the sight and shook her head. "Well if I'd left when your family did, I was planning on touring Israel. Even though I'd been there scores of times, it never grows old to me."

Emma took a ragged breath, "Yes, that's what daddy said. He was so looking forward to showing us around." She paused as if making a confession. "That all changed by Jamis being late." Her voice fell cold and empty.

Her mentor stood motionless. "I thought you were over it…that you'd forgiven him and you two were getting along okay."

Emma shifted uncomfortably, "avoiding eye contact. "So did I. But the other day at the reception, I got so tired of him calling me M and bragging about his family, comparing them to … well I blew my top."

"And?"

"And I lost it and said some things I shouldn't have. He left in a huff and hasn't called or stopped by since. I think I hurt him pretty bad."

"Badly."

"Badly?"

"Yes, badly, remember your grammar."

Emma slumped on the couch, "Oh brother, I forgot I'm traveling with a teacher." Her mood darkened. "Every once in a while, I am overwhelmed with feelings of anger. I blame Jamis for all that happened."

Nguyen sat down next to her and took her hands in hers.

"Don't you remember what the ancient writings say? 'All things work together for good to them that love God, to them who are called for his purposes.'"

"I know Miss Xhu, but it's just so hard." Salty tears rolled down her cheeks unhindered.

She nodded. "After I gave the president that cup of tea, I blamed myself for his death. I ran from the White House, from God…from myself. I felt guilty, so dirty …" She wiped a stray tear and stared ahead, unblinking. "I felt so lost."

Emma's mouth fell open. "I had no idea."

Nguyen leaned forward, elbows on her knees, and drew a deep breath. "I had to come to terms with the reality that I didn't know he'd have a fatal reaction to that mixture of tea-leaves. I couldn't have known. My actions were completely innocent, but I still felt terrible."

Emma froze, listening intently. "What did you do?"

Time held its breath as memories long banished to the past roared forward. "I hid for quite a while. Finally, I got the courage to come out of hiding. The first person I talked with was Saint Vincent. He showed me in the ancient writings, 'whenever you pray, if you have something against another person, forgive him, and your Father who lives in heaven will forgive you.'"

Emma sat, absorbing the meaning of the verse. Her face brightened, "Thanks, Miss Xhu. I needed that." The two women shared a warm hug and drew strength.

She smiled; her almond eyes turned into slits. "Now, as I was saying, before the feast begins we will do some sightseeing. You did invite Jamis to come, didn't you?"

"Yes ma'am, I did, but after our fight, I doubt he will." Her throat closed. She swallowed back an anguished tear.

Nguyen handed her a tissue. "Why don't you call him and tell him to meet us here at noon sharp? Rather than depart from the Providence Hover Port, I plan on taking the Anti-g tram to New Birth, and leave from there. The route to the Holy Land is much safer that way."

Emma's eyes widened. "I've never been to New Birth, that's so exciting." Her voice curled upward an octave. She pulled her sat-comm from her belt, "I'll call Jamis right now."

Her voice recognition responded and sent the signal. One ring, two rings and Emma began to wonder if he was ignoring her call.

"Hello?" his voice sounded distant, empty.

"Jamis?"

"Hey M, uh, Emma, everything alright?"

"Yes, I'm so excited. We're going to New Birth, can you believe it?"

"You mean *you're* going to New Birth." Icy crystals followed each word.

Emma put her hand to her forehead and fell back on the couch. *Oh no, I blew it this time.* "Uh, Jamis, about the last time we talked," she paused and watched Miss Xhu stand and leave the room. "I said some terrible things to you, and I shouldn't have. I was wrong, would you forgive me?"

Silence.

"Jamis? Are you there?" she shifted uncomfortably.

A rustle of movement caught her eye, and she swirled around.

"Jamis." She sputtered.

His smile and opened arms told her what she needed to know. She jumped to her feet and ran into his arms.

"Oh, Jamis." She buried her head against his pounding heart.

"Hey, I'm getting quite good at forgiving now days," he said. "But, I thought we were going to the Jerusalem."

She pulled away and gazed into his soul. "We are, but we're going to visit New Birth first, I'm so excited."

He released his hold on her, extending his palms. "Okay calm down before you jump out of your skin."

Emma paused a moment and thought how funny that would be. She took a deep breath in a failed attempt to slow her pulse. "Miss Xhu says to pack for at least two weeks. I can't wait to leave."

Shoving his hands in his pockets, he cocked his head. "Okay, tell me when and where, Emma."

She brushed aside a stray lock and inhaled. "We'll leave from here at noon sharp! Then we'll go to the Anti-g terminal, and take the north bound tram. She says we'll stay in New Birth for a day or two before joining the caravan."

"Alright I'll be there, and this time … I won't be late."

An impish smile danced in her eyes. "Oh and by the way … it's M, to you."

Chapter 26

Providence Population Center

Giant space-scrapers jabbed their spires through the thin atmosphere of earth, while the lower levels slept under a blanket of clouds. When the residents of Providence awoke, they were greeted with an unnatural haze that crippled the metroplex.

The new technology developed by Supreme Commander Christos, simulated a debilitating fog which engulfed the city, and blinded them to the danger that waited just outside the walls.

In a slow, deliberate pace, the low rumble of tanks and APCs echoed through forest the as an unseen army moved into position. Behind them, the commanders of the heavy artillery punched in the coordinates, plotted the trajectory of their missiles and double checked their munitions. Every square inch of Providence was marked and targeted. When they were finished, not one stone would be left standing on the other.

"I'm sure glad we are taking the A tram rather than flying this time," Miss Xhu said as she and her two charges hustled down the concourse. "I haven't seen this kind of fog in a long time." *Not since the days before the catching away, as a matter of fact,* she thought to herself.

Luggage in hand, the three gathered on the loading platform, waiting on the next tram.

"Miss Xhu, what is that long box you're carrying?"

Emma asked.

Nguyen looked down at the jewel studded case and rubbed her fingers lightly over its leather exterior. Looking up, she said, "This is Gideon, the Sword of the Lord. If you will remember, it was given to me many years ago. With this being a special occasion, I wanted to bring it along. The ancient writings say that one day we will beat our swords into plow shears and I have not done so. This might be the time," she said cryptically.

"Could we see it?" asked Emma, her heart skipping a beat.

Miss Xhu's forehead wrinkled in contemplation. This was no toy, its blade had been used to execute judgment against the infidels on many occasions and it was not to be trifled with. She herself had not handled it since the earliest days of the kingdom. With reluctance, she took a slow breath. "No, I'd rather not take it out. I hope never to look upon it again."

Disappointed, Emma sat back in silence. She wondered what secrets lay hidden inside that jeweled box. Seeing her quizzeled face, Jamis patted her hand to quiet her next question. A few uncomfortable minutes later and the tram slipped silently into the terminal. Its door slid open like two welcoming arms. Overhead, an automated voice herded the trio forward. They stepped up to the scanner, showed it their boarding passes and waited their turn to enter the tram.

"What was that?" questioned Jamis, as a slight tremor vibrated beneath his feet.

A wisp of dirt sifted through a fission in the ceiling and the lights swayed slightly.

Wide-eyed, Emma looked, her pupils searching for some unseen explanation. "Suddenly, I felt woozy."

"You mean wobbly? Kinda like back on Planet Edenica?" Jamis asked half kidding.

Emma shivered, "Don't remind me of that awful place." The lights flickered, and she grabbed his arm.

"Where did all this fog come from?" Joy asked as her hover-board lifted from the ground.

Timothy stepped on his and engaged the lift charge. "I don't know. This stuff is as thick as pea-soup. I hope we can find our way to the Sanctuary, I never had a chance to thank Saint Vincent for doing the memorial service."

Joy shook her head. "He did a wonderful job of honoring mom and dad."

"Yes, he did. I can't believe all the people who came out for the service. It was beautiful."

Joy waited for Timothy to get his equilibrium. She giggled as he teetered and fell off with a thud. "I already miss Emma and she hasn't even left yet."

"Well, I for one am glad we decided not to go to Jerusalem, especially after the last harrowing experience. The thought of flying makes me nervous." He glanced down at his leg. With the new technology developed over the centuries, they were able to regrow the burnt tissue, but he was still doing therapy to rebuild the muscle. He placed his feet on the hover-board and rose a dozen inches from the ground.

Joy giggled, "You know you're flying now?"

He weaved a little and caught his balance. A crooked smile tugged at the corners of his mouth. "I don't consider hover-boards as flying."

Joy reached out her hand and took his. Together they glided through the fog in the general direction of the Sanctuary of the Truth. With each turn, shadowed forms moved through the veiled atmosphere as pedestrians wandered aimlessly. The dark shapes of buildings emerged, then disappeared in the haze, and several times they had to adjust their course to keep from running into someone or something.

Finally, they arrived at the front door of the Sanctuary, their togas soaked from the dewy air.

"This weather has made a mess of my hair," Joy said, wiping the drips from her eyes.

Timothy nodded admiringly at his sister. Though only nine, she was already turning out to be quite a lady. They stepped off their hover-boards and shoved them inside their back packs.

Cloaked in the command center, Supreme Commander Christos nodded to General Hakeem. Like a plague of locusts, war hover-crafts rose and filled the morning sky.

Hearing something overhead, Joy cocked her head, and squinted through the fog.

A flash followed by the concussion of a building imploding knocked her and Timothy off their feet.

"Timothy, what's happening?"

He jumped to his feet. Another building exploded, sending him skittering across the pavement. His hands dug into the pavement sending fire up his arms.

"We're under attack," he cried amid twisting metal and falling debris.

In the distance, an echoed scream for help faded in the din. He grabbed her and covered her with his body, as a plasmic neutron missile raced overhead. Its heat signature punched holes in the fog giving it a ghastly ghost-like appearance. The missiles struck the crystalline zirconium space-scrapers with deadly accuracy. Razor-sharp glass rained down upon the

The Stranger Among Us

unsuspecting residents. As the towering giants fell, the heavy artillery opened fire, pounding the city with photon shells. Within an hour, the city was ablaze, turning the air into a toxic concoction of micro particles and poisonous gas.

Timothy grabbed the handle of a massive door, pulled, and led Joy into the sacred building. As they ran down the aisle, another explosion rocked the building.

Glancing up, he caught a glimpse of brilliant flashes reflecting through the stained-glass windows.

"It looks like New Year's Eve fire-works out there," he said between gulps of air.

Suddenly, one of the windows exploded. Shards of glass and metal framework showered down around them. He grabbed Joy and pulled her under one of the pews, shielding her from the burning debris. A moment later, he stood and pulled her out and led her toward the front. "This way," he cried, as the area where they stood a moment earlier ignited into flames.

Seeing an exit, they dashed through it and found a flight of stairs. The earth shook, sending Joy sprawling. Timothy grabbed her to keep her from toppling down a flight of steps. Cautiously, they crept further down until they reached the bottom. An iron door stood as the lone sentinel between life and death. He pulled, and the rusty hinges resisted.

"Here, let me help," Joy's small voice echoed through the dark corridor. Timothy smiled and put his back in it. The door squeaked open. "Get in," he cried.

He yanked the door closed just as the floor shook. Something crashed on the other side.

"What was that?"

Timothy peered into the darkness, his heart slammed against the walls of his chest like a hammer on an anvil. "I think it was the Sanctuary collapsing.

The moments turned to minutes, then multiplied. All he

heard was their rhythmic breathing and the constant pounding of explosions.

"It's so dark in here, isn't there a light?" Joy asked. "Oh, I know."

Timothy heard rustling, then a jar filled with lightening bugs appeared glowing in Joy's hand. The yellow glare painted her face with a soft glow.

"Smart girl, I'm going to give you an A for creativity."

"That would be a C not an A."

He shook his head, "Whatever, at least now we can see where we are."

Joy started rooting through the shelves."

"What are you looking for?"

"Bandages, you look terrible. Let me do something about those cuts. Where are we anyway?"

"I'm not sure. After you patch me up, let's explore."

Joy found a first-aid kit. Like a nurse, she began cleaning his wounds and putting BAND-AIDS on the cuts on his arms.

"There, that should hold you," she said as she kissed the last wound.

He admired the brave front she was putting on and hoped she didn't sense the fear he was feeling.

He lifted the jar of lightening-bugs and pushed deeper into the vault. He stopped along a wooden shelf. He picked up a can, and groaned.

"What is it Timmy?"

"These Baked Beans, are dated, January, 3020. Now I know where we are. We're in an old bomb shelter."

"Bomb shelter? What's that?"

"It's where we are and it might be the last place we'll be."

The Stranger Among Us

The horizon of Providence glowed orange as ash and cinders ascended in columns of black smoke. Commander Christos stood in the observation hover-craft and watched the attack unfold. For the first time, his face yielded to a fiendish grin and a guttural laugh percolated in his chest. With a quick nod, he gave the order for the ground assault to commence.

Tanks and foot soldiers began their slow advance through the defenseless city. Its mighty walls which once stood as silent sentinels now lay in ruins. Within hours of the initial attack, the city was overrun. Those few Eonians who resisted were quickly illuminated and by daybreak, the flag of the United Nations flew over the ruins of Providence.

The Anti-g Tram

"You would think after a thousand years of practice, the baggage handlers would have learned how to handle luggage the proper way," Miss Xhu mused. "I've seen better treatment back in the bad ol' days."

"I've got all my stuff," Emma said, looking around the compartment.

"Me too. I believe in traveling light."

"Yeah well, two togas and a fresh pair of BVDs don't fit my idea of packing light." Emma said with a nudge.

The mechanical voice came alive again. "Ladies and gentlemen, please take your seats. We have just been informed that Providence has come under attack by forces of unknown origin. Although this appears to be an isolated incident, we are not certain. The supreme authority has declared a state of emergency."

Emma's face paled. "Timothy, Joy, we must go back. We can't leave them." She stood just as the tram lurched forward.

"Please remain calm and in your seats, this tram is departing." The voice crackled.

Jamis grabbed her. She buried her face in his shoulder, sobbing. "We can't go back, M. It's too dangerous and this tram isn't stopping."

Her shoulders shook as she continued to weep.

"I thought something wasn't right. All those paramilitary men roaming the countryside were playing war games, and we walked smack-dab in the middle of them," Jamis said.

Miss Xhu looked up from her transponder, "Yes, and we nearly got killed for our trouble."

The tram shot through the tube at lightning speed. Behind it came a shock wave of fire. The rush of air from the collapsing tube nearly blew it off its rail. It shook violently.

"I wish I knew what was happening," Emma mumbled out loud.

Nguyen pulled Emma close and wrapped her arms around her. "We will, just as soon as we get inside the terminal in New Birth, I'll check on Timothy and Joy, alright?"

Emma's sat-comm vibrated. She looked at the caller ID. "It's Timmy!" She pushed the button. "Hello?"

"M, it's me, Timothy, something's happening. I think we're under attack."

"Timothy, where is Joy? Are you safe?"

"Yes, we're safe. We were in the Sanctuary when it all began. We ran to the basement and found an old bomb shelter. It's stocked with food and water enough to last us weeks. But I don't think anyone could get to us, even if they knew where we were."

"Why is that?"

Timothy coughed as a thin wisp of dust filtered through small cracks in the ceiling, "Because I think the walls collapsed outside the door. We're buried in here."

Emma's shoulders sagged. "Okay Timothy, You stay safe, we'll come and get you, as soon as we can."

Static filled the line and the comm went dead.

Chapter 27

New Birth Population Center

  The tram carrying Miss Xhu, Jamis and Emma glided to a gentle halt.
  "You have now arrived in New Birth Population Center. Please be aware of your belongings and your children. Disembark to your right and proceed to the luggage retrieval zone. And thank you for choosing the A. G. Tram for your transportation needs. We hope your stay in New Birth or wherever God leads you is pleasant. Have a blessed day." The automated voice gave no indication of the impending danger that awaited their city.
  The doors slid open and the trio exited the tram. Almost immediately a throng of panic stricken Eonians pushed in. Miss Xhu and her companions shoved passed them like salmon going up stream.
  "It is Hanoi all over again," Miss Xhu exclaimed, as mortals from all levels of society scrambled to leave the city. She led her charges up the steps to the street level.
  The scene wasn't much different. People scurried about carrying water and other provisions from the main distribution hubs. Emergency vehicles skimmed between space scrapers, their sirens blaring.
  "Oh my," Nguyen said, hand to her lips. "I had no idea."
  Wide eyed, Emma gathered close to her teacher. "I want to go home," her voice tinged with fear.

"Come on, let's get off these streets before someone runs us down," Jamis said.

He grabbed Nguyen's luggage and led the way toward a waiting taxi-craft. Emma raised her hand in protest, but was left standing. She snatched the handles of her carry-ons and raced after them, huffing.

After checking into their rooms, Emma and the others gathered in the lobby around one of two large plasma screens.

"The images coming from Providence are devastating," Nguyen said. "Any word from Timothy since the last time you talked?" she asked unblinking.

Not wanting to make eye contact, Emma shook her head, "No, nothing. What have you heard?"

Nguyen brushed a strand of hair from the corner of her mouth and smiled. "The authorities, the media centers, the solar-net are all saying the attack came from one of the rogue mini-nations, but no one has taken responsibility as of yet."

Emma lifted her sat-comm to her mouth,

"Timothy?"

Nothing. Exasperated, she ended the call. "The bank is overloaded with people trying to make or receive calls," a slight tremble in her voice.

She wrapped her arms around her waist and released a heavy sigh. "I wish I knew something, anything." She pinched the bridge of her nose, eyes closed in prayer.

Jamis, who had slipped into the crowd of gawkers, moved closer and leaned down to speak. Nguyen's finger rose to her mouth, stopping him mid whisper. Amid the rush of people pressing past them, the three stood in silence, waiting for an answer which would never come.

Moments turned to minutes, and Nguyen lifted her head. "Since there is nothing we can to here, let's do a little sight-seeing and try to not worry about what's happening in Providence for a while."

Emma's eyes popped open. "Miss Xhu, how can you suggest such a thing when my family, my grandparents, Timothy and Joy may be suffering or even dead?" Her protests resonated among the gathered assembly.

Embarrassed, Miss Xhu dropped her eyes and searched the floor for moral support. Jamis stepped closer. "M, she's right. There's nothing we can do here. No sense standing here staring at the screen." Heads nodded.

Emma huffed and stomped for the exit. "Okay, fine, but I'm still going to worry." She stepped to the street and crossed her arms. "Where can we go? This city is nearly in lock-down."

Miss Xhu gave a weak smile, "Oh, I know of a few places that will always be open. Let's start with the Bio. Dev. Center."

"The Bio-what?" her voice flat.

"The Biometric Development Center, the place is amazing. They are always coming up with new and innovative ways to use earth's resources. They have discovered certain trees produce leaves which, when properly prepared, can reverse the effects to aging." She paused and glanced at her reflection. "Not that it would help me, I'm the same age as I'll always be," she said over her shoulder.

Emma skipped to catch up to her and Jamis. "We need to tell them about the tree we found with eatable leaves."

"M, remember the ones that tasted like watermelons? We ate tons of them. Oh and don't forget the citrus fruit."

Emma, not wanting to stay upset for long, pushed a smile past her frustration. "Yes, and one day I'll get you back for the trick you pulled, too."

By noon, they'd finished the tour. Emma raced for the exit and pulled out her sat-comm. Disappointed, she stared at the device as if that would make the busy signal stop blinking. It didn't work.

"Let's get something to eat, and see if there's any news coming out of Providence from the Sat-net." Nguyen said, pointing to a sidewalk cafe'.

They chose a table with a white linen cloth and sat down. A waiter daftly placed three glasses of water on the table not taking his eyes off the plasma screen.

"Are you ready to order?" he said between glances.

The news footage looked like something from the War of the Worlds. Providence lay in ruins. Heavily armed hover-crafts moved above the city shooting randomly.

"I'm not hungry," Emma said, eyes glued to the screen.

"Honey, I know it's hard, but you need to eat," Miss Xhu said. "God will take care of Timothy and Joy. Remember, he led them to the bomb shelter just at the right time. When it's safe, I'll personally see to it that we send in a rescue team to find them. I promise."

Emma fingered her water glass and took a sip. "Oh, alright, I'm just so worried."

Jamis reached over the table and patted her on the back of the hand. "If nothing else, I'll go and bring them out."

She pulled her hand back and folded it on her lap. "And what? Get yourself killed being heroic? I don't think so."

"Yes, I could do it. Remember my old hover-craft? I tinkered around with it and discovered how the cloaking device works."

Emma wadded up her napkin and tossed it. "Jamis, aren't you forgetting that you left that stupid thing back in Providence? It's probably been incinerated like the rest of the city. And what is it about that dumb cloaking thing? Give it a rest," her voice tense.

Miss Xhu cocked her head with interest. "Now you've got my attention. Jamis, how does it work?"

Emma's mouth gaped, "Miss Xhu, don't encourage him."

She ignored her statement, eyes keen with interest.

At her raised eyebrows and obvious curiosity, he said, "Well, it's quite simple actually. The device is attached to the hover-craft's skin, which is covered with an ionic substance. The device reverses the effects light has on its outer shell. Instead of reflecting light, the ion coated surface absorbs the light, making it blend into its surroundings."

Nguyen shifted closer accidentally knocking over her glass. The water spilled and ran over the table, soaking Jamis' toga. He jumped to his feet.

"That's alright, I'll be okay," he said with a slight laugh. "Actually, this is the perfect time to demonstrate what I've learned. You see, I was able to scrape some of the ionic substance from the hover-craft. I mixed it with a neutral polymer and applied it to my body."

"You did what?" Emma's mouth gaped open.

His hands rose in mock surrender, "Don't worry, it's not harmful ... I think."

"What do you have to do to make it work?" Nguyen's interest piqued.

"This," he turned a nob on a small box, and vanished except for the wet spot.

"Jamis, you come back here right now!" Emma commanded.

A fiendish laugh echoed from behind Emma. Jamis reappeared. "Cool huh?"

"Jamis, stop fooling around with that stuff, it's dangerous," Emma whispered through tight lips.

His cavalier attitude irritated Emma.

"Anybody hungry besides me?" he asked.

Emma released a frustrated breath and slumped back in her seat.

Two men sat, listening, watching through darkened sunglasses. "Mic, did you see that?" asked one of the men as he peered over his menu.

"Yeah, I sure did. You think the boss would want to know about it?" his scruffy chin moved as he spoke.

"Why do ya think he sent us? Of course he wants to know. Now get a move on. We need to get this info to him before they leave New Birth." Unnoticed, they rose and left the restaurant.

"After lunch, I want to take you guys to the tallest building in the world. It's called Pisgah, named after the highest point on the Mt. Nebo mountain range. From there we'll be able to see the entire eastern seaboard and far into the unpopulated lands to our west," Miss Xhu said, her voice carrying a tone of hopefulness.

"Good, maybe we could see Providence…or what's left of it," Emma said over the rim of her glass.

The sun was still high when they gathered on the south side of the observation deck and scanned the horizon. An angry black cloud rose in the distance and formed the ominous shape of a mushroom.

"That used to be our home, M," Jamis said, a slight tremor in his voice.

"Yes, and it still is. We have got to find a way back and rescue Timothy and Joy." Her jaw set with determination.

"Don't worry M, we will," he stood and gazed at the rising column of smoke and shook his head.

"Let's go, there is one other place I'd like to see before it closes," Miss Xhu said leading to the return elevator.

The Stranger Among Us

By the time they reached street level, the sun shot amber spokes of rays between buildings. A brisk wind blew down the canyon of the city and nipped at Emma's cheeks.

Miss Xhu, who never seemed to get tired, looked at Jamis and Emma, "I've got one last stop to make if you guys are up to it."

"Where's that, Miss Xhu?" Jamis asked.

She pointed down the street, "It's the Museum of Ancient History."

Emma groaned wearily. "I can't wait until I get my glorified body. Maybe then my arches won't hurt," she said, rubbing her foot.

Jamis rolled his eyes.

"Come along you two, it's not far."

With a brisk pace, Miss Xhu led the way through the busy street. Window displays beckoned their attention with each passing store. Eonian models draped in gaudy apparel stood provocatively.

On each corner, vendors peddled their wares to passersby. Overhead, low altitude hover-crafts whizzed between buildings as if they were sent on some fiendish mission.

Emma noticed a singular man, dressed in an old-fashioned suit and tie, proclaiming the end of the world. A group of people gathered mocking at the sight.

On an opposite corner a well-dressed man in a toga, stood. His wavy hair parted in the middle and fell loosely over his shoulders. He carried a placard proclaiming one message… 'Freedom.'

"Citizens of the world, sign my petition urging the city fathers to ratify the declaration of independence from the United Population Centers." His voice resonated over the sound of the traffic.

"Blasphemy," Miss Xhu said, passing a group of

181

shaggy youths. Angry voices rose, and she quickened her pace.

"Keep going, I don't think they like the immortals right now." Her words came in short phrases.

Breathlessly, they arrived at the doors of a large building.

"Here we are." Miss Xhu's voice was light and airy.

Emma's mouth gaped open, "Are we going to tour this all in one day? This is bigger than the Smithsonian museum."

Nguyen shook her head, "Oh no honey, this would take weeks to s e e completely. I've been here dozens of time and have yet to see half of it. I just love to browse and take my time reading all the little plaques." She held up two fingers an inch apart. "So if you two want to explore on your own, go right ahead."

She paused and glanced at the clock on the wall. "It's three o'clock, why don't we meet back here at closing, get a bite to eat and head to our hotel rooms."

Emma nodded wearily.

"Come on M, let's check out the Pre-Historic Era." He took her by the hand, and tugged her down a wide corridor.

"Oh no, not more dinosaurs." Emma's pleas echoed. Nguyen smiled and kept walking.

The dark paneled walls sported a gallery of portraits by noted artists from the last century. They beckoned Emma's attention, but Jamis' grasp kept her skipping to keep up. He turned a corner led her down one corridor and stopped. Emma put her hands on her knees, her breath coming in gulps.

Pointing at the wall plaque, he said, "M, look, the Pre-Rapture Era. Let's check it out, we can see dinosaurs anytime."

Relieved, she nodded, "Good, I've seen enough of those things anyway."

They stepped into the anti-room and were greeted with the pungent scent of new carpet. Emma slipped her sandals off and wiggled her toes in the soft folds.

"Ah, this feels so good," she said, letting the carpet absorb her weight with each muffled step.

Defused light from recessed fixtures shone upward on tall columns, while narrow beams highlighted special points of interest. Wide displays held a menagerie of assorted historical items dating from as far back as the twenty-first century. They began walking around, looking at the many inventions.

"Would you look at those," Emma exclaimed.

Jamis leaned over the glass enclosure. "They called them 'Cell Phones' that's an interesting name."

"Look over here," Emma said, pointing at a free standing pedestal. "This is a Laptop Computer. You actually had to input information by pushing on those letters with your fingers, how archaic."

As they made their way around the room, pointing out the interesting inventions, they came upon a chamber.

"What is it," Jamis asked, leaning in.

The unit stood about five feet tall and about five feet around.

"This reminds me of an early version of a hover-craft," he said, pulling the handle. With ease, the door swung open. "That's interesting, a double seated outhouse." A wry smile played on his lips.

"Very funny, Jamis." Emma said, taking one of the two padded seats. Reaching over, she patted the other. "Come, sit, this is the thing I was telling you my great, great-grandfather invented." She pointed to the plaque overhead.

"It says; 'Time Chamber,' invented by Jeremiah Newton in the year 2547 A.D. Using the power of recollection, and projection one can transport themselves into the known past.'"

"What does the 'Known Past' mean'?" Jamis asked, stepping inside. The cushioned seat wheezed under his weight.

He grabbed the seat restraint and pulled it over his lap.

"Well I guess it means the part of history which, is within each of our memories. Look here, another plaque reads, 'The Known Past' is any part or parts of one's combined knowledge base. By meditating on your history, no matter how ancient, you can transport your physical form back into any period within that time zone. To return to the present you need only to focus on the time and place you were when you left.'

"So it's all done by mental telepathy?" Jamis asked.

"In a way," Emma kept reading, "The plaque continues and says, 'For a complete record of your Known Past you must study the ancient manuscripts located in Jerusalem."

Jamis straightened, "That's where we're headed. Maybe we can stop and visit the Cathedral of Ancient Manuscripts, and look up our histories. In the meantime, do you want to try it, and see if it really works?" Jamis asked, sliding the door shut.

Emma swallowed hard wondering what was coming next. "Yeah, I guess. Where do ya want to go?"

"I don't know, how about going to the Pre-Rapture Era. Let's see if it was as bad as Miss Xhu said."

"That's a great idea…where to, driver?" Emma asked, her voice filled with anticipation.

"Let's go to Beaumont, Colorado."

"What! Where on earth is Beaumont, Colorado?"

"You and Miss Xhu aren't the only ones who study ancient history. I've read a little about my ancestors, and they go way back to some town in the far west territory called, Beaumont, Colorado. That's all I know."

"Okay, if you say so. But is it in my known memory?"

"According to the history books, yes. So put on these four-dimensional goggles and begin focusing your attention."

Silence.

"Nothing's happening," a nervous giggle percolated in

her throat.

"Okay, let's try this." He reached out, his fingers interlocked with hers.

One moment they were sitting in a Time Chamber, the next they were sitting on a park bench in the center of Beaumont, Colorado.

Chapter 28

The Sanctuary of the Truth

Joy peered up, her eyes stabbing the ceiling in a failed attempt at seeing what was happening on the surface. The earth vibrated. "What was that?" Her voice wavered.

Timothy shrugged, "How should I know? They could be leveling the metroplex."

The ground shook yet again as another building collapsed.

"Look Joy, over there, it's a monitor screen. Let's see if it still works."

He flipped a switch and the screen flickered to life. Clouds of orange smoke drifted across the screen while phantom shadows moved in and out of view. Giant machines crawled along the surface spraying fire from long tubes. The blasts struck building after building causing them to burst into flames. People running from one building to another were cut down mercilessly by men with impulse weapons.

An angry face appeared, and Joy jumped back. "Oh, that guy scared me to death," her hand on her chest. "Oh, Timmy, who are those people and why are they doing this to our city?"

Suddenly, the face pulled back and an elbow smashed the lens. "Well that takes care of that." He stood, staring at the grey screen. "I don't know honey. Maybe it's better mom and dad didn't live to see these evil days. They would be so upset."

Joy laid her head on his lap. Maybe it would have been better had we stayed with the Forest Saints."

Guilt stabbed him. "I've thought that same thing. But who knows. They may have been the first to have felt the hand of those evil men."

She lifted her head and held his gaze. "Then we'd be in Heaven now too."

Timothy smiled and brushed the hair out of her eyes. "I thought about that too."

He shoved his hand into his back pack and withdrew the globe Andorra had given him. The arrow pointed west. "Are you thinking what I'm thinking?"

She returned an impish grin.

Timothy pushed himself up from his seat, and went over to the shelter's door. He slammed his shoulder against it. It's hard surface forbid their exit. Frustrated, he kicked it sending a bolt of pain up his leg.

"Ouch, that hurt," he said, rubbing his knee.

"Timmy, we can't stay here, try again." Her plaintive voice echoed in the flickering light.

He backed into the door and pressed his weight against it. The steel door groaned, then yielded. Dust swirled the musty air. He pushed again. The door moved another few inches and he slid through the tight opening.

"Joy, hand me your light," he called from the darkness.

A moment later, her hand pushed the illumination through the opening. Rocks and debris littered the stairwell through which they'd just come.

"I don't know Joy. The stairway is barely navigable." He returned, dust covered, but hopeful.

"Before we go, don't you think we should take a few things to eat, just in case we get lost?" Joy asked.

Timothy stepped back in the bomb shelter, his head and shoulders covered with a fresh layer of dirt. He eyed the shelves with interest.

"That's a good idea if we can find something that's edible. Let's see what they left us."

He picked up a can of peaches, and read the label. "Hum, some of this food isn't so old. I think someone has been keeping this place stocked in the event something like this happened."

"I want the peaches if you don't." Her words pierced the shadows.

"Take them. I've got my eyes on the corned beef."

Joy wrinkled her nose, "Yuck! You can have it."

After collecting a few necessary items, they slipped them into their back packs and crawled out. The air hung thick with dirt and shafts of sand filtered through fissions. The constant pounding above them vibrated the walls. An avalanche of rubble rolled down the stairwell.

Timothy climbed over a broken pipe, stumbled and fell against the wall.

"Be careful Timothy." Her voice echoed.

Cautiously, they got to the first level, and turned the corner, breathing hard. He reached into the pulsating light of the firefly jar and pulled her up.

"Come on Joy, let's keep going before this place caves in."

Suddenly, the door opened, and a man stood at the top of the steps. The blaze of his torchlight cast a white ray, temporally blinding Timothy. He and Joy ducked behind a concrete block.

With deliberate steps, the figure began a slow descent carefully picking his way down the steps. A slight whimper escaped Joy's throat. Instinctively, Timothy's hand grasped a rock and prepared to defend his sister. With a raised finger, he signaled her to get down and stay quiet. She blinked, the whites of her eyes flashing out a coded message.

Despite the chilled air which pricked his skin like a thousand needles, sweat ran into his eyes obscuring his sight. He swiped his hand over his face, feeling the slick mixture of soot and sweat between his fingers.

The torch stopped its downward motion and slashed a wide swath through the dust-laden air. It fixed its beam on Timothy's face. He recoiled under the blinding light. A gentle voice penetrated the darkness.

"Master Timothy?" asked the voice behind the light. "Saint Vincent?" he answered, shielding his eyes.

A sharp click later and the beam softened to a yellow glow.

"Why yes," he answered, his robe torn and stained. His gnarled hands, painted crimson from the blood of those he'd tried to save, held his trusty staff and the torchlight.

"I've been praying for you two. I thought it was you, and knew if you made it to the bomb shelter, you'd be safe. Why are you trying to leave?" His kind voice was a welcome relief.

"We didn't want to be buried alive," Joy confessed.

A soft chuckle echoed off the crumbling walls. "You needn't fear, the Lord is with you my child, and now, I am with you. Now come along, I know of a way out."

He pivoted and began a careful ascent. Halfway up, he stopped, his fingers followed an unseen line on the wall until they found what they sought.

Swoosh

A secret panel popped open. "Follow me." His dry voice carried a sense of urgency.

Timothy glanced at Joy. She shrugged her shoulders, and scampered after the stately gentlemen. The rhythmic beating of condensation bounced off the stone walls. With each warm breath their exhalations came in short puffs. The slick floor glistened orange in the dim illumination.

"Watch your step," he said over his hunched shoulders. Three shadowed figures trudged in thoughtful silence for what seemed miles.

Finally, the elderly gentleman paused to listen. The pounding on the surface which dogged their labored steps had softened to a distant rumble.

"Where are we?" inquired Timothy.

Saint Vincent held up the light and scanned the walls. He smiled. "We are directly under the great walls surrounding our city. Of course, those walls now lay in ruins."

"How much farther," asked Joy.

He ran his fingers through his beard. Specks of dirt joined the littered floor. "Oh, not much. This tunnel was carved out by my father and the other priests of the Sanctuary. I was but a lad back then, his face brightened. Father feared this day would come and we, I would need a way out." His eyes twinkled with wisdom. "He was right." Each word yielded puffs of condensation which formed and dissipated in the cool hallway.

Timothy rubbed the chill from his arms. They continued through the darkened passage until they reached a flight of stairs.

Saint Vincent's voice grew ominous. "This will take us to the surface. But who knows what awaits us up there. The last time I checked, the enemy had breached the walls and was

pushing toward the center of the city. I'll check to see if it's clear."

In a pace which surprised Timothy, Saint Vincent double stepped it to the top. He cringed as the rusty door opened and poked his head out, scanning the area.

"Psst, come on, the coast is clear," he whispered and waved them up the steps. They stepped from the door into the moonless night. Billows of thick black smoke wafted across the open ground between their lair and a stand of young trees.

Gathering his soiled robes, Saint Vincent plunged into the night. "This way," he called over his shoulder.

Timothy took three paces and glanced back. Like Lot's wife, he froze in his tracks, staring. "Providence is gone," he gasped.

Smoke and ash ascended as the first sacrifice to the god of war. A thick cloud gathered overhead raining shards of ash, the size of snowflakes on the blackened landscape. Occasional flashes from exploding cooling stations punctuated the night sky, and the drone from military hover-crafts gave an ominous warning. Their spot lights cut swaths through the smoke in search of survivors. It was all he could do to keep from running back into the city in search of his family.

"Timothy!" called a voice from behind him. He turned and saw Joy waving franticly. "Someone is coming."

Overhead, a large battle-craft swung its beam on the ground. Almost on cue, it began moving in his direction. He tried to run, but his feet refused to move. Without warning, the weight of another body slammed into him, sending him sprawling. Saint Vincent rolled to the ground and leapt to his feet. Bullets chunked up pieces of turf as the battle-craft strafed the area. It made a tight U-turn and came back for a second pass.

"Run!" cried Saint Vincent, and shoved Timothy toward the woods.

He dashed toward the door leading to the tunnel, waving his arms franticly. "Over here," he cried at the approaching spot light.

Timothy ran into the thicket. Tripping over a fallen log,

he rolled to a stop next to Joy. He climbed to his feet, and watched in horror as the hover-craft bore down upon the defenseless man. One blast from it impulse weapon, and Saint Vincent was gone.

"Nooo!" cried Joy. Timothy clung to her barely able to keep her from running into the open. The hover-craft swung around. It's bright beam scouring the rugged ground, looking for more targets. In a flash, the beam passed directly over their heads, then cut to their left.

Grabbing Joy by the arm, he tugged her to her feet, and ran deeper into the forest. Thorny vines scratched like cats paws, clawing at their thin togas and exposed flesh. Timothy barehanded one thick vine and yanked it over his head. Blood trickled from his perforated hand. He ran until his legs burned and his lungs craved oxygen. Finally, he slowed his pace and leaned against a tree, panting.

"I think we made it," he said between gulps.

Joy collapsed on the uneven ground, her mind broken, too frightened, too traumatized to speak. She stared blankly at her brother.

Timothy pulled his sat-comm from his pocket. Concerned that his signal would be picked up by the enemy, he sent a text. 'Going to Nickolas,' and pressed send.

"Okay Joy, let's go," he said. Then he pulled their hover-boards from their back packs, and linked them together. "Here, lay on this." Using her globe for guidance, they rose above the trees and headed west.

Chapter 29

Beaumont, Colorado

Emma opened her eyes, "The air—it tastes so dusty."
"Yeah and it smells like fumes or something," Jamis said. A large vehicle belched a smoke drive past them. "Would you get a look at those earthbound forms of transportation, M."

"They're called automobiles or cars," pointing at a large SUV, its wheels squealing as it rounded the corner. "I feel rather exposed, sitting here in this toga," she said, rubbing her shoulder and glancing at a couple of onlookers. "Let's walk."

"I agree, maybe we can get an idea about this place."

Jamis helped her to her feet and began walking down the sidewalk when an elderly man stepped from behind a tree. He stuck out his hand. It was weathered with age but the deep crevices gave no indication that they were accustomed to hard work. "Say kids, could you loan a guy a few bucks?"

Jamis gaped at him. His torn overalls, unshaven face, and strong scent of alcohol, repulsed him.

"No sir. We can't help you." He took Emma by the hand, and quickened his pace. "What are bucks?" He whispered.

Her hand covered her mouth, trying to keep from laughing out loud. "I have no idea."

He guided her down the tree-lined avenue, peering in the storefront windows. The autumn sun pushed rays of light through the barren limbs. Children jumped into piles of colorful leaves under the watchful gaze of their mothers.

"This is an unusual time of the year," Emma said, looking at a picture of a witch on a broom painted on a storefront window.

Jamis read the accompanying inscription, "'Happy Halloween.' That's funny, she doesn't look too happy."

Passing a store named, J. C. Penny, Emma glanced at a display. "I've never seen so many naked women in my life."

"Uh, M, I don't think those were actually real people. They looked kinda stiff."

The next window, filled with a variety of tools and gadgets, held Jamis' interest. "Now there's a place I'd like to spend some time," eyes wide, taking in the sights.

They followed the sidewalk around a corner and entered an alley. A discarded newspaper tumbled across the narrow passage. An old man bent over, rummaging through a dumpster. They quickened their pace. Suddenly, a door opened and a man staggered out and fell off the curb. From inside came laughter, mingled with a loud metallic throbbing, punctuated by an uneven rhythm. A gray haze wafted out, making Emma's eyes water.

Out of curiosity, Jamis stepped in. Emma followed.

"Achoo," she sneezed.

"God bless you young lady," a scantily dressed woman said. Her arm hung loosely around a man's shoulder.

What's God got to do with it? Emma questioned as she and Jamis peered through the blue haze.

Men and women sat at a bar, drinking a brown foamy liquid from mugs. Others sat at a table playing a game of cards, while smoke curled upward in ever growing concentric circles. A man sat at an old piano plunking some unfamiliar tune. The room seemed to sway with an undulating beat. Emma's hand rose to her gaping mouth. A couple snuggled in a booth, acting inappropriately, captured her attention.

"Come on Jamis, let's get out of here. I've heard and seen enough."

They scurried back to the street. Shooo, my clothes smell like burnt trash," Jamis said, sniffing his toga.

Emma lifted her sleeve to her nose, "Mine too. I hope Miss Xhu doesn't get very close to us," she snickered.

Further down the block a set of doors beckoned. Above them flashed a sign in a multitude of blinking bulbs. Movies.

"What is a movie?" Emma asked, attempting to decipher the scrolling words.

"I don't know, let's go in and find out."

He pulled the door open. The chilled air bit into their skin like a thousand pin pricks.

"Burrr, this place is like freezer," Emma said, rubbing the goose-bumps on her bare shoulders.

Jamis gave her a gentle tug, and they pressed further inside. It took a few moments for their eyes to adjust to the dimmed light. Soft carpet absorbed each step until they reached the seating area. On one wall, flashed images of men and women.

Jamis grabbed her arm and yanked her into the corridor. Together, they quickly scampered through the door, red-faced and panting.

"Now I feel hot," fanning herself. "That was awful."

"This really is a wicked place," Jamis said, looking down the street. "I don't think I like Beaumont after all. It's every bit as bad as Miss Xhu said it was."

"Worse, can we go home now Jamis?" her eyes pleaded.

"Okay, but let's make one more stop."

"Where? I've seen enough evil in this place for a lifetime."

Hand in hand, they headed to the park. As they rounded

the corner, Emma stopped, and stared. "Look Jamis, a church."

The sign read, The Community First Church.

She grabbed the handle, "Shall we?"

Jamis shrugged his shoulders, "Why not."

They stepped into the foyer. The pungent smell of new carpet greeted their noses. Except for a large, circular table adorned with a flower display, the entry was empty. Cushioned seats invited the weary travelers to sit and rest, while soft music emanated from some unknown source. In the distance, an elderly gentleman pushed a machine on the floor. He looked up and waved. The whirl of the machine ground to a halt. His halting gait told Emma he was a man well stricken in years, yet his piercing dark eyes communicated an inner zest for life.

"Hello, may I help you?"

Emma held his gaze. "Uh, we are just visiting and wanted to stop in."

The fatherly figure stepped back and scanned them. His furrowed brows relaxed into a smile. "Well, we are closed for the day. Our services begin tonight at 7:00 o'clock and again tomorrow at 8:30 in the morning. We have contemporary and traditional services. However, I think you might like our blended service at noon."

"A blended what?" Emma asked.

The elderly man's gaze fell and he scuffed the carpet, nervously. Lifting his head, he took a quick look over his shoulder as if he expected some unseen spirit to leap from behind a curtain. "It's a mix of the old and the new…sorta."

Jamis glanced down at Emma. Her forehead wrinkled with a question.

"Well, we're not planning on staying that long," he said looking around.

The kindly older gentleman smiled warmly, and turned to go. Emma reached out and touched his arm, "Sir, may I ask you something?"

He hesitated then nodded.

"Now don't get me wrong, I'm not judging you or your church, but how is it that you have a church right in the middle of a town filled with all this wickedness and not make a difference?"

His eyes misted as he shifted uncomfortably. "I'm afraid you have a point young lady. On second thought, I don't think you'd like our blended service either."

He slowly turned and padded back down the corridor. A slight sniffle echoed off the dark paneled walls.

Emma and Jamis stepped outside. A cool breeze whipped past them on some unseen mission, scattering leaves in its wake.

"I don't like it here," she said.

"Neither do I, it gives me the creeps. But let's check out one more place."

Taking her by the hand, he led her across the street and down a brick path through a tree-lined park. On either side, a lush carpet of green grass invited their bare feet. Yielding to the temptation, Emma pulled off her sandals and skipped along the pathway. Suddenly, she stopped.

"Ouch!" she said, holding her foot while balancing on the other like a ballerina.

"What's wrong?" Jamis inquired.

"I don't know. I stepped on something," picking a sandspur from between her toes. She put her sandals on.

"Even the grass has bad things growing in it."

They continued their foray, smiling at the children who

played chase while doting mothers warned them not to get too close to the road. "Some things never change," she said.

Above a weathered door flashed the words, "Open."
"This is interesting," Jamis said, "especially if it is what I think it is."

The rusty knob yielded to his touch. With a groan, the rugged door swung open revealing the warm atmosphere. A bell chimed in silver ringlets as he shut out the cold.

Scattered throughout the room were tables and chairs boasting of salt and pepper shakers and napkin dispensers. Other than one lone person, Jamis and Emma were the only patrons. He led her to one of the tables in the back and took a seat.

"I think they serve food here," he whispered."

Music played from a machine in the corner. Its colored lights danced to the rhythm of the beat.

"M, what do you think these are?" He held up several greenish, rectangular pieces of paper. The number five imprinted on each corner.

She inspected them with interest. "I think these are bucks. You know, what that guy was asking for?"

A portly woman sporting a soiled apron waddled to their table. "What are you having?" her voice course, her face unfriendly.

Emma glanced at Jamis. He stared blankly back. "Having?"

"I, I'm not having anything," Emma sputtered, barely able to contain a giggle.

The woman cocked her head and placed a pudgy hand on her hip, glaring. "Well, we don't cater to no loitering. So order something or leave."

Emma lifted the proffered menu and quickly scanned its listings. "Um, we'll take this." She pointed to the apple pie al a mode.

The waitress huffed, wrote on a pad, and marched away.

As they waited, the bell above the door chimed, announcing the entrance of yet another customer. Two people entered, laughing at an unknown story which hung just out of the reach of Emma's hearing. They pushed past the empty tables in search of one particular seat. It was their table, marked by time and claimed by eminent domain. The guy nodded at Jamis, who took his cue and nodded back, wondering if it was some secret sign.

The waitress emerged from behind the counter carrying a tray. On it, were two plates of apple pie al a mode. She placed them on the table, and slid them in front of her customers, eying their garments.

"That'll be five dollars, Miss."

Emma fingered the fives dollar bills which lay on her lap. Guessing she was referring to the money, she handed them over as if she were being robbed. The old women's face brightened. "Thanks Miss."

The aroma of the hot apple pie wafted up, invigorating their senses. "Umm, whatever it is, sure smells good," Jamis said as he picked up his fork.

Shoveling a hearty bite into his mouth, he sat, savoring the warm doughy mixture of baked apples, cinnamon, and ice cream. "This is a whole lot better than those leaves you had me eating a few weeks ago," he said out of the corner of his mouth.

Emma lifted her fork and chewed thoughtfully. "You're right. I wonder what it is."

Keeping his voice low, Jamis looked around. "This place may be evil, but they sure know how to make a meal."

She studied her slice of pie, "I don't think this is a whole meal. I think this is like the first dish, or something," she whispered.

Jamis opened his mouth to speak, when Emma raised a finger. "Listen."

Chapter 30

The Outer Zone

Timothy clung to his sister as they laid on their hover-boards and skimmed along the tree tops. A light breeze blew across the upper branches causing them to wave in an undulating rhythm. Stars beyond count sparkled in brilliant splendor.

With Joy's jar of lightening bugs held high enough for him to see the needle, they navigated the jagged terrain. Chased by a crescent moon, they swung around one mountain and down into a valley. The orange illumination scattered its amber rays on a narrow creek, which cut its way through the woods.

"It looks so different at night," he said, pointing below.

Joy blinked and clung closer. "I don't like flying so high. It scares me."

"Well, we can't fly any lower for fear of being seen by a scout or some creature coming after us."

The hover-boards rose and fell with each nuance of the terrain, like a pair of dancers. He glided over a crest, and a wide field, bathed in pale shadows welcomed the weary travelers.

"Hey, this looks familiar. Let's go down and check it out," Timothy said. He leaned to his left, and circled around, bring their boards to a gentle stop on the mossy turf.

In the distance, a lone owl asked the eternal question, "Whoo, whoo?"

Silently, Joy tucked behind a shrub. Moments later she returned smiling. "I'm glad we stopped when you did, or you might have gotten wet."

Timothy pushed his hands in his pockets and scuffed the ground. "I understand. I had to go too."

A stray cloud skittered past the shadowed moon and a hollow breeze stirred what few dried leaves that clung tenaciously to a branch.

"Okay, now that that's taken care of, let's see if this is the right place."

"It is," Joy said, confidence rang in her childish voice.

Timothy pulled his hand out of his pocket. "How can you be so sure?"

"That's easy." She walked over to a low blackberry bush. Steaks of silver glimmered on its broad leaves. "See this?" A triumphant smile pinched her cheeks.

A wristband dangled lightly from her fingers. "I left it here just in case we came back." Her bright face gleamed in the moon light.

"Clever girl."

She grinned.

Timothy scanned the sparse landscape. "I wonder how I'm going to start a signal fire."

In the dimness, he watched Joy shift out of her backpack and begin scavenging through it. She pulled out a box of matches and held it out.

"Where did you get those?"

An impish smiled tugged at the corners of her mouth, "You gave them to me when we were running from those men, remember?"

Timothy's eyes widened in surprise, "Like I said, clever girl."

Eagerly, he gathered a stack of twigs and dried leaves in the center of a bare patch of ground, and lit a match. Guarding the new-born flame like a hen protecting her chicks, he knelt over the pile, and touched a dry twig. It caught and began to creep from one leaf to another, a wisp of smoke swirled upward and joined the light breeze. Cupping his hands, he knelt, and gently blew. The infant embers grew, and within moments, a small flame erupted into a raging fire which demanded to be fed. He threw in a few larger twigs and watched the embers ascend like a thousand glowing souls.

"If the Wood Saints are still alive, they should be here pretty quickly."

"Or those men with guns," Joy said, looking around the circle of light.

Timothy tossed an unwilling branch on the fire. "One way or another, we'll know in a few minutes."

As they stood staring into the flames, a shadow moved. Five figures emerged from the darkness, dressed in green, carrying bows and arrows. So silently had they arrived, that Timothy didn't notice until he was completely encircled.

"I see you have returned, my friends," said Andorra.

Timothy whirled around, mouth gaped.

"Andorra, I didn't hear you."

The warrior extended a weathered hand. A broad grin spread across his face. "Rose will be pleased. She has prayed every day for your return. Now you have."

Timothy swallowed, not knowing if he should run or surrender to the inevitable. He gripped the proffered hand and returned a crooked smile. "We are your prisoners, take us to your leader," he quipped.

The last warrior kicked dirt over the fire, it sputtered, sending up smoke signals.

Chapter 31

The Beaumont Cafe'

"It was so hard for me to live out my faith in my home," the young lady began.

"My father took a rather open view of religion when I made the decision to trust Christ. Back then he believed, 'I'm Okay. You're Okay,' that all religions lead to the same place. He would often say, 'who's to say if your view is better or worse than someone else's.'"

"That's what your dad was preaching the other night. Don't you agree with him?"

"Actually no," she said softly. She brushed a short crop of hair behind her ear. "I don't agree with him. All religions are not the same, and all roads don't lead to Heaven. The Bible says in Matthew 7:13, 'Enter ye in at the strait gate: for wide is the gate, and broad is the way, that leadeth to destruction, and many there be which go in there at.'"

"You see," she paused, "there's only one way to get into Heaven, and that is by trusting Christ as your Savior."

"What about your mom?"

"Mom was different. She hit the ceiling, wouldn't talk to me for weeks, and made fun of me all the time."

The young man sat back, and pinched the bridge of his nose.

"Why? I mean, you just prayed a prayer, what harm could there be?"

"You don't' get it, do you? You see, I was raised in

private schools with strict Muslim teachers."

Jamis narrowed his eyes, "What's she talking about?" he whispered.

M put her finger to her lips. "Shush!"

"I heard their teachings, memorized large portions of the Qur'an and frankly agreed with a lot of their thinking. Then a missionary to the Muslim people came to my school to give a counter view in my debate class. He said things I'd never heard before; that Jesus was the Son of God, that He and Allah were not the same. The way he described Allah, and the teachings of Jesus, I knew there was no comparison."

Jamis lifted a finger but Emma glared at him. "Listen."

"Then, when he showed the class from the Bible that Jesus came to earth to die for other people's sins, frankly, I was shocked. Allah would never have done that, nor would any other deity. To top it off, he showed us from the Bible that Jesus' death, burial and resurrection were all part of a master plan, prophesied centuries before it happened, I was hooked! I had to learn more. So over the next couple of weeks I met secretly with the missionary and then one day it happened."

"What happened then, M?" At his raised eyebrow, and obvious curiosity, she plunged ahead.

"I put my trust in the Lord Jesus Christ, that's what happened," she said with a smile.

"It was that simple? No tongues, no water, no laying on of hands?" He asked

"No silly, I simply put my faith in Jesus to forgive my sins, and take me to Heaven."

"M, how do you know it's real, you're not in Heaven yet?"

"God gave me the confidence through His Word."

The verse she quoted seemed strangely familiar to

The Stranger Among Us

Jamis, he knew where she was going with this conversation.

Pointing to her Bible she read, "He that believeth on the Son of God hath the witness in himself: he that believeth not God hath made him a liar; because he believeth not the record that God gave of his Son."

While she read, Jamis sat up straight and stared. *Who am I to be calling God a liar? I know what this lady is saying is true. It's time for me to get serious about this.*

He blinked and continued to listen ...

"... that ye may believe on the name of the Son of God."

Emma pushed her plate back and placed her elbows on the table. Leaning close, she said, "I feel like this has happened once before. Just look at them, they're so in love, she speaks with such passion about the Lord. She was telling him the same things I've been telling you."

Something inside of him yearned to believe, begged him to yield, to trust. When he saw the young man bow his head to pray, so did Jamis.

That day, the diner became a birthing center, as two people, a thousand years apart, were joined as brothers in Christ. The miracle of the new birth spanned the centuries, and touched their lives.

"Jamis, did you notice anything strange about those two?" Emma said, watching the young couple leave.

He cocked his head. "Beside the way they were dressed? No."

"I did, he kept calling her 'M,' that's what you call me."

His eyebrows rose. "Well, it's a small world, isn't it?"

"I wonder who they were, and what she meant when she said her mom was a Muslim," Jamis said.

Emma finished her pie. "I don't know, but did you catch the part about her father? The way he talked, he sounded like Professor Christos. He even had the same World-View."

The waitress came over and cleared the table. She jammed the greenish pieces of paper into her pocket, and walked away.

Emma glanced down at the crinkled paper, and wondered.

"That young lady really made the gospel of salvation clear to her boyfriend, didn't she?"

Jamis ran his fingers through his hair in exasperation. "This is really important to you isn't it, M?"

"Well yea, for us to be more than friends, you need to get this thing settled, plus, remember, we're both mortals. We aren't going to live forever."

Jamis smiled, "This truly is an evil place, except for the food," he said trying to change the subject. He scraped the last bite from his plate, and wiped his mouth. "I think we have seen enough. Do you want to go home?"

Emma nodded, "Do I ever." She tossed the paper bills on the table, took Jamis' hand and closed her eyes. A moment later, they were sitting in the time chamber, still holding hands.

Emma's sat-comm vibrated. She stepped from the time chamber, and pulled it out and looked at it. 'Going to Nickolas.'

Emma stared at the device.

"What is it M," Jamis asked, seeing her face blanch.

"It's from Timothy. I just got the text saying they were going to Nickolas the Wise and the Wood Saints."

Jamis breathed a sigh of relief, "That's good news. I just hope they're still alive."

"I don't know," Emma's fingers scrolled over the key pad looking for the proper response. "At least Timothy and Joy are out of that horrible bomb shelter. I'd hate to think of them cooped up in a concrete tomb."

The soft footfalls of Miss Xhu's slippered feet caught her attention.

"Oh Miss Xhu, I just got a text from Timothy."

She stepped close, and slipped her arm around her waist and gave her a hug.

"They'll make it Emma, I'm sure of it. In the meantime, try not to worry."

Her shoulders slumped and she stifled back a tear.

Nguyen glanced at her time piece. "It's getting late and they'll be closing soon, why don't we find a nice restaurant, relax over a hot meal before heading to our rooms."

Emma rubbed her belly, "I think I'll pass on eating." She cut her eyes in Jamis' direction, "As a matter of fact, we just got up from the table." An impish twinkle danced in her eyes.

Miss Xhu leaned closer; a quizzical look shaded her face. "Girl, you smell like smoke, where have you been?"

Emma's cheeks pinked. Jamis lowered his eyes and he pawed the floor.

"Hum, we kinda took a detour," she said, biting on her thumb nail, eyes wide.

Miss Xhu stepped back, crossed her arms, clearly unhappy.

"Well, you know I'll have to report this to the head master, we can't have you two sneaking off. Now let's go, I think we've had enough touring for the day," she huffed. Making a quick about-face she headed for the door. "Come along you two."

Emma took two steps and glanced over her shoulder, "Coming Jamis?"

He froze ... his eyes switching between Emma and his

teacher. "I, uh, I have a hunch," he said, backing toward the time chamber.

"Jamis, what are you doing?" Emma demanded.

Jamis disappeared into the chamber.

Before she could react, he slid the door shut and threw the lock.

Miss Xhu raced to the side of the time chamber and beat on the port hole.

"Jamis, you get out of that thing immediately," her voice taut.

Emma cupped her hands, and peered through the thick, dark glass window. She gasped and pulled away, eyes wide with terror.

"He's gone!"

Chapter 32

Millennium Research and Development Facility

The pristine halls of Millennium R and D Facility shone bright with fluorescent lights. Men and women, dressed in white lab coats, carrying clipboards scurried from one cubical to the other. With deliberate gait, they moved through their routine full of purpose and direction. Small carriages supported machines with dangling tubes, rolled with squeaking wheels at the behest of orderlies. Importantly dressed Eonians talked animatedly on sat-comms.

Jamis appeared in the shadowed corner and stepped to a kiosk at the intersection of two corridors. A young lady, clipboard in hand, approached with an even pace, head down, reading a print-out.

Thud!

Jamis bounced and fell to the floor. Its cold hard surface sent a chill up his backside. Eyes wide, he looked up.

"Oh, I'm sorry sir. I absolutely didn't see you," she said, eying her clipboard from the floor.

Jamis scrambled to his feet, and stepped out of the flow of traffic. Grabbing the clipboard, he handed it to her and smiled. Her cheeks flushed as she smoothed out her smock. It was not an unexpected reaction whenever he turned on the 'charm machine,' as he called it.

"It's okay, no harm done, except to my ego."

The young technician scanned him, starting at his legs. A moment later their eyes met. With an involuntary move, she fanned her flushed face.

"Uh, Miss, would it be possible for you to direct me to Professor Damien's lab. I've only been here once before, and that was a while ago. *Over a thousand years ago,* he thought.

She buckled slightly at the knees, and gave a faint smile. "Sure, I was headed that way. Walk with me." She returned to her quick, short-gait, her heels clicking an even cadence.

Jamis did a double take and skipped after her.

"Are you one of his students?" she asked without turning her head.

"Uh, well no, not exactly. I'm his son."

Her feet froze, glued to the floor, "You're Prof. Damien's son?" hand to her mouth. "But of course, I should have known. You look just like him ... only better." Her voice trailed off. She turned a corner without looking.

"Thanks, I think," Jamis called after her between breaths.

She resumed her trek with mission and purpose. "I don't think the prof's in, but of course, you probably knew that. Every Tuesday, he meets with his sponsor to give him an update."

Jamis' eyebrows knit together. Occasionally, he overheard his father and mother discussing some top-secret project he was working on, but he had no idea he had a private sponsor. In the kingdom, all R and D labs were supported by the King, not by individual donors.

"Here we are, do you have authorization to enter his lab?"

His heart jumped into overdrive. The palms of his hands slicked, and he struggled to maintain control of his breathing.

"Uh," he patted his pockets, "I seemed to have lost it, probably when you ran me over. Could you just let me in? I'll only be a minute."

Her eyes cut in both ways, and she licked her lips. With a quick swipe of her magnetic key, the door popped open. She pulled him in and slammed it behind them. Before his eyes adjusted, two warm lips pressed against his. Like an ember, the heat from her body radiated against his, taking his breath. He fell backward striking his back on the wall. Streaks of light flashed across his mind. With effort, he squirmed from her grip, but her advances were unrelenting. She pressed closer, her hot breath coming in short gasps. Finally, he placed his hands on her shoulders, and pushed, gasping for air.

"What are you doing? I don't even know your name," he sputtered. His hand searched for the light switch and flicked it on.

The young lady stepped back, brushing her hair from her eyes. "Oh, well that can be remedied. My name is Keisha. Now, where were we? She leaned toward him, lips pooched.

With a quick side-step, he dodged her advance. "Look Keisha, all I wanted to do was see my dad, none of this kissy, kissy stuff." He brushed her hand from his shoulder.

"But I thought that was what you wanted," she pressed, hands reaching out like a phantom siren.

Jamis' heart pounded in his ears so loud he was sure she heard it. His breathing shallowed and sweat beaded on his forehead. "Like I said, I just came to see my dad and get out of here. Now if you don't mind ..."

Keisha crossed her arms, lip pouched. "Well, if you aren't going to play by my rules, you'll have to pay." Her hand reached for the alarm.

Jamis, knowing how much trouble he'd be in if he were caught, grabbed her arm and spun her around. She started to scream, but he covered her mouth. Things spun out of control. If he let her go, she'd scream. His options grew thin.

The longer he held her, the more she struggled to break free. He had to do something. With a quick move, he placed her in a sleeper hold. She slumped to the floor.

With seconds to spare, he found his dad's computer and punched in the code CD2176.6-Damien. The monitor sprang to life. He began reading through a series of coded phrases. The combination of numbers, symbols and abbreviations meant nothing.

Desperate, he scrolled further down. His eyes fell on the properties. With a click, he followed a series of prompts. He smiled to himself. He stumbled over the section listed as Global Engage/Disengage Sequence.

"Uh," she groaned. His time was up.

Quickly, he stuck in a nanochip in the slot and hit, 'Export.' A green progress line appeared. Its slow crawl from left to right made his stomach knot. He wiped his brow and counted the seconds.

Uh!

Three, two, one.

Keisha roused, and pushed herself up from the floor. Leaning against the desk, she held her position. As her mind cleared, she blinked. Her eyes scanned the empty lab. A monitor scrolled lines of meaningless numbers.

Outside the lab, Jamis stood, panting. His mind raced as he tried to calm his palpitating heart. His thoughts fluttered like a moth to a flame.

An alarm sounded, clearing his mind. Instinctively, he broke into a full run. He slammed against the exit door, it refused to yield.

"Shoot, this place is in lock down," he said through

clenched teeth.

He dashed down the hall amid flashing lights and the beat of the alarm. Interns and technicians jumped to get out of his way as he scrambled from one corridor to another.

Seeing a door slightly ajar, Jamis smashed through it and tumbled to the floor. The smitten door struck the bumper and slammed shut. In the darkness, he lay, panting. His heart slammed against the walls of his chest like a hammer on an anvil. As he regained control of his breathing, he heard voices. He followed the source to a door separating the two rooms. Though muffled, they were audible and one was strangely familiar.

With effort, he held his breath, and leaned his ear against the door, listening.

"Yes sir, I assure you it will be completed on or before schedule," Professor Damien said.

Jamis squeezed closer. "You know, in order for us to have the element of surprise, we must control the cloaking ability from a central hub. I don't want some yahoo accidentally hitting the deactivate sequence. If that happens, my plan will go up in smoke."

"I understand General Christos. And I assure you, with my Midas-touch program, we will be able to maintain complete control over the entire battle theater."

Jamis nearly swallowed his tongue. He pulled the nanochip from his pocket and looked at it. *I hope I got it all.* He closed his eyes, and thought of Emma.

Chapter 33

The Time Chamber

Emma slumped against the frame of the time chamber. Her petite body curled in a tight knot, knees wrapped in her arms, head down. She buried her face in her arms and sobbed.

"He is *so* frustrating."

Nguyen slipped down next to her and wrapped her arm over her shoulder. Neither spoke.

The ticking of an ancient clock somewhere in the room was the only measure of the passage of time. Emma lifted her head, eyes puffy and red. She took a ragged breath.

Handing her a tissue, Miss Xhu asked, "You love him, don't you?"

Emma bit the side of her lip. "I know I shouldn't, but I do," she paused, and dabbed her eyes. "And I hate him. I adore him, and at the same time, want to run from him. He's the most stubborn, conceited, pompous, adorable, thoughtful, guy I've ever known." Her head fell back against the time chamber, letting her eyes wander the ceiling like a lost sparrow.

Miss Xhu nodded knowingly. "You got it bad, girl."

Emma let out a weak chuckle, "Yeah—I know, but I also know that if Daddy were alive, he'd die if he knew I was in love with an unregenerate Eonian. What do I do, Miss Xhu?"

Nguyen took her by the hands and drew them close. "Now I'm really going into the past, and you must swear never to repeat what I'm about to tell you."

Emma gulped, not knowing what to expect.

219

Nguyen plumbed a part of her mind she'd not visited since before the millennium began. Her eyes looked to a distant time, and fixed on a far-off place. Her face brightened.

"I was a senior at UC. He was a grad assistant, I was twenty-four. He was twenty-seven. I was a believer, and he wasn't, but we were in love." She smiled as if she were looking into his eyes. She blinked and sighed heavily.

"One day, in the spring of the year we took a walk along the beach. The golden sun sat low on the horizon; sea gulls played lazily in the salty air while children chased sand pipers. All along the shore surfers rode the waves in and swam back out. I can still feel the warm breeze caressing my cheek as if it were today. Then, exactly at three o'clock, he stopped and knelt on one knee in the sand. He pulled a small box from his pocket." She paused, a single tear coursed from the corner of her eye.

"Miss Xhu, you're an immortal. I didn't think you could cry."

She nudged it aside, wiping her glistening fingers on her robe. "Oh honey, we still cry, believe me, and get angry, and love just like before."

Emma clasped her hands under her chin like a kid listening to a bed-time story. "What happened next?"

Nguyen inhaled and held it momentarily before releasing it as if it were her last.

"He asked me to marry him."

Emma straightened. Her jaw dropped. "Oh Miss Xhu, I didn't know you were married."

Nguyen's shoulders slumped, "I, I'm not," she sniffed and blew her nose. "I told him I couldn't."

"Miss Xhu," Emma croaked. "What did he say? What did he do?"

She cupped her hands, buried her face. Through muffled

lips, she spoke, "It broke his heart. He begged me, but I'd made a promise to my parents that I would not marry an unsaved man. It was the hardest thing I've ever done." Her body shook, weeping.

Emma sat, stunned. "Do you think I should end it with Jamis before it goes that far?" her voice barely above a whisper.

Nguyen lifted her face. Her eyes were puffy. Red blotches streaked her neck as if she'd been clawed. She forced a weak smile. "Honey, I can't live my life through you. All I can do is tell you what the ancient writings say."

Emma braced herself.

"From what I understand, the ancient writings are clear, they say do not be unequally joined to an unbeliever."

Emma nodded her head, trying to absorb the news. "What did you do after you turned down his offer?"

She closed her eyes and recited the story by memory. "A few weeks later I graduated and got a job in Washington D.C." She paused and took a sharp breath. "I never heard from him since." She blew her nose in a tissue.

"A few years later, he did marry, but it didn't last. Rumor had it that he left her for another woman and was living in southern California at the time of the catching away."

An uncomfortable silence settled over the two women as each considered their decision.

"So when are you going to tell him?" Her somber question hung in the air like a black cloud.

Emma sighed deeply, "I don't know, the sooner the better. I suppose."

Nguyen gave her a reassuring hug.

The swish of the time chamber's door brought them back to reality. Emma jumped to her feet. A bright smile greeted Jamis then evaporated like the morning dew.

Chapter 34

Millennium Research and Development Facility

Sirens blared, and lights flashed red throughout the lab. Technicians held their ears and tried to scurry past the klaxons. Armed guards held their weapons at the ready while K-9 units began a floor to floor sweep in search of one man ... Jamis.

"What is going on?" demanded Professor Damien as he stepped from his meeting. An aid stood white faced.

"Would somebody shut off those infernal sirens," he bellowed.

Moments later the corridors fell silent and everyone breathed a sigh of relief. "Now what the blazes is going on?" The veins of his neck bulged as he scanned the circle of young faces.

"I don't know sir," one of the technicians said. "Some guy came running down the corridor and ducked into that room." He pointed to the room next to the conference room. The professor nodded, and two armed guards took up a stance on either side of the door. Professor Damien strode over and turned the knob. It resisted.

"Kick it in," he ordered.

A guard lifted his foot and kicked. The door splintered, and fell back. Professor Damien stormed into room demanding answers.

Sheepishly, Keisha broke through the crowd of white smocks. Her eyes searched the floor, hands tightly jammed into her pockets.

223

"Uh, sir, it was your son. He used me, took advantage of me and got into your lab. I, I—"

He cut her off with the wave. "I don't give a rip how he got in, what did he want?"

Keisha shrank back under the judgmental eyes of her colleagues. She had a reputation, and it wasn't good. All the guys knew what kind of girl she was, so did the ladies, and they hated her for it. It was her way of advancing up the corporate ladder. That was then…now she began to doubt.

"Sir, he said he wanted to see you, but I told him you were in a meeting. So he tricked me into letting him into your lab."

Heads snapped as the professor unleashed a string of expletives.

"You didn't tell him who I was meeting with, did you?" his gruff voice grew ominous.

Cringing, she raised her hands in defense. "Oh no, sir, I didn't even mention you were with General—"

"Shut up, you idiot. He may still be in the building," his stretched lips white with rage.

Like a caged animal, she scanned the gawkers; looking for sympathy, hoping someone would come to her defense … none came. She raised an accusatory finger. "He attacked me. Your son attacked me. It was terrible." Her voice broke into a manufactured cry.

A slight chuckle percolated from among the guys, and except for one, her female colleagues sneered, and turned their backs, heading for the dining common.

Damien crossed his arms. "He's my son, what did you expect?" he spat. "So why the alarm?"

"Well, after he got me into the lab, he demanded that I let him see your OMFP, your Omega Mind Fusion Processor, and then he knocked me out. When I came to, your console was on and a bunch of numbers were scrolling on your monitor."

The professor's eyebrows knit; he pushed her aside and rushed to his lab. He slammed the door back and stomped deeper into his lab.

"I want everyone out," his voice boomed. Glass trays vibrated. He stood in front of his plasma screen, fists clenched, his breathing coming in short gasps. One glimpse and he knew. Mechanically, he pulled his transponder from his pocket and pressed a pre-set number.

"Sir, we have a problem ..."

Chapter 35

New Birth Population Center

The first rays of morning crested the horizon like golden fingers as day dawned over New Birth Population Center. Thin serous clouds skittered past the gleaming towers of steel and crystalline. On the street level, doves cooed while vendors opened their kiosks for another day of business.

"Miss Xhu, wake up, this is the day that the Lord has made."

Emma spent a sleepless night anticipating their trip to the Holy Land.

She rolled over, her long black hair a tangled mess. Sitting up, she looked bleary eyed at Emma. "Couldn't sleep?"

She smiled eagerly, "Nope, not a wink. Let's go."

Though Nguyen was eternally young, Emma's enthusiasm for life always amazed her.

They found Jamis standing at the breakfast bar, munching as he filled his plate.

"Didn't your momma ever tell you it's rude to eat while you're in line?" Emma chided, a half-smile parting her lips.

He swallowed the last piece of bacon. "I was just making room for more food."

Emma shook her head, condescendingly.

After a quick breakfast, the three took a hover-cab to the bustling air terminal and were directed to the right gate. By ten o'clock, they were waiting for their intercontinental hover-craft.

"Just look at this thing. At mack plus two, we'll be in Israel within a few short hours," Jamis said as they neared the loading port. "That's the largest hover-craft I've ever seen. How many can it hold?" He asked to no one in particular.

"Over three hundred," Nguyen suggested. "That will be on the test, you can count on it," she said with a smile.

They descended the tube and found their seats.

"Isn't this exciting Jamis, we're finally getting to go somewhere," Emma said as she snapped on her harness. "I've always wanted to say that, ever since I read the play, 'Once to Die.'"

Jamis clicked his harness in place and cocked his head to his right. "Well, I read it too, and I didn't like the way it ended," he observed.

Emma shot up a flare prayer. "It ended fine for the people who were believers, just not so good for those who weren't."

"So it's that final?" Jamis questioned, pinching back a smile. "No second chances, no way to work off your bad deeds?"

"No, the ancient writings say we are all destined to die and after that ... well you know, the judgment."

The flight attendant took center stage and proceeded through the pre-flight announcements.

Seated to her right, Miss Xhu leaned over, and whispered, "When are you going to tell him?"

Emma glanced to her left; at the guy she'd known all her life, her nemesis, her tormentor, her best friend and the love of her life. She swallowed hard and turned to the right. "I will ..." *Eventually.*

"M, you'll never guess where I went last night." Jamis' words cut her attention in two.

The idea of him using the time chamber in such a

cavalier way, made Emma's blood boil. A thousand thoughts lodged in her throat. Nothing came out. She narrowed her eyes. "I couldn't care less. You shouldn't have gone gallivanting around the time warp without, uh, without ... permission."

He smirked and shook his head.

She hated it when he did that. Following his movements, her eyes widened as he reached into his pocket and pulled out a small box. Suddenly, everything Miss Xhu said came rushing through her mind. Her heart pounded in her chest. *So this is it, the big proposal.* It was all she could do to keep from running for the exit.

He lifted the box. She put her hand on his and pushed. "Not now Jamis, I'd rather not talk about it. Not here." Her voice cracked, and she buried her face in her hands sobbing.

Miss Xhu placed a tender hand on her shoulder. Her eyes narrowed and glared at Jamis. He sat—mouth gaped open.

The pixel screen located on the back of each seat sprang to life. Jamis sat, staring. The images flashed across the screen, but none of it made any sense. *What's gotten into M? Why the sudden change? I wonder what Miss Xhu has been telling her?*

By the time the show ended, Emma was sleeping deeply, her head leaned on Miss Xhu's shoulder. During the credits, she rolled over, and mumbled something incoherent. Strands of her golden hair drifted his direction like feelers from an unseen creature. They tickled his nose. He resisted the temptation to brush them aside, preferring rather, to have her close, even for a few minutes.

After what they'd gone through; running for their lives through the AG-tube, getting shot down, burying her parents and wandering through the restricted district, he'd never seen her get mad. Her faith was like a rock, and he admired her. No, it was more than that. It was ... *love.* He admitted to himself. He loved her and the desire to tell her was insatiable.

The hover-craft hit an air pocket sending cups and loose items flying. He swallowed hard and smiled, glad for the decision he'd made.

An hour later, they touched down. Emma lifted her head. The red spot on her cheek, glowed, and her hair was smushed on one side. She fluffed it with her fingers to no avail. "Oh I'm sorry," she said sleepily. "Hope you didn't mind me using you as a pillow."

Jamis smiled, "A pillow?"

"A lumpy one at that," she corrected.

The craft bumped to a halt, and the stewardess toggled the comm. "Welcome to the Ben-Gurion Intercontinental Hover-craft Port and Jerusalem. We hope you enjoy your stay in the World's Capital," pride carried her voice. "But if you are connecting, may the peace of God rest upon you, Shalom."

Jamis, Emma and Miss Xhu emerged into the bright sunlight and gazed at the emerald Mediterranean Sea.

"Would you look at that? It's as green as your eyes."

Miss Xhu cut a glance at Emma and shook her head. "He's got it bad," she whispered.

Emma covered her mouth and stifled a giggle.

They trudged through the bustling concourse. Everywhere they looked there were Eonians from all walks of life, some coming and others going. In one line stood a group heading to one of the territories to do some evangelistic work. In the arrival section were pilgrims from all over the world coming for the Feast of Tabernacles, many carrying palm branches.

They passed a tour guide giving his introduction to

Israel; spiel, "Throughout the millennium ... all nations have paid honor and tribute to Israel. For the first time in history, her borders extend from the Mediterranean Sea, across Syria and Iraq to the great Euphrates River. Her northern border extends from the mountain ranges of Lebanon, as far south as the river of Egypt. There is even a highway built, which extends from Egypt to Assyria to Israel. As a matter of fact, you can see it from a hundred miles up."

Miss Xhu smiled as they passed the tour guide. "I should get a job doing that."

"Yes, you know a whole lot more about Israel than he does," Emma chirped.

The trip time from Ben-Gurion Intercontinental Hovercraft Port to Jerusalem took less than twenty minutes by overland tram. The trio emerged from the tram station to the aroma of fresh flowers. A welcoming party stood at the Damascus Gate with rings of fragrant flowers and hung them around the necks of each new arrival, then placed a gentle kiss on each cheek of everyone as they welcomed them to Jerusalem.

Preparations for the celebration had been going on for months. Banners with the various names of God hung across the wide walkways. Streamers fluttered in the breeze over the many spires throughout the vast city.

Emma and Jamis followed Miss Xhu along the crowded streets of Jerusalem. He grasped her hand but she pulled away. *What is wrong with her?*

"Notice all the new construction," Miss Xhu pointed out. "It's everywhere—new cathedrals, symphony halls, and great arenas." She was breathless. "I can't believe the changes since the last time I was here," she spoke over her shoulder as they cut through the art district.

New Museums, Art Galleries and Sculptures dotted the

city streets. Music resonated from every corner from hidden speakers. The rebuilt walls engulfed an ever-growing portion of land.

At the center of Jerusalem sat Solomon's rebuilt Temple; its white stone walls gleamed in the morning sunlight. The magnificence of the Temple Mount was more resplendent than anyone imagined. No more Mosque of Omar. No more Dome of the Rock. It was dedicated completely to the Holy Temple. Its doors stood open to the thousands who gathered daily to pay homage to the God of Heaven.

"There is just something magical about this wonderful old city," Miss Xhu said. "There is nothing like it in the whole world. It is the apple of God's eye. This is truly an enchanted place," her eyes danced from one building to the next.

"Let's take our time and walk through some of the colorful markets and narrow alleyways, and try to get a feel of the city's history," Emma suggested.

"Don't your feet hurt?" Jamis asked.

She shook her head, "Nope. I feel invigorated."

"Come to think of it, I feel rested and anxious to get started too."

As they passed a shadowed corner, Miss Xhu caught movement. She took a quick glance, but it disappeared. A cold breeze sent goose-bumps up her arms.

Chapter 36

Jerusalem

A light breeze blew in through the open doors on the third-floor hotel room. Emma woke early and tread across the tiled floor. It was cold to her bare feet, but she didn't mind. She parted the thin curtains and stepped onto the veranda. The morning sun rays kissed her cheeks and brought a smile to her lips. She stood, arms around her waist, enjoying the dawn. Fixing her hand over her eyes like an Indian searching for smoke signals, she looked over the vast city. It was quite different from Providence. There were no hover-crafts whizzing about, only foot traffic, no buildings taller than the Temple and certainly no exoscrapers, yet the city was a mix of old and new. Her thoughts turned to her brother and sister. *Oh Lord, keep your hand on Timothy and Joy wherever they are.* She prayed.

A slender arm slipped around her and gave her a gentle squeeze.

"Good morning Emma, sleep well?" Miss Xhu asked, her voice light and airy.

She nodded.

"Why so glum, did you tell Jamis why you could only be—"

Emma waved her off. "No, not yet," she gave her a weak smile and took a ragged breath. "Every time he comes near me my heart does flip flops."

Nguyen nodded knowingly. "I know how hard it is, but you must tell him and the sooner the better."

Emma furrowed her brow, "Yes, I know, I know. I'll tell him today, right after breakfast. But actually, I was thinking about Timothy and Joy and that infernal war. It has already consumed Providence, my home and my family. We could be next."

Nguyen took Emma's hand and gave it a gentle squeeze. "Don't you think the Lord God knows all about your home and family? He knows all things, and is working them for your good and His glory. Try to relax and enjoy your days here. Things will work out. You'll see." Her words warmed her like a cup of hot tea. Emma brightened and smiled through the tears.

"Now, let's get dressed. I can't wait for you to taste the feast they put on every morning." Miss Xhu said.

Thirty minutes later, Emma pranced down the steps and into the dining area, Miss Xhu at her side. "Am I famished! What smells so good?"

Jamis cocked his head, squinting in the bright sunlight. "If you're so hungry, why did it take you so long to get down here?"

She looked at her watch and groaned. "That's right; I'm still on Providence time. What time is it here?"

"Breakfast time," he handed her a plate. "Now eat, we have a full day ahead of us."

Miss Xhu picked up a plate and stepped in line.

"Do you have any particular place you want to go to first, Miss Xhu?"

She picked up a falafel and spread hummus over it, then began adding scrambled eggs, cheese and slices of bell pepper. "I was thinking of mixing shopping with a little sight-seeing."

He spoke over his shoulder while he piled on a slice of cantaloupe and some strawberries. "That's fine for you, but with your permission, I need to get to the Temple Mount and see the King."

Emma dropped her plate. It struck the floor sending shards of glass and vegetables skittering in every direction.

"Jamis, you can't just go walking up to the king without a special invitation," she said. *This is either a bad joke, or he's out of his mind.*

"I know, but I have information about the cloaking system he needs to know."

Emma stomped her foot. "Jamis! Would you give it up? He couldn't care less about that stupid cloaking whatever," her hands flailing.

The room fell silent, mothers shushed their children, and old men laid aside their forks as all eyes turned upon her. Emma's color darkened, and Jamis held his breath.

Sheepishly, he slunk to an empty chair and hung his head. The room returned to normal with the exception of one set of ears.

Emma took a seat across from him, and lowered her forehead. "I think your obsessing over that thing," she said in a tight whisper.

Jamis pushed his food around with his fork. "It's important M."

She sat up straight, crossed her arms. "Not as important as knowing him as your personal Savior." Her words assaulted him like in a withering attack.

He loved to taunt Emma, especially when it got under her skin but this was getting out of hand. He slammed his fork down.

"Okay! I give up," his hands rose in surrender. He stood on a precipice—caught between telling her the truth or telling her off. He chose poorly. He turned and headed for the exit.

"Jamis, don't go."

He paused, hand on the door frame. Seconds passed. Then, without looking back, he stepped across the threshold, and was gone.

Emma buried her head in her hands, broken hearted. Miss Xhu took a seat next to her and tried to comfort her.

"No!" she shook off her warm hand. "You did this. I see the way you look at him. You just want him for yourself." Her words cut like a razor.

Nguyen's face paled, she swallowed hard, trying to think of something to say. She liked Jamis, but not that way. She was an immortal saint, incapable of human feelings...or was she?

Movement caught her attention and Nguyen glanced up expecting to see Jamis return, smiling. Instead, she noticed a shadow receding through the door. Her heart pounded within her chest like a jack-hammer. The still small voice of the Lord prompted her, and she knew what she had to do. She stood and dashed from the dining room, tears streaming, her heart beating wildly.

"Jamis!" she called after him.

When she reached the street...he was nowhere to be seen.

A lone figure stepped to the curb and glanced both ways. Being unfamiliar with Jerusalem, Jamis soon found himself wandering through the narrow streets. A shadowed figure dogged his every step. Fingering the small box containing the nanochip, he hoped to get the CD2176.6-Damien code to the King before it was too late. By mid-morning he'd finally found the steps leading up to the Temple mount. He took a deep breath and approached the entrance. A dozen armed guards rushed forward, encircling him.

"Halt in the name of the King," one burly temple guard

shouted.

Jamis quickly abandoned the idea of making a run for it. "This is no James Bond movie," he muttered.

"I just want to speak with the King. I have an important message to give him," Jamis said as the guards patted him down.

"What's this," a short, stocky guard asked through a thick beard. He held the small box.

For a moment time stood still as he hung between truth and deception. "It's a…it's a nanochip."

The guard opened the box and fingered it. "And you do what with a nanochip?"

Jamis reached up and took it from his hand. "You store tons of information on it, information that the King needs to know."

Another guard placed the butt of his weapon against his chest and shoved him back from the steps.

"Well, the King is busy making preparations for the feast. You'll have to get an appointment and come back later, now go."

Miss Xhu sprang from the hotel restaurant and out into the bustling sidewalk. She peered to her left and to her right. A shadow receded, and she knew. Making a quick about-face, she dashed back inside and up three flights of stairs taking two at a time. Her fingers fumbled with the key, finally succeeding in finding the right one. A moment later she was inside. Looking around as if being watched, she threw the deadbolt, and threw the curtains. She wasted no time and knelt beside her bed. With trembling hands, she withdrew a foot locker. Then carefully dialed the lock and slipped it off the hasp.

Taking a deep breath, she gently lifted the lid. Inside, wrapped in a purple velveteen cloth lay Gideon, The Sword of the Lord. Its jewel studded handle welcomed the daylight. Each gemstone glittered like the day it was first given to her. Her fingers shook with adrenaline as she pulled it from its scabbard. The finely crafted blade rang with delight as it greeted the morning. Its duel edges were as sharp as the day it was made.

Nguyen strapped the golden belt around her waist and slid the sword back into place. Pulling her robe together, she stood, smoothed out her hair and ran from the hotel room. Time, like sand, slipped between her fingers.

A moment later she was back on the street, in search of one person.

Chapter 37

The Throne Room of Heaven

Thunder rolled like a distant timpani, and Michael the archangel appeared in the western sky. With two mighty outstretched wings, he swooped down from the heavens and took his place at the foot of the great stairs. His golden hair shimmered in the radiant light of the throne with a face that shone like the sun at noonday. Two eyes, like embers, glowed with the zeal of God. He adjusted his buckler, flexed his muscles and prepared to ascend the wide staircase.

Like an eagle, Gabriel lighted next to him, and straightened his robes. "What news, my friend?"

"Grim are the days we face," Michael said, his brow furrowed, jaw set. "Lucifer is on the move. As I speak he is leveling the Population Center of New Birth. By day's end, he will have destroyed Antioch and Bethesda. New Europe is in flames. The southern hemisphere is in total rebellion. Within days, he will be marching on the Camp of the Saints."

Gabriel stood fingering his sword. "We must alert the Master," his voice somber.

"He knows and yet he waits."

"You should know that the Mighty Lord is never early, neither is he ever late. His ways are not our ways, his thoughts higher than the heavens."

Michael lowered his head in agreement. "It is true. However, I grieve for my beloved city. She has suffered so much at the hand of that tyrant," his breath came in short snatches. As he spoke, his fingers gripped the silver hilt of his sword. He longed to be called into service.

"I remember the day we drove him and his kind out of Heaven." Gabriel said, his shoulders squared, chest swelling.

"Yes. That was a glorious day, one that I will not soon forget. He did, however, put up quite a battle. It took my entire legion to dislodge him and drive him to the brink of Heaven," Michael said.

"But it was I who gave him the final shove sending him hurling to earth." A triumphant smile parted Gabriel's lips.

"Don't get too smug, my friend. Remember what pride can do."

"You are right, I stand corrected my friend. Now, with your leave, let me sound the trumpet and marshal the hosts of Heaven. We can withstand the Evil One indefinitely, cause his troops to scatter in fear, or turn inward and destroy themselves. We've done it before," Gabriel pleaded.

"Yes, we have, but that was under the command of Lord Sabaoth, but as of now, he has not given me permission to move."

"You have at your command a myriad of the heavenly hosts encircling Jerusalem and the Holy City. Why not summons them or at least put a hedge of protection about this city until the Mighty King chooses to act."

Michael shifted his stance. His resplendent vesture shimmered with every move. The hilt of his sword bespangled with gems glistened in the amber hue of Heaven. He looked at his friend.

"I will ascend the stairs of Heaven and illicit as much grace and power as is necessary to hold off the onslaught until our Lord and King is ready for the final solution. Be ready to sound the alarm."

Gabriel bent at the waist and stepped back.

Michael outstretched his wings and with one powerful thrust, rose to the top of the staircase. He bowed his head, and waited to approach the throne of grace.

"Enter in," a voice thundered, its rich tones were full of love, and ringing with authority. Michael stepped into the thick cloud and was not seen.

"Oh Lord, our Lord, how excellent is your name in all the earth. The whole world is full of your glory." He bowed low.

"Arise my trusted servant. What is your request?" the Lord God asked.

"As you know, the enemy is very lively. Even as we speak his deception has spread like a plague. He has marshaled the world's armies to attack the resting places of your people. Soon the wicked one will bring to bear his power and might against the Camp of the Saints and the Holy City."

"I, who have decreed the bounds of the sea that it not pass, have determined the times before appointed, and set the boundaries of mankind's habitation, that they should seek the Lord, have also set them in slippery places. There will come a day in the which I will judge the earth by that man whom I have appointed. Then I cast them down into destruction. They will be brought to desolation, as in a moment, they will be utterly consumed with terrors."

"And so we wait, My Lord?"

"We wait. The spirit of jealousy is at work, let him work until harvest is at the full. Then I will rise from my resting place. I will lift my mighty arm and will save gloriously my anointed. As for the Camp of the Saints, marshal your forces, keep them safe."

"And what of my young charge? Even now his life is in danger. A dark shadow dogs his every move."

Lightning flashed, and the temple shook as the

Almighty held him in suspense.

"I have dispatched someone to help him and at the right moment, will act on my behalf."

Michael clasped his fist to his chest and bowed on his knee. "Yes My Lord. I await your command."

Chapter 38

The Camp of the Forest Saints

Shadowed figures chased by the waning moon passed silently through the foliage. Boston ferns brushed Joy's ankles, tickling her with each step. There was no need for the hood as the night obscured any trace of their passing. A wispy blanket of snowflakes drifted in lazy patterns through the chilly air, painting the barren limbs in soft layers, and lighting on the weary traveler's heads. Evergreens swayed with the rhythm of the night while in the distance the howl of a lonely wolf sent chills up Timothy's back.

Andorra paused to get his bearings, and then pressed on like a homing pigeon. By then, the snow fall had deepened, making walking difficult. A stubborn vine grabbed Timothy's foot causing him to stumble headlong into a patch of briers. Vines clung to him like a spike-laden web. Without condemnation, Andorra held out his hand and pulled him from his entanglement. He nodded to his men to continue. "You have forgotten how treacherous it is to pass through our forest without proper attire."

Timothy brushed the snow from his toga and hastened to catch up.

An hour later, weary and soaked, the hunting party broke through the perimeter and into the camp.

Rather than finding a well-ordered society, they found a camp preparing to move. There were no fires, no women hunkered over boiling pots of stew, no children playing tag.

243

Instead, they saw groups of men hastily breaking down tents, and folding them up. Women gathered their cook pots and prepared to leave. A somber atmosphere permeated the camp.

"This place gives me the creeps," Joy whispered as they were ushered to the Meeting Tent.

"Me too. By the way they are staring, I get the distinct impression, they think we betrayed them."

Joy's mouth gaped, "But we didn't. We didn't betray anybody." Her voice etched with pain.

Timothy tried to calm her, "I know honey. We just need to convince them."

From the shadows, Rose emerged and sidled up next to Timothy. "I have prayed for your return ever since you left us." Her eyes glistened with tears of joy.

She unfolded two large blankets and laid them over Timothy's and Joy's shoulders.

"There, that should help until we find you some dry buckskins," she said.

Andorra nodded approvingly and led them to the center of camp.

A thin layer of snow painted the dark tones of the meeting tent in whitened hues. Andorra pulled back the flap sending an avalanche down its sides.

Reluctantly, Timothy and Joy stepped inside. The air was thick with tension. Nickolas, the Wise, stood in the midst of his councilors—arms folded, fingers rubbing his beard, listening.

"Lord Nickolas, we should take our people to the south where our fleet awaits us. From there we can take the river to the great sea, then on to the City of the King," Arthures argued.

"And be cut down by the enemy in the open sea? I'll not expose our people to such danger."

Cush rose to his feet. "My Prince, we could move by

night to the west, to the grand canyon where our fathers took refuge in the centuries before the coming of the man of sin."

Nickolas nodded, deep in thought. He stopped pacing and looked into the eyes of his men. These were his councilors, his advisers, and yet they spoke unadvisedly. "No, I will not allow our people to be caught on the open ranges. It's far too dangerous."

"And so we sit and wait for the inevitable?" questioned Arthures.

Time passed at a snail's pace while Nickolas sought a word from Heshem. "My friend," Nickolas said, placing his hand on his counselor's shoulder. "I know you speak your heart, but your heart is clouded with fear. I have a word from the Lord God."

"Then speak, my chief," Andorra said, as he ushered in his guests.

His grey eyes brightened. "Ah, we have guests. Our friends from the outside have returned. Please, sit and tell us. How goes it out there?"

Suddenly, all eyes were on Timothy. He stepped back, uncomfortable being in the limelight.

"Please, step forward. Are the cities of Providence and New Birth still standing?" Nickolas' face bore a deep interest in the plight of the outside which warmed Timothy's heart.

Timothy cleared his throat, "I cannot speak to the condition of New Birth, but I can tell you Providence is no more."

His words had a ripple effect. A low murmur spread among the men within the circle. Heads bobbed in agreement to some predetermined notion.

"Go on my child. What of the armies of the enemy? How are they armed?"

Timothy looked nervously from side to side. He licked

his lips, wishing he could tell them more. "Well sir, it's like this. They encircled Providence and attacked us with giant hover-crafts, and mighty machines of war. The devastation was quick and complete."

Voices rose. Tensions mounted. Nickolas lifted a weathered hand, and the meeting tent fell silent.

"It is as I thought." His voice carried an air of resolution. "We have no choice but to fight. Let us flee to the great mountain. There we will take our stand."

Somber faces lightened, a rustle of excitement spread like wind driven snow.

"My chief, is this the word of the Lord?" questioned Andorra.

He nodded slowly, "I will lift up my eyes unto the hills, from whence cometh my help. My help cometh from the Lord who made heaven and the earth. Now, let us gather our wives, our children and our weapons, we only have a short time."

Chapter 39

The Temple Mount

    The crisp morning air crackled with excitement as all around the Temple Mount priests moved with deliberateness. The white flagstone piazza glistened, while large banners flapped lazily in the breeze. The aroma of baked bread mingled with the morning sacrifice and wafted through the open space. Clusters of priests gathered at a water wheel holding silver pots, waiting for their turn.
    Jamis, seeing a discarded robe, grabbed it, and quickly donned it. Finding an empty pot, he lifted it to his shoulder and stood in line. Suddenly, he felt vulnerable, exposed. His heart raced. The urge to run was palpable. He glanced around expecting to see a temple guard or a soldier charging him.
    Nothing.
    "My mind is playing tricks on me," he muttered to himself.
    He filled his container, and followed the man in front of him up the steps to the Temple Mount. In the distance stood the Holy Temple of God. He figured, if he walked slowly at first, he wouldn't draw anyone's attention, then bursting into a mad dash, he could make it before the guards fired upon him.
    Keeping his head down, he delivered his supply of water, then turned and began a measured pace toward the temple. Angry voices shouted after him, but still he continued. His heart pounded, yet he maintained an even gait. Leather soles slapped against the pavement as temple guards and priests gave chase.

Peering over his shoulder, he knew he had one chance. He broke into a full run. Every muscle in his body strained and cried in protest. His lungs burned, yet he pressed on. Panting, he counted the closing distance. Twenty yards, ten, five and he reached the stairs leading to the throne room.

He bent at the waist, gasping for air, when a shadow leapt from an unseen corner.

It held its position between Jamis and his goal. The soldiers and priests skidded to a halt and began backing away. One soldier lifted his weapon. A bolt of lightning flashed, striking him. His charred body fell to the pavement, smoldering.

Suddenly, the apparition began to materialize. Its shadowed form swirled in a dazzling whirl of wind and light. Thunder cracked, rocks split as the shape of a great red dragon coalesced and towered over Jamis' shivering body.

He tried to run, but his feet refused to obey. He tripped and fell, striking his head on the tile pavement. A knot formed and warmth seeped down his forehead. Touching the wound, his trembling fingers returned, tinged with his own blood.

"Well, well, well, master Jamis. What have we here? You think to be a tattle-tail?" smoked curled. "I'm impressed. Sadly, but no one is home today." The dragon swung his wing in grand fashion, displaying an empty throne. "It looks like the doctor's out to lunch," a wicked laugh crackled through his throat.

Trying to regain his footing, Jamis stood, trembling.

"Now, if you would kindly return what you stole from me, I won't have to kill your girlfriend." He held up a looking glass and Jamis stared in amazement. Emma dangled over the precipice by a thin rope, its twine unraveling.

"My girlfriend, she's not my girlfriend. She hates me," he spat.

"Au Contraire, she is madly in love with you. But alas, you'll never be able to share your love with her if you don't give me that nanochip." He swooped down. His feet clawed at the steps as he descended to the lower level. Jamis crab-crawled backwards, panic gripped every muscle.

The temple guards fired, but the bullets fell harmlessly like snowflakes to the earth. The dragon reared his head and bellowed in rage. With one blast from his nostrils, he singed the armed men, leaving them smoldering embers.

Then he pounced upon Jamis, his clawed foot pinning him to the pavement. Jamis struggled to free his hand but was held immobile under the weight of the creature.

If I give it to him ... all is lost. If I keep it ... I'll never see Emma again, he thought.

With effort, he willed his hand loose and fished the nanochip from his pocket. In the struggle, it slipped, and clattered to the pavement inches from his reach. The dragon shifted his weight, and Jamis made one last desperate attempt to move. He snatched the small box and held it up.

"Here, if you want it, come get it…"

He tossed it as far as he could.

Movement caught his attention, and he cocked his head around.

Miss Xhu ran toward the creature, sword in hand. Her scream echoed with each advancing step. With two hands, she swung the silver blade; it blazed as if it were on fire. The dragon recoiled at the sight. His grip loosened, and Jamis squirmed free. He crawled behind the stair railing and peered out, heart pounding wildly. He gulped for oxygen and stared wide-eyed at the battle.

The dragon raged, exhaling blue flames.

Miss Xhu held her mighty sword up, and cleaved the flame asunder.

Frustrated, he lifted his wings.

Swoosh!

The sword found its mark, slicing bone and muscle. Black ooze seeped through his leathery hide.

"You have seen this sword before haven't you, Lucifer, son of the morning. It was you whom I exorcised and dispatched to the underworld."

The dragon bowed his neck and billowed.

"And that's not the first time either, is it? This is Gideon, the Sword of the Lord." Again, she swung, chopping his other wing. "I proclaim the blood of the Lamb, and the victory that is in the Lord Jesus Christ. I demand that you depart, immediately," she said with a loud voice.

Two glowing embers set in a mask of black leather flashed, his nostrils flared, and flames shot out. Miss Xhu danced to the side.

Spying the little box, he made one last attempt to claim his prize. His claw closed around it. With a guttural laugh, he began to lift off. Jamis sprang from his hiding place and grabbed the dragon's leg. The creature shook him violently, but Jamis held on with all his might. He gritted his teeth, fearing he would take off with him hanging on.

Miss Xhu, seeing the death struggle, stepped closer. She swung her sword in a high arch, and brought it down. Bones cracked, and muscles peeled back as the sword sliced through the dragon's leathery neck. With a sickening thud, its head fell to the pavement and rolled. The decapitated body flapped mindlessly, legs kicking.

Jamis sprang to his feet, while a pool of black ooze formed in an ever-widening circle.

With one triumphant move, Miss Xhu stepped on top of his head, its eyes wide, mouth gaping. Lifting her sword with two hands, she rammed it through the dragon's skull. A wild laugh echoed in the distance. It was little consolation. She had only destroyed Lucifer's outer manifestation.

And Satan fell as lightning to the earth, having great wrath, because he knew he had a short time.

Miss Xhu turned to Jamis, "Go to her, she needs you."

Chapter 40

The Cathedral of Ancient Manuscripts

Two large oak doors stood guard in front of the Cathedral of Ancient Manuscripts. Aged ivy vines grew up its walls. The white stones peeked between its branches like children playing hide and seek. Emma took hold of the gold leafed handle and pulled. The door creaked under its own weight yet swung with more ease than she'd expected. She stepped inside, letting her eyes adjust to the dim atmosphere.

Through an overhead window, a shaft of gilded illumination filtered through particles of dust, painting the atmosphere in golden hues. Her feet remained constant, eyes shifting from side to side, while corridors disappeared into the distance.

Dozens of saints dressed in silk robes moved about the corridors carrying large books under their arms.

"Who are all these people and what are they doing?" Emma asked to no one in particular.

A tall, gaunt gentleman stepped to her side. His stance was that of an old butler from some southern mansion. "Most are doing family research, ma'am," his voice level.

"Oh!" she jumped, hand over her mouth.

"Don't do that Sir, you nearly frightened me to death."

The lines on his face deepened. "Hardly that my lady, in here, no one dies."

"Sir, what are the angels doing? Aren't they supposed to be in Heaven, singing or something?"

253

The elderly gentleman's lips parted at her innocent question. His grizzled hand rose to cover a deep chuckle.

"No my child, not all angels are charged with praise. Many have other responsibilities. For example, some watch over the young of your society, others carry messages…answers to prayer. These are busy with family archives, updating the latest births and deaths. There are others who record the latest entries into the Lamb's Book of Life." His keen eyes saddened. "But alas, those angels have had little to do of recent times."

"The Lamb's Book of Life." Emma repeated. "What's that?"

The man locked his fingers behind his back and lifted his chin. "To put it simply, it is the book King Jesus will one day consult. All those whose names are written therein will enter Heaven's eternal rest. Those, whose names are not found written in the Lamb's Book of Life, will be cast into the Lake of Fire as punishment for rejecting the offer of God's forgiveness."

Emma's heart sank, "Oh Jamis," sorrow gripped her throat.

"Sir, could you direct me to the room of my family's history?"

The man nodded, "But of course, young lady, follow me."

With a smooth gait, the elderly gentlemen led her down one corridor. They stopped at an open doorway, and gave a slight bow.

"Here we are, the Archives of Family History."

He turned and disappeared in the shadowed hall. Emma stood gazing at rows of large mahogany tables, their polished surfaces shown like mirrors. Comfortable chairs supported angels of all sizes as they scribbled in the ancient tomes.

Emma stepped inside. The pungent scent of leather bound manuscripts mingled with dust lingered in the air. She sneezed.

"God bless you my child," said the docent. "May I be of some assistance to you?" The elderly woman, dressed in stoic attire, held her gaze.

"Oh yes ma'am, absolutely," she said with a slight bow. "I would like to see my family history," her voice light and respectful.

"Very well, my child, follow me. What is your name young lady?"

Emma studied the elderly woman. *She must be a mortal; she looks as old as the hills.* She wore a heavy shawl and was stooped with time, yet there was no bitterness in her voice.

"My name is Emma, Emma Newton," her eyes wide, full of anticipation.

The docent nodded and quietly led her passed the 'A's and 'B's down to the section marked 'N's.

"Alright, here we are," her sing-songy voice rang out. "Now, let me pull this volume down." Her bony hand grabbed the four-inch thick volume with the name Newton worn with age.

"Here, my child, is the genealogy of the family known as Newton. This is the 'Book of Known Past' of your family. For your purposes why don't you start in the section marked Pre-Rapture and come forward in time."

She opened the book. The pages crinkled with each turn. Pointing to the most recent entries, she nodded and backed out of the way.

"Now I will leave you. If you need me, just call. I'll return to assist you."

She backed away and quietly slipped out of the room. The impact of Emma's loneliness struck her in full force. She wished she had Jamis to comfort her, and then upbraided herself for thinking such a thought.

Slowly her fingers ran over the yellowed pages. Some were torn, others dog-eared, waiting. Her finger stopped at the column titled, The Generations of the Families of Chase Newton.

Emma began reading, "Chase Newton the son of Ben and Martha Newton was born-again in the year of our Lord 2010, and married Megan Roberts, the daughter of T. J. Roberts, the deceiver.

Chase and Megan walked with God, and they were not for God took them up leaving behind their first teenage son Ben, who entered Jacob's Week of Trouble as an unregenerate mortal.

Ben Newton, the son of Chase and Megan Newton, whose name was written in the Lambs Book of Life in the year of our Lord 2018 entered the Kingdom of God as a believing mortal and married Phoebe Berkowitz, the daughter of Stan and Joyce Berkowitz, also being a believing mortal. They lived fifty years and begat John Newton and had many sons and daughters. He died at the age of 279 years old.

John Newton, the son of Ben and Phoebe Newton, whose name was written in the Lambs Book of Life in the year of our Lord 2250 and as a believing mortal was granted permission to marry Lydia Randall, also a believing mortal. They lived 78 years and bore twin sons, Jeremiah and Carl. These were the days when man ceased to use Godly names. It is noted that John Newton made war against a large stronghold of unregenerate mortals hidden in one of the restricted zones and conquered them. He died at the age of 527 years old.

Jeremiah Newton, the son of John and Lydia Newton, whose name was written in the Lambs Book of Life in the year of our Lord 2439 was granted permission to wed Rhonda Tomlinson also a believing mortal. They lived 74 years and bore

The Stranger Among Us

Paul Newton and had many sons and daughters. It is also noted that Jeremiah Newton is the father of Time Travel. He died at the age of 691 years old.

Paul Newton, the son of Jeremiah and Rhonda Newton, whose name was written in the Lambs Book of Life in the year of our Lord 2634 was granted permission to wed Victoria, whose last name failed to be verified, who was also a believing mortal. They lived 91 years and bore Charles Newton and had many sons and daughters. At the present time, Paul and Victoria remain among us.

Charles Newton, the son of Paul and Victoria Newton, whose name was written in the Lambs Book of Life in the year of our Lord 2776 was granted permission to wed Andréa of the Stevenson clan. Andrea being a believing mortal, bore Michael Newton in their 84th year of marriage and later bore many sons and daughters, and at the present still lives among us.

Michael Newton, the son of Charles and Andréa Newton, whose name was written in the Lambs Book of Life in the year of our Lord 2915 was granted permission to wed Joanna Berkowitz. Michael Newton being the fifth generation from Ben and Phoebe Newton and by Kingdom Law – in League, thus were married. They bore Emma, Timothy and Joy.

Emma Newton the daughter of Michael and Joanna Newton, whose name was written in the Lambs Book of Life in the year of our Lord 3015 lives among us and is awaiting marriage.

"That was very interesting M."

"Oh, Jamis. You scared me," she sputtered.

The twinkle in his eyes told her it was intentional. "Let's do a quick review of my family history while we're here."

Her eyes narrowed. "Where did you come from?"

A heart-stopping smile spread across his face. "Oh, I

was in the neighborhood and thought I'd do some reading. That old butler guy said you were back here."

Emma held his gaze, not sure if she wanted to hug him or slap him. Her hands froze at her side. "I thought you were going to see the king." Sarcasm rolled from her lips.

"Oh that, well, the king wasn't in, and so I figured it could wait."

Her eyes scanned him. "You're filthy, you smell like sweat." She drew closer, and reached up. Her thumb rubbed his lower lip. "Where'd you get the lipstick?"

Instantly, a knot formed in his gut. "I, I can explain," he stuttered.

She crossed her arms. "Yeah, right! How'd you get so dirty? The last time I saw you, your toga was white."

He shrugged his shoulders sheepishly. "It's a long story. I'll tell you later. Mind if I do some research of my own?" he smoothed out his soiled toga.

"Go ahead, knock yourself out," she huffed.

He took a short step and pulled out another large tome. Emma's eyes bulged as his finger coursed the ancient lines. Starting at the Pre-Rapture days, he walked through the pages of time from as far back as his great grandparents.

"Would you look at this M, my great great-grandmother married your great great-grandfather's brother, Carl Newton."

Her widened eyes beckoned him to continue.

"Did you know we are cousins?" he asked.

Emma leaned in close, sending a wave of perfume wafting around him. His heart skipped a beat as he felt her warmth.

"No, we're not actually cousins, silly. Not in the way you think of it. We're fifth generation cousins."

"Well yeah, that's what I meant to say. And it means we are 'In League'" Jamis' eyes danced with an impish glee.

"Jamis, we can't be 'In League' it is against Kingdom Law for an unbelieving mortal to be 'In League' with a believing mortal. That's what I've been trying to tell you."

He stepped back and crossed his arms, "Well, who says I'm not a believing mortal, look here in the book of the archives under my name," pointing, barely able to cover his smug grin.

Emma ran a quivering finger down the long list of names and dates. It stopped at the name, Jamis.

Her voice trembled slightly as she read. "Jamis Newton, the son of Damien and Jolie Newton, whose name was written in the Lambs Book of Life in the year of our Lord 3020." Her breath caught in her throat.

"See M. The ink is still wet."

She touched the ink. A tiny dot of black marked the point of contact.

Emma took a quick breath, "Oh Jamis ... when did that happen?"

A broad grin tugged at the corners of his mouth, "Oh, about a thousand years ago when we were in the diner. When that girl told her boyfriend the gospel story, and he bowed his head, that's when it happened!"

"That's when what happened?" she repeated, her hand covering her mouth.

"I put my trust in the Lord Jesus Christ, that's what happened."

"It was that simple? No tongues, no water, no laying on of hands?" Emma kidded.

"No silly, I just put my faith in Jesus to forgive my sins and take me to Heaven."

"Well, we aren't there yet, but it won't be long."

Her cheeks colored. She lowered her eyes and fidgeted with the fringes of her toga.

Jamis slipped down to one knee. He took her by the

hands and looked up.

"Jamis, let go of my hand. What on earth are you doing?" she said, pulling away.

His grip tightened. "Emma ..." his throat closed. He cleared it and tried again.

"Emma Newton, will you join the heritage of your fathers, with the heritage of my fathers?" his eyes pled.

Emma held her breath. Those were the words she'd longed to hear, dreamed she'd hear, even prayed to hear, and now heard. She leaned forward and threw her arms around his neck. "Oh Jamis, I have always wondered why our last names were the same. Yes, I will marry you. I love you so much."

They held each other, savoring the moment.

"Alright you two, I leave you along for thirty minutes and find you doing what?" Miss Xhu said as she came out of the shadows, the hilt of her sword still visible.

Emma released Jamis and jumped, hand to her chest. "Oh Miss Xhu, I have the most wonderful news, Jamis just told me ..."

"I overheard it all and I say congratulations are in order for both decisions. The ancient writings tell us that there is joy in Heaven over one sinner who comes to repentance. I, for one, am so happy for both of you. This has been a most eventful day."

Jamis stood, still holding Emma. He wiped his brow. "Well I, for one, am worn out," he said.

He winked at Miss Xhu hoping she'd not reveal their last encounter. "I have been waiting days to break the news and for a time, thought I'd never get the courage to ask you to marry me. If it's alright with you guys, I think I'll head back to the hospice and rest for a while. I'm still on Providence time."

Emma narrowed her eyes, sensing something but unwilling to spoil the moment.

The Stranger Among Us

"Why don't you go back to the hospice and get cleaned up. We'll meet you downstairs for dinner. Emma and I have some serious shopping to do."

With a sheepish smile, Jamis backed away, and the ladies headed to the first bridal shop they could find.

After a quick shower, Jamis was back on the street looking for the first diamond jeweler he could find. The scents of leather, fresh falafels and flowers permeated the air as Jamis walked the narrow streets. He joined the flow of other pilgrims whose movements were akin to a school of fish as they moved in and out of the quaint shops. At last he found his quest on Ben Yehuda Street. Since the Feast of Tabernacles opened with a mass wedding, he was anxious to get started preparing for their wedding. Couples from all over the world came to Jerusalem for the sole purpose of getting married in the traditional mass wedding ceremony. He stepped into the shop and perused the glass cases. Within an hour, he'd made his selection.

"Do you want us to size it and if so what size is your fiancée's finger?" the jeweler asked.

Jamis stepped back and scratched his head. "I'm not sure, but it's small. That's all I know."

She offered him a few suggestions, and he nodded. "Yes, that's about her size. I'll take it." Using his PAA, his personal appropriation account number, he transferred the funds and waited.

An hour later, he walked out of the jeweler's store with a small box tucked in his pocket. As he made his way to the restaurant, he met a traveling band of musicians who began to play an unfamiliar tune. He stood mesmerized by their music and before he realized it, he was late for dinner.

Emma and Nguyen's contagious laughter resonated throughout the restaurant as they reminisced over the earliest memories of her and Jamis. Even before he arrived, Jamis could hear them over the din. Barely able to stifle their giggles, they eyed him warily as he dashed in, still breathing hard. He scratched his head in bewilderment as he drew near.

"What are you two giggling about?"

In mock sobriety, Emma took a halted breath and assumed an innocent face.

"Oh Jamis ... we were just talking about you," she snickered.

He crossed his arms feigning an offense. "Talking about me or laughing at me?" he probed.

Emma squeezed down a chuckle with a sip of water from a bottle. "Miss Xhu simply mentioned in passing that you were such a pest when you were growing up. That's all."

He acted crestfallen. "That's because I was, but that seems a lifetime ago."

"It sure does," Emma said, fingering her water bottle.

"Well if it's any consolation Jamis, you acted very much like your father when he was your age ... energetic, impulsive and the quintessential pest. This time, Jamis joined the rolling laughter.

After a light dinner, they stepped out on to the busy street. Emma pranced with excitement. Her musical voice caused Jamis' heart to skip a beat.

"Besides the Muristan Bazaar, there are several sites I'd like to visit before all the festivities begin," Emma said, her hands clasp under her chin.

"Where should we start? I want to see them all," Jamis said.

The Stranger Among Us

Nguyen reassessed the tourist map. Red circles indicated the major tourist stops. "Let's begin at the Garden of Gethsemane and follow the steps of Jesus during His last week before the Crucifixion," Miss Xhu suggested.

Jamis snatched Emma by the hand and tugged. "Let's go, we don't have all day," he said, smiling.

Led by Miss Xhu, the three trudged east, until they reached the place called Gethsemane.

Patchy sunlight shone through the ancient olive trees on to the paved walkway. A warm breeze brushed Emma's face as she strolled in silence. "I love looking at those trees and thinking what it must have been like to have been here when Jesus prayed all night," she whispered to Jamis.

He nodded thoughtfully. As a babe in Christ, this was all new to him…and he savored each moment.

After spending some time in the Garden of Gethsemane, they crossed the viaduct, and passed through the Eastern Gate. By evening, they'd checked off many of the red circles.

As they entered Antonio's Fort, Miss Xhu stopped. "This is the place where the soldiers beat our Lord prior to His crucifixion."

The low ceiling and glassy floor, made smooth by the millions of feet, intrigued Jamis. He stopped and knelt, rubbing his hands on the stones. Warmth coursed down his cheek, as he whispered, *Thank you Lord. I could never repay you for what you did for me. But I want to live for you the rest of my life.*

In the distance, Miss Xhu continued her lesson, "Then they forced Jesus to carry his cross out of the city," she paused and scanned the crowd. "Where's Jamis?"

Emma scanned the crowded room, her heart palpitating.

"Sorry," his voice slightly ragged. "We must have gotten separated." He wiped his face with the back of his hand

and pushed out a crooked smile. "What?"

Emma smiled. She knew he'd been crying. Her heart was touched at the scene as well. "Where to next?"

"Follow me," Miss Xhu said, pointing to the exit.

The three of them strolled the narrow Via Dolorosa along with a large contingent of other pilgrims. It led through the Damascus Gate, to a flat place with a wall of rocks its backdrop.

The hollowed shape emphasized by deep shadows brought a chill to the warm air. "So this is Mount Calvary," Emma said, eyes wide.

"Jamis took her by the hand. "That sure is ugly. It reminds me of a skull."

"That's why it is called, Golgotha…the place of the skull."

Three empty, rugged crosses stood in front as silent reminders of the suffering and the victory that was won on the middle cross. A reverent hush settled over the assembled gathering of pilgrims.

Suddenly, a dove landed on the center cross and cooed. The amazed crowd broke out in jubilant song, singing one of the old hymns of the faith, "Victory in Jesus."

As the last strains faded, Jamis, Emma and Nguyen passed quietly along the walk. Jamis took one more glance over his shoulder trying to burn it into his memory.

"Just think, Jesus did that for me," Jamis said, his throat closing with emotion.

"He did that for all of us, Jamis," Emma said, "for the whole world past, present, and future. He died for the sins of the world. That's what I've been telling you."

They loaded the tram and rode the short distance to the Garden Tomb. Emma's eyes glistened while Miss Xhu hummed softly. Jamis snapped pictures at every turn hoping to capture every moment.

Beneath an azure sky, pilgrims from across the globe gathered at the opening of the empty tomb as they had for thousands of years. The giant stone stood in the same place as it did the day the mighty angel rolled it aside. Over the door was a sign announcing to the world 'He is not here. He is risen.'

The air crackled with emotion as Jamis gathered Emma close and whispered, "Thanks for never giving up on me." Salty tears scalded his cheeks as he thought what Jesus had done for him. Emma wrapped her arms around her soul-mate and gave him a gentle hug, joining the celebration, singing and worshiping their risen Savior.

Chapter 41

The Mountain of the Forest Saints

The sky above Jerusalem reverberated with a clap of thunder as Michael the Archangel and a host of his mightiest angels took to flight. They streaked across the sky from east to west like a bolt of lightning. Moments later, he and his hosts descended through the clouds like the earliest offerings of snow, and gathered above the Camp of the Saints.

Orifiel folded his wings and floated through the evergreens to the rugged ground next to his leader.

A few grey columns of smoke wisped from smoldering embers and gathered in the barren limbs overhead. An armadillo scavenged through a pile of trash, looking for its next meal, while ravens fought over a few crumbs of bread. All around the camp an eerie veil shrouded the atmosphere.

"It looks like we're too late, captain." Orifiel said.

Michael crossed his arms. "No my friend, this camp hasn't been overrun by the enemy. They left here in an orderly fashion, under the guidance of Nickolas the Wise. He has taken them to the Mountain Fortress. That's where they will take their stand. We must go there at once."

"How do you know they arrived safely?"

Michael folded his hands behind his back and began to pace. He followed the trail leading from the camp as far as the tree line studying the foot-falls. In the distance stood the majestic mountains of Nouveau. He fixed his keen eyes on one dark form among the thousands and smiled. "They have, but they won't last the week if we don't make haste."

Like a majestic bird, he lifted his wings and swooped. His attention was fixed on the distant mountain range to his west. From his vantage point high above the forest, he saw the last of the refugees entering their stronghold.

He knew it wouldn't be long before the mountain fortress would be surrounded by the forces of the enemy. They covered the landscape like the smoke from a raging forest fire. Michael led his forces across the sky and took up their positions high above the tree-line. Amid the snow-covered peaks, they looked down keeping constant vigil.

"Stand alert. We will know when the time is right," he commanded.

Supreme Commander Christos gathered his generals together after the destruction of New Birth.

"Our forces in the southern hemisphere are reporting complete victory. The Far East is united and on the move. The cities of Antioch and Bethesda lay in ashes. New Europe fell weeks earlier. Now it is time for us to focus our energies on Israel," he said, looking at his Hover Force Commanders.

"Take your hover-crafts and fly to the Valley of Megiddo and wait for my arrival. Once I have dealt with the Camp of the Saints, I will return and gather the inhabitants of the world together and lead them in one final assault against Jerusalem."

His underlings cried, "Hail, Christos," and made an about face. In lock-step, they marched from his presence.

He looked at the commanders of his ground forces. "Now we go to the Mountain Fortress of the Saints. Show them no mercy!"

The Stranger Among Us

Andorra stood, a lone sentinel on the peak of the Mountain Fortress. He squinted and lifted his hand to his eyes and saw a cloud appear on the distant horizon. Columns of tanks, trucks and APC's slashed through the forest, leaving a path of destruction a mile wide. Thick billows of dust and debris rose into the air as the first offering to the god of war. The earth shook as the armies ground to a halt.

"Why are you stopping?" demanded Commander Christos.

General Hakeem climbed from his command vehicle, adjusted his belt and approached. Although Christos was his supreme commander, he was a military man, seasoned and hard. If he knew anything, he knew how to command an army. As for Christos…he was just another politician looking for power. *If I play my cards right, I could be the real force behind the power, or I could have it all*, he thought.

"Sir, may I suggest we divide our forces, half to the north and the other half to our south. That way we will leave them no way of escape."

Christos eyed his general warily. "I had already taken that into account you idiot. Why do you think I am standing here? I was prepared to personally handle that detail myself until you stopped our advance. Have you no idea how long it will take to get this army on the move again?!" he billowed. "I should shoot you where you stand. Now get this army moving," he ordered.

White faced, Hakeem saluted and backed away.

Andorra receded into the shadows, unseen by the approaching army.

"They are here, my lord."

Nickolas glanced up from the map he'd been studying. "I know, I felt the ground move. There must be millions of them."

"How long do you think we can hold them off?"

The lines in the great chief's face deepened, "It depends on how many of them there are and how many arrows we have."

"I have instructed our warriors to remain out of sight until you give the signal."

Nicholas returned his attention to the map. "Good, General Christos will throw everything he has at us. I pray we will be able to sustain the punishment he inflicts."

Andorra took a step toward the door, and turned, "As do I, my lord, as do I."

The chief fixed his gaze on Andorra. Years of service to his King etched deeply in his face. "How are the women and children faring?"

Andorra stood at ease. He'd known Nickolas for unnumbered centuries, fought many battles with him and even defended this very mountain against the unruly hoards to their west. He always cared for the least fortunate.

He smiled at his chief, "We have provisions enough for the entire tribe to last us months. By then the battle for Jerusalem should be decided."

The wise old chief nodded and plopped down on a stool. "Good, I'm weary my friend. These bodies are just not made to last forever." He stretched his hands behind his head, and leaned back. "I long for the days when I will sleep with my fathers."

Andorra held his gaze, "The journey this time was particularly arduous, I agree. Only now are the last of the stragglers getting settled in."

"And as to our young friends?"

Andorra smiled. "Thanks to Rose, they are well taken care of. Her special energy bars will keep young Timothy alert for days," he said with a chuckle. "From what I've heard, as many as our young friend has eaten, he could whip the enemy single handed."

A wry smile creased the old chief's face.

Drops of condensation formed on the ceiling of the old cave and fell with rhythmic cadence as Nickolas led his people deeper into the Mountain fortress. The chilled air hung thick in the shadowy recesses and coalesced. Ghostly apparitions danced in the torch-light on the glistening walls. With each wave of new-comers, the ruts deepened. Walking became treacherous.

"Ouch!" Timothy said, picking himself up from the gravel floor. Shards of rock cut into his palms. He grimaced and rubbed the growing knot left from an unseen stalactite. With each step, a throbbing pain stabbed his head.

"Stop laughing, it's not funny. It's not my fault I'm not as short as you."

Joy held her jar of fireflies higher, "It's not my fault you're not leaning over enough," she kidded. Her breath came in short puffs of steam. "I don't like this place."

"Be grateful. You are as safe as possible down here."

"It reminds me of that bomb shelter," she said. The cold air cut through her thin garments and stung like a thousand bee-stings. She wrapped her arms around herself and rubbed vigorously tying to chase the goose-bumps.

Rose appeared from behind and threw a new blanket over her shoulders. "Here sweetie, this will help until we reach the central meeting area."

She handed Timothy another energy bar, and smiled sheepishly, "I made these especially for you."

Timothy took it and tried to smile, "Thanks."

He waited until she was out of sight and tossed it into a caver. "If I eat another one of those things, I'll puke."

Joy giggled, "She likes you, you know that, don't you?"

He nodded, "Yeah, but I don't like her, at least not that way. Besides, I'm not of the marrying age."

Looking back over the line of weary travelers and seeing the young mothers juggling their babies, Joy whispered, "By the looks of it, I don't think they stick too close to that."

"Thanks," he gulped.

They walked in silence until they reached the central chamber and took their seats at stone tables. Small candles flickered in chiseled recesses, giving the room a yellow pallor. Whispers echoed off the slick walls, making secrets a thing of the past.

"This waiting is killing me," Timothy said, rubbing his wounded hands.

Joy looked up from the sheet of paper. Her little fingers gripped a primitive writing instrument as she scribbled a letter to Emma. "How do you spell energy bar?"

He ran his hand through his hair. "What are you writing?"

She shrugged and returned an impish smile.

"Give me that, you little vixen," he grabbed for it, but she was too quick. In a move that surprised him, she snatched the letter and dashed around a tight circle of women, with Timothy giving chase.

The room broke into laughter.

A shadow filled the stone entrance. Arthures stood, arms crossed, the lines of his face deep with anxiety. A hush swept over the assembled.

"I need all able-bodied men to come with me," he announced.

His message sent a ripple throughout the torch-lit room. Mothers held their sons close, fear and pride defining their faces. For one last time, they kissed them and released them to Arthures' command.

Timothy watched as the adolescents were transformed into men. He took his place in line. Joy's cold fingers filled his hand and tugged at his heart. "Timmy, don't leave me, I'll be scared," her face awash with fear.

Kneeling, he wrapped his arms around her and squeezed. "I'll only be gone a short time, honey."

"But I'll miss you," she said, hot tears glistened down her pinkish cheeks.

An elderly woman slipped her arm around Joy's slender waist. "You needn't worry my child. Your brother is being very courageous. God will be with him."

Timothy straightened and looked at her. "What is your name ma'am?"

The older woman smiled. I am the wife of Andorra, Rose's mother. My name is Sasha."

Timothy fought back a grin. "Thank you, Mrs. Sasha." He held Joy's gaze. "Now Joy, you stay with her. I'll return before you know it."

He took his place with the gathering of elderly men and younger boys. He inhaled deeply, trying to steady the queasiness in his stomach. As he did, he glanced over his shoulder. Joy stood erect, and saluted.

Arthures led them to the armory and handed Timothy and the others crossbows and a stack of hand carved arrows. After a crash course on loading and firing the primitive weapon, he stationed them along a ridgeline high above the trees.

"Keep your heads down and remain out of sight until I give the signal."

Timothy squatted behind the rock wall, short puffs of condensation gathering and dissipated in the cool night air as he panted and waited. *What have I gotten myself into?* He thought.

Above him, hung a velvety black sky studded with diamonds. A stray cloud whisked passed the slivered moon as if it sought a place to hide. Timothy counted the moments. It wasn't long before the night sky lit up with the streaks of incoming missiles. The earth shook beneath his feet as impulse charges detonated. Further down range, fires burned out of control sending columns of thick smoke up to where he and the others hunkered.

Deep within the bowels of the mountain, Nickolas and his warriors waited. The pounding continued through the long hours. When the morning sun broke over the horizon, not one tree stood, and every stone had been pulverized.

Nickolas remained at his post; a look of determination painted his features. A shadowed messenger raced along the narrow passages to the command and control center.

"They are coming!" his message echoed.

Like a black cloud passing over the mountain, a million men began their slow climb.

"Now?" asked Andorra.

Nickolas, the Wise furrowed his brow. *All those souls, all those men, doomed the day they vowed their allegiance to Commander Christos,* he thought.

His conscience ached at the thought of sending them into eternity, yet it had to be done. He took a slow breath and let it out.

"Wait until they are within range, then let the arrows fly."

His warriors emerged from their hiding places. Each bearing quivers filled with titanium arrows, tipped with a hydrogen charge.

Timothy, along with hundreds of other archers, aimed their crossbows at a 45 degree angle, and waited. Despite the cold, sweat beaded on Timothy's face and his body shook. Suddenly, a surge of adrenaline released and his heart palpitated with new energy.

The advancing line of soldiers crossed a line of rocks painted orange.

"Loose!" Andorra ordered.

Like a flock of quail, the arrows shot into the thin morning air. They reached their apex, arched and began their decent.

Two thousand yards downrange the army stood, watching. Some laughed at the primitive weaponry. Others backed away, only to be shot in the back by their commanders. The rest held their ground, gritting their teeth.

When the reality of their fate struck them, it was too late. Each arrow found its mark. The hydrogen charged tips exploded on impact. Small radioactive mushroom clouds spread across the open slopes. Everyone within a hundred meters of the blast was incinerated.

Joy and Sasha stood next to Arthures when the command was given.

"I can't bear to watch," Joy said, covering her eyes.

The motherly woman held her close and cradled her head. "That's okay; it will all be over in a few minutes."

The mountain shook with new concussions. Thunder rolled as its sides gave way, sending an avalanche of rock and ice down its rugged slopes. It seemed to Timothy that the mountain wept as it covered the corpses of the fallen in a blanket of dirt and debris.

The archers pivoted and released another volley of arrows. This time the advancing hoards scattered in fear, some trampling the few who stood to fight. The arrows rained down, and the devastation was vast and nearly complete. Mushroom clouds of radioactive gas mingled with burning timber and smoldering corpses. Ghastly phantoms staggered like lost spirits through the toxic clouds. Those who survived raged up the mountain in one final suicide attack.

Michael, the archangel, watched the enemies advance. He rose to his feet, and gave the signal. His angelic army drew their swords, spread their wings and swooped down the mountain. The air scintillated with energy.

The advancing soldiers flailed wildly, battling the unseen forces. Arthures leaped from his hidden position, and threw himself into the fray. He drew his laser-saber, its blade glowed green in the morning haze.

Swoosh!

With a wide swing, he lopped off one man's head.

Andorra stepped from his hiding place and stood on an outcropping. He raised his laser-saber high above his head and led his warriors down the slope, screaming like a band of banshees. Singling out one soldier, he sliced him in half, and kept running.

The angelic forces joined the Forest Saints and slashed through the advancing enemy. Blood flowed down the mountain and mingled with the streams and formed a river of crimson.

Commander Christos jutted his chin out and cursed. "Retreat!" he demanded.

General Hakeem turned his chiseled face toward him, ashen faced, eyes wide with fear.

"Sir, there is no one left to retreat. They are all gone."

Christos drew his side arm, pointed it at the frightened man and pulled the trigger. Then he pulled out a small device from his pocket and typed in a code. A red light began to blink on large, unmanned hover craft flying high above the mountain fortress. A nanosecond later a flash of light, as bright as the sun, lit the sky and the earth shook.

Chapter 42

The Shalom Hospice, Jerusalem

Streaks of golden rays streamed through the lace curtains painting the hospice sitting-room in soft amber tones. Jamis roused. He cracked an eye open enough to allow his mind to begin processing information.

"Where am I?" he muttered to no one in particular. He'd returned and fell asleep waiting for Emma and Miss Xhu to finish their shopping spree. A light breeze gently stroked his face, and he stood, stretching out the kinks from his limbs.

Across the room, Emma lay curled in a tight ball and purred like a kitten. He closed the distance and brushed the hair from her face. Her eyes opened, and she smiled. Jamis' heart stopped as he caught himself staring.

Emma's cheeks colored, and she turned away. "You were sleeping so soundly on the couch. I didn't want to wake you."

Jamis stretched and yawned. "When did you come in?"

She unfolded herself, knotted her fists and screwed them into her eye-sockets. "Oh, about two in the morning. I plopped down and started to check my messages and, wham, it hit me. I curled up and was gone."

"Yeah, you were pretty out of it, too."

She brushed the bird-nest of hair aside and headed up stairs. "I've been on such an emotional roller coaster. I feel like I could sleep all day."

277

Jamis nodded. "Me too, but there's a lot to do before the festival begins. I'm going to run upstairs, get a quick shower, change and be back down here in a half hour," he said, a twinkle in his eye.

Taking a challenge, she pranced to the stairs and placed her foot on the first step. "Well, that maybe all you need, but a girl needs more than a half-hour to get ready. Give me thirty-five minutes," she said and double stepped it up to the third floor.

"Deal," Jamis said, close on her heels.

Thirty minutes later he rushed down to the waiting room, clothed in a fresh toga, his hair still wet. A pair of smiling eyes met his.

"How did you do that?" he asked. For the first time, he took notice at how pure her skin was.

She returned a coy smile, "Less is more, in my book." She spun in a tight pirouette.

Jamis bowed at the waist and held out an elbow. "Shall we go, my lady? We should get our marriage license first before the line gets too long," Jamis said. "Miss Xhu said we should get started early."

Emma checked her lips in a small mirror, gave him a heart-stopping smile, then grasped the proffered elbow. "Okay, so where to?"

"I think it's in the same building where they keep the Archives." With a skip, they set off in the direction of the Cathedral of Ancient Manuscripts. A broad grin stretched across Emma's face, and she chattered with nervous energy.

Judge Antonio, a thin aristocrat type, peered over his wire rimmed glasses. After reading their application, he leaned back in his seat, and cleared his throat.

"Let's see now, Mr. Newton, you are the son of Damien Newton, the son of Mark Newton, the son of Carl Newton, the brother of Jeremiah Newton, the father of Paul Newton, the father of Charles Newton, the father of Michael Newton the father of Emma Newton. And you Miss Newton are the daughter of Michael Newton, who's the son of Charles Newton, the son of Paul Newton, the son of Jeremiah Newton the brother of Carl Newton and so on. Alright now! I think I got that straight." He paused and adjusted his glasses.

"Since you are of age and In League, meaning you could marry without parental consent, I will waive the one-year waiting period and state, for the record," he raised his right hand. "By the authority vested in me by King Jesus, the King of Glory, Mr. Jamis Newton, I now do swear that you have legal claim to the hand of Miss Emma Newton and may join your two-family heritages at the first practicable time." Then he slammed down his wooden gavel.

Emma jumped. "Sorry," she giggled, "I wasn't expecting that."

The Judge of Family Ancestries drew out a quilled pen and scribbled his name on the Warrant of Marriage. "May the Lord bless you and keep you. May He make his face to shine upon you and give you peace. May you be fruitful and multiply and fill the earth with a Godly heritage." He smiled and handed it to Jamis.

Emma and Jamis left the office of the Judge of Family Ancestries, giddy as children on the playground.

"Now let's go to the Temple Mount to reserve a place for the wedding reception," Emma said. "Since many of my family are here to celebrate the Feast of Tabernacles, they might as well come to the banquet."

"I'm sure they'll be delighted to come. I only wish some of my family were here to celebrate too."

Emma nodded, not knowing what to say.

When they arrived, Jamis stopped and stared. "Oh brother,

this may take all day," he said, looking at the line to register stretching down the street.

Emma grabbed him by the arm and tugged. "Nope, over here, they just opened another line."

A fresh parchment sheet attached to a clipboard, flapped lazily in the breeze, waiting for the first signature. Jamis grabbed the quilled writing instrument and signed their names. Emma pranced and clapped her hands, as she watched him sign their names on the 'Notice of Weddings.'

"There, it's official. There's no backing out now," Emma said, an impish grin.

Jamis scooped her in his arms and squeezed, "I wouldn't think of it for the world."

Chapter 43

The Temple Mount, Jerusalem

A blast from two ram's horns broke through the cool morning air, and echoed, in the distance. The first day of the Feast of Tabernacles began and with it, an air of expectancy.

"Come along Emma," Miss Xhu said, her white toga flapping in the breeze. "I have an appointment for you at the Mikvah. It's the last act of purification before the big ceremony. I'm so excited for you."

Emma had been awake for an hour reading the ancient manuscript's instructions concerning the wife. Even though she'd been brought up knowing the writing, she'd never taken the time to read that portion.

"This is amazing," Emma said, "I never knew the Lord God had such a wonderful plan for the home. I mean, I knew my father loved my mother. They were so in love." Her eyes glistened at the memory. "I just thought that came naturally. I never knew that they were following God's commands."

Nguyen smiled, "I've known your family for as far back as the beginning of the golden age. And yes, they have always followed God's commands for marriage, but it doesn't come naturally. Agape love comes from God himself. But in their case, there was always the passion, the romance, the love that the men of the Newton family had for their wives. It's what kept them together for so long, and I see it in Jamis as well. Remember, he gets it from both sides."

"Can Jamis come and watch my baptism?" Emma

asked.

"Oh no honey, he must not see you until the time appointed, besides, he has his own to go to."

Jamis gathered his toga as he stood allowing the cool waters to swirl around his ankles. He waited for his name to be called, and then stepped down into the Mikvah. Next to him stood Saint Demetrius, one of the earliest believers in Europe. He raised his right hand, closed his eyes and began, "Brother Jamis Newton, because you have placed your faith in the finished work of Christ on the cross, I now baptize you my brother, in the name of the Father and the Son and the Holy Spirit. You are buried in the likeness of Christ's death and raised in the likeness of his resurrection."

The godly Saint, well acquainted with the practice took Jamis by the hands, covered his mouth and nose and lowered him back. The cool water enveloped him causing him to consider gasping, but he quickly dismissed the idea. He came up out of the water feeling invigorated, committed, and dedicated to God. Stepping into the changing room, he downed a pure white robe and tied a golden sash around his waist. He ran his fingers through his hair and shook it loose, then ascended the narrow flight of stairs to the Temple Mount, his wet soles slapping on each step like duck's feet.

A group of anxious men of all ages gathered in a waiting area, shivering in the morning air. Jamis took his place among them and glanced around. *Where is M?*

His heart quickened as a priest, robed in white apparel, climbed the stairs to the pinnacle. With angelic grace, he lifted a silver trumpet to his lips and blew a clarion call.

As the last refrain echoed off the distant buildings, a

rustle of movement stirred behind him diverting his attention.

A single ray from the sun descended from heaven like a spot light, surrounding Emma. She stood, back straight, shoulders squared, her hair shimmering in the illumination. A light wind blew, stirring her garments of pure white. Two emerald eyes glowed with warmth.

As she moved with the grace of a swan, Jamis took her by the hand and stepped forward. The urge to take her in his arms and kiss her was insatiable. With great effort he resisted the moment.

"Isn't this the most exciting day in your life, M?"

Her lips glistened in the morning light like dew on a polished apple. She smiled and his knees buckled. Giggling, she placed her arm around his waist and tugged.

He blinked, "I guess I got a little wobbly, I'm so happy and thankful to God for using all the events in our lives to bring me to salvation."

She wrinkled her nose in reflection. "I just wish Mom and Dad were here to celebrate with us."

"Your parents would have been so surprised to discover they had a fifth-generation cousin marrying their daughter."

As they spoke, a golden gate opened and the assembly surged forward. They were ushered to the designated area reserved for the wedding couples. Thousands of couples, young and old, smiling and holding hands, pressed into the area and waited.

The fragrance of the Rose of Sharon wafted through the cool morning air. Jamis broke his trance and glanced around, savoring the moment.

The High Priest of the Temple strode to the center of a large raised platform. His baritone voice, carried by the breeze, had a musical tone. "It is my great pleasure to announce the commencement of the Year of Jubilee. As you know, this celebration is only recognized every fifty years. And this marks the twentieth and last of such celebrations."

With a grand sweep, he opened a cage releasing a flock of pigeons. From all around the piazza, priests opened their cache of their cousins. Soon a large cloud of birds gathered in the azure sky and circled the Temple Mount in playful movements.

On the far end of the piazza, a choir and orchestra began to sing the Song of Moses. As the last strains echoed off the nearby buildings, it seemed the heavens joined the 'Amen' chorus.

The multitude broke into thunderous applause cheering and calling for an encore.

Another official stepped up to the podium, catching Jamis' attention.

"As Mayor of the great city of Jerusalem, I greet you in the name of the Lord," he said.

Jamis cupped his hands and joined the assembly in saying, "Greetings in the name of the Lord."

A grin tugged at the corners of Emma's mouth as she enjoyed Jamis' enthusiasm.

"Look Jamis, I can see right into the Holy of Holies," Emma said, pointing in the direction of the magnificent Temple. Its white stone wall shimmered in the bright sunlight.

Jamis craned his neck trying to catch a glimpse. Looking between heads, he saw the throne made of ivory and overlaid with fine gold.

Seven steps led from the pavement level to the top. On either side fourteen golden lions stood in quiet repose. Upon the throne sat the Lion of the Tribe of Judah, the King of Kings and Lord of Lords, Jehovah God, robed in purple, and girded with a golden sash. On the side of his regal garment was a name.

Jamis squinted to read it, but the letters were unknown

to him. Upon the King's noble head were many diadems studded with jewels which danced in the golden sunlight.

With great pomp, the King rose to his feet. His robes gathered loosely on the ivory platform. In his right hand a golden scepter glittered. Its knobbed dome, be-speckled with diamonds, rubies and sapphires reflected the glory of God, like a thousand gilded suns.

He beckoned the wedding parties to approach the throne. Jamis drew Emma close and stepped forward. The light fragrance of her freshly anointed body quickened his senses. His heart pounded with desire. Together they neared the throne and bowed lying flat on the stone plaza.

The air reverberated with the thunderous voice of King Jesus. "Arise, my darling, my beautiful one, and come with me. See! The winter is past, the rains are over. Flowers appear on the earth for the season of singing has come. The cooing of doves is heard throughout our land. Behold, the fig tree forms its early fruit, and the blossoming vines spread their fragrance. Arise, come, my darling, my beautiful one, come with me."

The words of comfort which flowed from the Masters lips brought a chill of delight to Jamis' heart. He yearned to look at Emma, knowing she was as thrilled as he was. But he couldn't tear his eyes from the beauty of the Lord's holiness.

"In the beginning of time I said, it is not good for man to be alone. I will make a helper suitable for him. So I caused the man to fall into a deep sleep, and while he slept, I took one of the man's ribs and closed up the place with flesh. And I made a woman from the rib that I had taken out of the man. I didn't take a bone from his head that she might rule over him, nor did I take a bone from his foot that he might tread upon her. I took a bone from his side, close to his heart that he might love and cherish her, and brought her to the man. And the man said, this is bone of my bones and flesh of my flesh. She shall be called woman, for she was taken out of my side. For this reason, a man will leave his father and mother and be united to his wife, and they will become one flesh. So you will no longer be two, but one."

Jamis and Emma joined hands and said, "Amen."

King Jesus continued, "Come, blessed of the Father; take your inheritance, in the kingdom prepared for you since the creation of the world. For the Almighty blesses you with blessings of the heavens above, blessings of the deep that lay below, and blessings of the breast and womb. Mercy and truth have met together; righteousness and peace have kissed each other. Therefore, what I have joined together, let no man put asunder. You may now kiss your bride."

Jamis broke his trance and gazed deeply into Emma's eyes. Her lips pooched slightly, waiting. The urge to draw her close overwhelmed him. He leaned down and tenderly kissed her. Heat from her body penetrated his robe, and radiated throughout every fiber of his being.

"Now let the Wedding Feast begin. Let us celebrate the Feast of Tabernacles for I, the Lord God Almighty, have chosen to dwell with you this day."

"Can you believe this Jamis? I could never in my life have imagined such a wedding or reception."

He glanced down with a mischievous smile, "Or such a honeymoon."

Emma cupped her hand over her mouth, giggling.

"Come on M, check this out." They clasped hands and he led her through the assembled crowd to a table with a giant ice sculpture of a mighty angel slaying a dragon in the center.

"Wow, that's cool," she said chuckling.

Located throughout the Temple Mount, were tables of every kind of delicacy imaginable; fresh fruit, apples, oranges, tangerines and grapes the size of baseballs, bowls of raisins, and nuts of all kinds.

Emma emerged from the serving line. Her plate heaped with sliced watermelon, cantaloupe, and honeydew melons. She laughed out loud as she watched Jamis balancing his cup of grape juice on top of a double stacked plate. He set it down on a small circular table and glanced around. "What?" he asked between bites.

"Oh, I don't know. I just can't get over how happy you look."

He took a swig of punch, and wiped the corners of his mouth with a napkin. "It's amazing M. That day when I prayed, was like the first day of my life. It's like I was born all over again. I wanted to tell you but ..." he let his voice trail off, as another couple neared. They stood munching and chatting, each sharing their love-stories.

Across the piazza drifted a light grey cloud. "What is that I smell?" Emma asked.

"I don't know, let's follow our noses and find out. They clasped hands and worked their way to the other side of the Temple Mount.

"Wow, get a look at that," Jamis said, peering at the large grills with fresh meat searing over open flames.

He smiled, "Now we're getting somewhere. This is man food," he said, pounding his chest.

Emma rolled her eyes. "Oh brother, just like my dad."

By evening, Jamis sat rubbing his swollen abdomen. "I think I ate too much."

Emma gave him an unsympathetic smile and shook her head.

A hush quelled the festivities as the Lord stood and raised his hands to Heaven. "And the evening and the morning were the first day, now go to your tabernacles in peace. Shalom."

The feasting ended and Jamis held Emma's gaze. An unasked question knit her brows. "Umm, what's next?"

Miss Xhu, who'd been enjoying the wedding festivities, overheard her question and came to Emma's rescue. She smiled sheepishly. "Well, under Kingdom Law, it is required for you to dismantle your tabernacles and reassemble them as one. It is there, you will spend your first nights together."

Jamis looked at Emma's rosy cheeks. He touched his own and felt heat. She giggled and tugged him down the steps.

Chapter 44

The Temple Mount, Jerusalem

Shafts of morning light filtered through the makeshift tabernacle and onto a bed of straw. The construct had been quickly thrown together as neither Jamis nor Emma had any foreknowledge of its necessity. Despite the last-minute effort, their tabernacle became a love-nest for the two newly-weds.

Emma awoke to the sound of children playing in the street. Their laughter and free spirited play pushed a smile across her face. She lifted her head. "I love to hear the children at play. I can't wait for us to have a whole house full of them," she said, picking straw from her hair.

Jamis rolled over, his bare chest rising and falling in a gentle rhythm. "Yes, well, if they're anything like me, they might get into a few fights along the way."

"Yes, and who won most of those fights?"

"Don't remind me," he said with a groan.

Emma lay back on his chest and listened. The even beating of his heart brought her a sense of comfort and joy. "That's because most of those fights were with me," a devilish grin tugged at her lips.

Jamis lifted her face to his, brushed the hair from face, and kissed her passionately. Then, looking deeply into her eyes he said, "It seems like I've known you all my life, and yet, I am just now really getting to know you."

"And that, my love, will take you the rest of your life," she said with an impish twinkle in her eyes.

He cocked his head, "Well let's get started," and threw the covers over her.

The sun beat a path across an ocean of blue in its race to the horizon. By noon the festival was in full-swing and Jamis and Emma joined the gathering of happy celebrants. Again, the aroma of fresh bread filled the air mingling with bouquets of aromatic flowers.

King Jesus arose from his throne, his pure white robe gird about his waist with a purple sash. He lifted his arms heavenward and declared; "This is the Acceptable Year of the Lord, I proclaim this blessing; The Lord is the Spirit and where the Spirit of the Lord is, there is liberty, so stand fast, therefore, in the liberty by which I have made you free."

Jamis and Emma joined the assembled in enthusiastic song. After an hour of singing, servants in multi-colored robes entered the crowd carrying silver trays. At the king's signal, they lifted the shining lids.

Wisps of steam rose from the warm rolls; their aroma filtered throughout the morning air and activated Jamis' senses.

Then, the king lifted his hands to Heaven and spoke in warm tones. "To him who overcomes, I will give the hidden manna."

Jamis stood. His jaw dropped open, eyes wide.

Emma faced him, and followed his gaze, "What is it Jamis. You look…surprised."

He lifted his hands and pointed at the king, "When King Jesus raised his hands, I saw scars, great big old ugly scars," he caught his breath. "I thought he had a resurrected body."

Emma turned back, her eyes wet with tears. Sorrow and joy mingled together and streamed down her cheeks. "He does have a perfect resurrected body," she said.

"Yeah well then, why does he still have those scars, M?"

Her gaze fell, and she scuffed the pavement. A pained expression washed over her features and she choked back a sob. "This is supposed to be a happy occasion, why am I acting like such a twit?" She took a halted breath and stared at her hands. "Because that's the scars our sin inflicted on him. He bears those scars as a constant reminder of the tremendous price he paid for our redemption."

Jamis held out his hands, staring. "I had no idea," he said in awe. "Oh, what grace!"

Moments passed in which neither were aware of the other. Jamis stood, his mind fixated on the old rugged cross.

A gentle squeeze brought him back to reality as Emma embraced him warmly. Tears of joy streamed down his face.

The aroma of the bread wafted through their tabernacle as Jamis and Emma dressed for another day of celebration.

"Mm, what smells so good?" he said, cinching on his sandals.

Emma threw open the cloth door and inhaled. "I know, let's eat. I'm famished ... again."

Jamis grinned like a Cheshire cat, "You wouldn't be eating for two, now would you?"

She returned his smile, "Jamis, whatever could you mean?"

After a day of feasting, singing and worshiping, the King dismissed everyone to go back to their tabernacles to rest.

Jamis grabbed Emma by the hand and dashed through the crowd. Down the steps they ran in a race to see who could get to their tabernacle first. Jamis won, and arrived at the door panting, hands on his knees. Emma, close at his heels, dove headlong into the tabernacle. "I win ... again," her musical voice called out, and Jamis dove in behind her.

For the next three days, the Temple Mount was a cathedral of praise as King Jesus displayed his creativity and power. Every day was a feast dedicated to a different aspect of God's grace.

The fourth day began as the third ended. The chilled air guided by the fragrance of pine greeted the young couple causing them to snuggle closer. Again, the Ram's horn sounded announcing the beginning of a new day of worship and festivities.

"Come on M, let's see what the Good Lord has for us today," he said as he quickly threw on a fresh toga. "Last one to the Temple Mount is a rotten egg."

She smiled and playfully held something behind her back. "Not so fast, you forgot your sash." Jamis halted and looked down.

She danced to the side as he made a failed attempt to grab what it was she held. He countered and snagged her as she dashed for the door. "Not so fast, you forgot your head-covering. She returned and tied the sash around his waist and sprang for the door, veil in hand. "Wait," Jamis said looking at the small box which had fallen from his pocket. Emma picked it up a quizzical look crossed her features. "Jamis, what's this?"

He plopped down on their bed and sighed heavily. "Now don't get mad at me, but that's the thing I went back and got that day we were in the time chamber."

Emma bent down next to him, a flood of emotions washed over her. "I know it's none of my business why you did that, and I've forgiven you, so if you don't want to tell me, you don't have to."

Jamis nodded. "Well at the time, it seemed really important, but now, I don't know. You see, I was so focused on finding out the code for the cloaking mechanism that I lost all objectivity." He paused, opened the box and lifted the nanochip. "I discovered that my father had something to do with its invention, and I went back in time to see the connection. I stole the code, and in the process found out my father was working directly with Professor Christos."

Emma's face paled.

Jamis lowered his head and stared at the floor. "I didn't tell you this, but after that argument we had over breakfast the other day, I was determined to see the king and give him the code, and—"

"And what?" Emma placed a warm hand on his forearm.

"And well, I was attacked."

"Attacked, by who?"

"Not who ... what? That's why I was so dirty. I nearly made it to the throne when this giant dragon leapt from a shadow and started clawing at me. It said if I didn't give the nanochip to him, he'd kill you."

Emma sat unblinking, riveted to every word. "What did you do, I mean you didn't give him the code did you?"

Jamis wiped the sweat from his upper lip and tried to smile. "It was then I realized how much I loved you. I was willing to do anything to save your life, even if it meant throwing away the only chance I had of saving Jerusalem. I pulled this box from my pocket and started to hand it over."

Emma buried her head in his chest and clung to him, "Oh Jamis. I don't know what to say."

Jamis pushed the hair from her face and kissed away a tear. "Just tell me you love me. I love hearing you say it."

"I love you Jamis...and I think you're the bravest man I've ever known." She held him absorbing his warmth, giving him hers. Suddenly, she pulled her head from his chest and faced him.

"What is it M?"

"I have an idea, every day the king invites us to come and to sit with him and we haven't gone yet. Why not do it today, and you give it to him then?"

Jamis gave a weak shrug. "I don't know, M. Somehow I don't think it's that important anymore."

Emma put her hands on her hips and eyed him warily, "Now Jamis, if you're going to wimp out on me now, after all we've been through, I'm going to crown you."

Jamis closed his hand around the nanochip, his jaw set, his eyes burned with renewed determination. "Let's do it."

They dashed from their tabernacle with Emma leading the way.

In a flash, he caught up to her, and together they ran to the top of the steps.

"You never told me what happened to the dragon," Emma said between gulps of oxygen. He slowed his pace as they crossed the wide expanse of the Temple Mount.

"Man, I forgot the best part. When he pounced on me, he knocked the box from my hand, and pinned me to the pavement. I fought to get free but couldn't. Out of nowhere, Miss Xhu showed up with the sword she was telling us about. She was absolutely fearless. You should have seen her. She fought like some wild banshee."

"What happened?" Emma's eyes wide with expectancy.

"The dragon made one last attempt to grab the box when she swirled in a great arc and chopped off its head."

"Oh Jamis, that's so exciting." Her face beamed.

I sure hope she never asks about where the lipstick came from, he thought.

They approached the Temple and slowed their pace, hesitating.

"You know Jamis. The ancient writings say to come

boldly to the throne of grace to find help in the time of need. Let's claim that right now and go before I chicken out."

"Good idea," he said. Clasping hands, they stepped into the thick cloud.

"Welcome my children; I see you have come after all." The voice of God echoed through the mist. "How I long to have fellowship with my beloved children. Sit and enjoy my presence."

Through the haze, a large ivory bench appeared but instead of it being cold and hard, as they sat, it felt warm and comfortable.

"There now, isn't that better than those old hard stone benches?" the Lord God said with a chuckle.

"Yes sir," Jamis barely eked out.

"Oh no! You mustn't call me sir. I'm your Father, your Elder Brother, your Comforter and Friend. Not some capricious, distant entity that must be feared," he said with a belly laugh, deep and resonant. "I understand you have something for me Jamis."

Jamis stiffened. "How did he know that? Did you tell on me?" he whispered, catching Emma's eye.

She feigned locking her lips and throwing away an invisible key. "I didn't say a thing."

Surrounding them came a jovial laugh. "My children, there is nothing hidden from my eyes, for all things are open and naked before him with whom you have your being."

Jamis sighed and fished his hand in his pocked. He produced the nanochip and held it in an open palm. "Sir, uh, uh. I mean, Father, I confess I stole this from my earthly father, but, but I thought it was important at the time," he stuttered.

The cloud billowed, then thinned. "Oh, that, I've already covered your sin with the blood of my Son. Now as to the cloaking mechanism, I, who know the end from the beginning, who understands the witty inventions of my creations, know all about the plan of my enemy." A thunderous laugh shook the temple. "I have said in my wisdom why do the heathen rage and the people imagine a vain thing? I, who sit on the circle of the earth, will laugh and have them in derision." The thunder subsided. "But thank you my child for your courage, I understand you were willing to risk your life for the one who sits next to you."

Jamis swallowed and clasped Emma's hand.

"That reminds me of the story of the Pearl of Great Price, I wrote about. You should read it. It would do your heart good. But I digress. I do have everything under control. Now go in peace my children. Enjoy the last days of the festival together. Oh, and about that lipstick …"

A moment later the haze disappeared, and Jamis and Emma stood in the middle of the Temple Mount. A crowd of happy people surged around them.

A servant appeared carrying a tray.

"Jamis, I have never seen so much bread in my life," she said, lifting a warm morsel and popping it into her mouth. "Look, there are tables of flat bread and yeast bread, wheat, rye, corn, pumpernickel, and bran. I want to try them all." Her eyes danced with delight.

He faced her and his heart did a somersault. He was so proud to call her his wife.

"M, you gotta try this one," handing her a slice of cranberry walnut bread.

"Umm, it's still warm," she said and took another bite.

They grazed the rest of the day, sampling the breads and chatting with the other newlyweds. From time to time, they would run across Miss Xhu, who filled them with wonder as she recounted her fight with the dragon.

By day's end, their hearts were full as well as their

bellies. Jamis led a weary Emma back to their tabernacle. He flopped on the bed and patted it.

She smiled, "I don't know how much longer I can keep up this pace."

He nodded, a smile tugged at the corners of his mouth.

After a few minutes, Emma cocked her head; a questioning expression filled her eyes. "Jamis, what do you think the Lord meant about lipstick'?"

Jamis' light snoring told her she was getting nothing from him tonight.

Taking her place next to him, she wrapped her arms around his chest and dreamed of the coming day.

Chapter 45

Outside of Jerusalem

Like a giant python wrapping itself around its prey, Satan's power encircled the globe and began to squeeze. For over a thousand years, the earth enjoyed her Sabbaths, but not anymore. Now, she was feeling the heavy hand of her former taskmaster. She reeled to and fro like a drunken sailor. Since his release from his imprisonment, he'd worked to deceive the nations. The population center of Celebration was the first to own his wrath, then Providence and New Birth fell into his hands. Pressure began to build, and the earth groaned under its weight.

While the saints were celebrating in Jerusalem, Supreme Commander Christos was quietly gathering his forces from around the globe. Iron clad men from Rome with their war machines, black-robed men from Babylon and beyond the Euphrates River bearing weapons of mass destruction, and soldiers from Gog and Magog traveling in bands numbering in the millions, moved with determination. They descended through the land bridge of Georgia, from the Mediterranean Sea and across the Sinai desert.

Using their cloaking devices, and moving under the cover of darkness, the armies filled the plains of Megiddo, and took up strategic positions around Jerusalem. Then, they waited.

Supreme Commander Christos stood among the olive trees in Gethsemane peering through a set of field glasses.

"Is everything in place?" he asked his general.

"Yes my lord. We await your orders."

He lowered the viewers and adjusted his stance. The white stoned walls of Jerusalem glistened in the sun. Colorful banners hung in angles from its ramparts and flapped lightly in the wind. Joyful music drifted across the valley, while celebrants danced and moved about the Temple Mount with a steady cadence.

That celebration should be for me, he seethed. *Those people should be singing my praises, not his. I should be the one sitting on that throne, not him.* He thought.

"Jerusalem is ripe for the picking. They are so preoccupied with having fun, they won't know what hit them until it is too late."

Raising his arms high above his head, he inhaled, expanding his chest beyond his vestments. The military uniform began to tear apart, one button at a time. His outer shell peeled back, and a ghastly red dragon emerged. Its scales rippled and shimmered in the sun. Its snake-like neck, still bearing a bloody gash, bowed as the great beast lifted its head. Standing erect, it lifted its head above the trees and exhaled fire and brimstone, scorching the ancient foliage. With one powerful thrust of its leathery wings, the dragon rose skyward.

"To war!" he cried, and the assault began.

The pilots of hover-crafts released their impulse charges; the commanders of the artillery units gave the signal to open fire. The earth shook. Contrails from a thousand missiles streaked across the azure sky like cat-claws.

And the world held its breath.

Silence.

Like the first offerings of a winter snow, the missiles disintegrated and fell harmlessly to the earth.

Lucifer cursed.

Suddenly, a single flare, high in the heavens appeared

and held his attention. It rose to its zenith, and then began a slow descent. In a grand moment, it burst into a thousand sparkling embers of color, and spread in an ever widening circle. Another one appeared, followed by another like the early promise of a grand finale yet to be unleashed. Then, the windows of Heaven opened, and fire and brimstone poured down.

Lucifer hung in mid-air and watched the drama unfold, helpless to stop it. As the wrath of God engulfed him, his knees buckled.

"My Lord, and my God."

At the epicenter of the universe, a low rumble began and rolled through the vast regions of deep space. Like a giant stone, thrown into the center of the sea, its energy spread, consuming everything in its wake. Within a nanosecond, it enveloped the universe. Atoms split, the elements melted with fervent heat, and the old gave birth to the new. The heavens, once the domain of Satan disintegrated and The New Heaven emerged, pure and clean.

Jamis and Emma felt the vibrations and lifted their eyes to the heavens.

"What is happening?" asked Emma, clinging to Jamis.

His chest heaved; his heart racing. He wrapped his arms around her and held her close, and whispered, "I don't know, but keep your eyes on Jesus."

The golden sky above Jerusalem ignited in a dazzling display of light and color, as the Lord God of the universe demonstrated His power and glory. The finale of the ages blazed across the sky, and thundered throughout the heavens.

"This is beautiful," Jamis said, his heart beating wildly.

Emma lifted her head from his chest. Her eyes turned upward. "I've never seen fireworks like this before."

They stood wide eyed like two children in Walt Disney World. When the grand finale ended and the last echoes of thunder faded, Emma lifted her arm and pointed. "Jamis, what is that?"

Miss Xhu, who'd been standing nearby, stepped next to them. "It's New Jerusalem coming from God out of Heaven prepared as a bride for her husband."

Emma's screams of joy were drowned out as the mighty voice of God echoed from eternity.

"It is finished! I am the Alpha and the Omega, the Beginning and the End. To all who thirst I will give to drink of the water of life freely. He who overcomes will inherit all this, and I will be his God, and he will be my son. I will make my home among these people. You will be my people, and I will be your God. I will wipe every tear from your eyes. Death will no more haunt you; neither will there be any more crying nor pain, for the old things have passed away. Look and see ... I have made all things new."

Jamis and Emma joined the cheering throng, dancing and singing praises to God and to the Lamb.

They watched the golden gates of the New Heaven swing open. A multitude of people, robed in white, waving palm branches flooded out.

"Jamis, I see mom and dad, Timothy and Joy."

Taking him by the hand, they ran through the crowd.

"Mom, Dad, I missed you so much." They embraced, tears of joy streaming down their faces.

Michael brushed the hair from her eyes and kissed her forehead. "We missed you too honey."

Emma lifted her head. "Daddy, I know this may come to you as a bit of a shock, but—" She paused, wondering how to tell him. "Daddy, you won't believe it, but I'm married to Jamis. He's my cousin, five times removed."

Michael smiled and held her close. "You don't say."

Her mother stepped next to her. "Honey, we've always known you two would marry. Why do you think we sent you to Edenica? And as far as knowing he's your cousin.—we've known that too."

Emma stood, grasping for words. Scanning the plaza, her eyes searched for Jamis.

He stood talking to a young couple. His outstretched hands moved with animated energy. His face beamed with joy. Though their backs were turned to hers, there was something about the young lady's stance that was familiar.

"Jamis," she called as she neared the trio.

The young couple shifted around to face her.

"M, it's them, the couple from the café. She looks just like you," he said, his eyes dancing between them.

One glimpse and Emma knew.

"Chase, and Megan!"

Epilogue

Imagine what it will be like, living in a world without the effects of the curse ... a world under the direct reign of King Jesus. Just think of the technology, the progress we'd make. Think of the progress our society has made in the last one thousand years. Now multiply that exponentially by the factor of God.

The ancient manuscripts are rather sparse when it comes to explaining the final days of that coming golden age. They simply say, "After the thousand years have expired, Satan will be released from his prison for a season."

We don't know how long that season will last, but it won't be long. But during that period of time, he will gather the unregenerate people from the four corners of the world. Gog and Magog, the perennial enemies of God, will willingly join together for one final showdown. The ancient manuscripts simply say, "And fire came down out of Heaven and consumed Satan and his host of rebels and they were cast into the lake of fire."

Pretty simple, pretty direct, giving me a lot of room for imaginative speculation. I hope you've enjoyed our little excursion into the future.

CPSIA information can be obtained
at www.ICGtesting.com
Printed in the USA
LVOW01s0455300916
506778LV00002B/7/P

9 781681 426549